About the Author

Lexie Winston has been an astronaut, rock star, princess and time traveller. In her dreams. But none of the dreams have lived up to what becoming an author has been like. She gets to live in a world of pure imagination, and her heroines get to do the things she's always wished she could.

When not writing books, Lexie is a mother of two gorgeous teenagers and the wife to a patient and understanding man. They live in Western Australia and are lorded over by a black toy poodle. She loves camping, reading and if her iPad was stolen, her world would explode. (It has the kindle app on.)

And check out my website at lexiewinston.com

Also by Lexie Winston

The Collectors Division

(Reverse Harem Series)

Guardian

Guardian's Blood

Guardian Ascending

Collectors Division Omnibus

Arbor Vitae Coven

(Paranormal Romance Series)

Candy Conniptions

Dreamy Delights

Fangtastic Fireworks

Neighpalm Industries Collective

(Adult Bully Reverse Harem)

Abandoned Girl

Broken Girl

Tormented Girl

Wanted Girl

Cherished Girl

Loved Girl

Superficial Girl - Jacinta's Story

Seductive Sins Collection

(Reverse Harem Series)

Glorious Gluttony

Gangs, Guns, and Glory

Galaxy Circus

(Sci-Fi Reverse Harem Series)

Apprentice

Stagehand

Broken Promises

(Dark Poly Romance Series)

Secrets Kept

Lies Untold

Secrets Kept

BROKEN PROMISES SERIES

LEXIE WINSTON

First published by Neighpalm Publishing in 2022

Secrets Kept - Broken Promises Series

Mobi : 978-0-6450988-0-8
Print: 978-0-6450988-7-7

Cover design by Infinity Cover Designs
Content Edited by SCW Editing
Copy Editing by Elemental Editing

Content Warning

This books contains scenes of a sensitive nature and
readers are advised to continue at their own risk.
Theses scenes include and are not limited to
Drug Use
Violence
Non Con
Dub Con
Blood and Knife Play

The Broken Promises series will contain MM and FF
and is considered a poly romance as opposed to a
traditional reverse harem romance.

Prologue

Present Day

The sound of the little pill baggie hitting the desk echoes loudly in my soundproof office. "That's what you wanted when you came in here, isn't it?" I ask the girl on the other side of my desk, waving to the bag with a couple of ecstasy pills in it.

Her eyes widen, and she fidgets in her chair as I close and lock the desk drawer I'd just gotten them out of and push my chair back from the desk. Leaning back, I light the joint I also removed from the drawer, inhaling deeply before blowing out smoke rings. I can see her biting her plump lip like she isn't sure if I asked a trick question or not.

Grabbing the bag, I shake one of the pills onto the desk and pull out the little mortar and pestle I have in another drawer. I drop the pill in and crush it before tapping it onto the desk, my movements slow and precise to draw out the anticipation. The more she wants it, the less likely she'll be to ask any questions. Using a razor blade, I cut it up nice and fine before forming it into two lines. One of her hands is twitching now as she holds onto the arm of the chair like she wants to reach for the short plastic straw I place next to the two piles.

While she thinks about it, I run my eyes over the length of her body. She's not really my type. She's skinny with fake boobs, and her long hair looks like it's been bleached blonde one time too many, but her face is pretty enough, I guess.

"But what about payment? You said we could come up with something." She has the desperate gleam of an addict in her eye that I see all the time around here. The old me probably would have taken pity on her and sent her on her way without the drugs, but the old me died a gruesome death the day my best friend turned on me. It took me a year to recover, but the new me blossomed, and I'm pretty happy with the way I am now.

I stand up from my desk, joint in hand, and grab the baggie with the remaining pills before heading over to a nearby couch and coffee table. "Why don't you snort that and then take a seat over here, and we can discuss my terms," I tell the girl, grabbing a bottle of water out of the nearby mini fridge. I put both it and the bag on the coffee table before throwing myself back onto the leather couch, lounging like I don't have a care in the world. Her eyes light up and she moves to my desk, her long legs bare under her tiny skirt and her feet encased in five-inch stilettos. She leans forward, her skirt rising with the movement, exposing a peek of a thong-clad ass as she grabs the straw. I watch as she holds it to one nostril while blocking the other with a finger as she runs it along the line. Her sniff is loud in my otherwise silent room. She quickly swaps nostrils and does the same with the other line before throwing her head back and riding the quick rush that flows through her body.

I feel a smile cross my face. So fucking easy. I reach down and pull out the Glock 9mm that is wedged into the side of the couch, putting it down on the table next to the little baggie now down one pill. Her eyes widen, and she looks from the gun to me, the fear in her gaze causing a thrilled shiver to course through my body and goosebumps to pepper my skin. "Now let's discuss payment."

"But... But..." She stumbles back into the desk.

"But nothing. You didn't think to negotiate before snorting those lines, you silly bitch," I growl. "Now if you don't want me to put a bullet in your brain, I suggest you get down on your knees." She looks between me and the door, but I locked it when we first came in. If she tried to make a break for it, she wouldn't get very far.

"Ticktock, honey, time's running out." I spread

my legs and watch her gulp, but I can also see that the ecstasy is kicking in. Her pupils are dilating, and goosebumps cover her skin. Her nipples have tightened and look like Hershey kisses tucked down her top—there's no bra to hide her reaction. I wonder what color they'll be. "If you're a good girl and can get me off, I'll let you take the rest of the bag for nothing," I cajole, and I see the moment she decides to do what I ask.

God, I love the feeling of power that courses through me as she gets down on her knees on the polished concrete floor. I remember how powerless I felt that day, how betrayed, and I swore from then on that I would never feel that way again. Circumstances handed me a way to achieve it not long after. Karma really is a bitch, and I'm going to get my revenge.

She shuffles over to me and hesitantly lowers herself to the ground, her gaze locked between my legs.

"Take your top off. Let me see those perky nipples," I order, and she shrugs out of the scrap of material she is using to keep herself covered. She holds it in front of her chest, but I growl, so she throws it to the side. Her nipples are a pretty rose pink that I actually wouldn't mind getting my lips on. I reach out and run a finger over first one nipple and then the other, and she shivers from the light contact. Pinching one between my thumb and forefinger, I squeeze, and she moans quietly, shoving her breast forward into my hand, her eyes narrowing with desire.

My gaze leaves her nipples and returns to her face. "Well, come on, get on with it. I don't have all night."

She looks a little nervous as she runs her tongue over her lips, making them glisten. They are going to glisten even more in a moment. Her manicured hands reach up and shove my dress up high, exposing my dripping folds. I love corrupting straight girls.

I spread my thighs wider, and she leans in and licks my clit like it's poison.

"Oh no, honey, you either eat me out like it's your last meal on earth, or you'll be sorry. Just do to me what you like having done to you," I suggest, not hiding the hint of steel in my voice, before I grab her hair and shove her face down. A grunt leaves her mouth, but her tongue slides through my folds before she goes to town, licking and sucking. Her hands grip my thighs tightly and just on this side of too hard, and the pain in contrast with the delicious pleasure she's wringing from my cunt has my breath increasing. I slide my hand up and start to caress my own nipples through the fabric of my dress as she slides her fingers through my dripping pussy before ducking her head back down. Her fingers are a little awkward as she tries to find where to put them—it's a different angle than she's probably used to when she's doing it to herself—but she gets it right, and I've soon got two fingers pumping in and out, giving me something to clench on.

A moan leaves my mouth as I lean my head back against the sofa. "Oh yes, you dirty slut, I knew just looking at your mouth that you would be good at licking my pussy." I can see her chest heaving in reaction to my words, and I decide she needs a reward for such a superb effort.

Leaning down, I grab her hair and pull her face out of my cunt. She looks up at me in a daze, the X in her system doing an excellent job of keeping her horny. She removes her fingers when I pull her to her feet as I stand.

She blinks a couple of times in surprise, but before she can say anything, I lean down and lave one of those rose pink nipples with my tongue. I circle it once, then twice, before blowing air on it. My gaze goes back to hers. Her pupils are blown, and there are beads of sweat forming across her forehead. I move over and help her lie down on the couch, pushing her skirt up and pulling down her panties. Her pussy is bare and glistening with her juices—just the way I like it. She starts to say something, but I just lean in and place my mouth over hers, coaxing her into a kiss. It doesn't take her long to respond, and I can taste myself all over her lips as she twines her tongue with mine.

Like I said, the corruption of straight girls is a hobby of mine, and nothing brings me more satisfaction than having one respond like this one is. I really did turn into a monster a year ago.

Pulling off my body-con dress, I stand naked before her, her eyes scanning my body before she licks her lips. I watch her swallow nervously again before I lean in and brush her hair back from her face. "You've been such a good girl. How about I return the favor?"

I push her backward so she's spread out along my

leather couch that has seen many a girl providing payment for drugs the same way. My brother laughs and accuses me of being a sick bitch, but he's just as bad. We have a tally of how many girls we've both fucked.

Going around to the end where her head is, I kick my shoes off and gently climb over her until I'm positioned above her in my favorite sixty-nine position. The only problem with this is I find that once I get them to a certain point, not many of them can continue to work my pussy and orgasm at the same time. We'll see how this one can do.

Lowering my face as I lower my pussy onto her mouth, I wait for her to continue before I begin. I don't even have to say anything. Her arms wrap around my hips, and she pulls me down onto her mouth, plunging her tongue into my hot center.

My eyebrows fly up in surprise, and a grunt leaves my mouth, followed by a long, drawn-out moan. Oh yeah, she's got the rhythm now.

I breathe in deeply, and the musky scent of woman greets my senses as I flick my tongue out to taste the bitch. She tenses up and then relaxes as I suck lightly on her clit before groaning into my body.

I continue to lick her pussy, alternating between her clit and her center, swallowing her cream. I can feel my orgasm start to tingle at the base of my spine, and my toes flex with the sensation. Her fingers join the party, and she pounds in and out just how I like it. I return the favor, fucking her with two fingers. The sensory extravaganza of what we're doing is almost enough to tip me over the edge. The sounds of fingers squelching, the scent of pussy in the air, and the sight of her pretty pink folds are just about perfect. I couldn't really ask for a better way to start the night.

Her hips start to thrust up and down, and her moans get louder, but she continues to go to town on my pussy with her teeth and tongue, providing the right amount of soft and hard. As I tip over the edge, two things happen—she cries out, her orgasm squirting all over my face as I try to drink down everything she gives me, and the door to my office bangs open, meaning one particular person is standing there now.

"Oh, for fuck's sake, Tori!" My brother sounds annoyed, but I hear him snort in amusement before the door bangs closed again as I shudder through the rest of my orgasm. The girl is too far gone, the drugs riding her system hard, to care about someone being at the door. I flick the girl's clit a couple of times with my tongue as I feel her thrash underneath me, oversensitive to my touch, before removing my fingers and licking them clean. Rolling onto the floor, I quickly stand up and look around for my dress. I grab the girl's top off the ground and wipe my face and fingers clean on it before throwing it at her and pulling my dress over my naked body. I pick up the remaining pills and throw them in her lap.

"The next time you come into my club and want drugs without coughing up the green stuff, I'll have you beaten so badly, those plastic tits will pop." I pick up my gun, and her lust-filled gaze quickly turns frightened as she scrambles to her feet. The only problem with dresses like this is I have nowhere to put my gun. I wave it in her direction, and she shrieks. "Now get the fuck out of my office, and if you tell anyone about this exchange, someone will be coming for you. Otherwise, everyone will think they can score without having to pay."

She teeters toward the door, still a little shaky from me rocking her world. I mean, it's only fair that she got something too, especially because her fear makes the orgasm I just got so much better. The thrill of forcing someone to do something they normally wouldn't is intoxicating. I follow behind her and stick my head out, talking to the roided up goon waiting on the other side.

"Follow her and make sure she doesn't cause any problems."

He nods and lumbers after her as my brother shoves his way past me.

"God, it smells like pussy in here, which would be fucking hot if you weren't my sister." He screws up his nose in disgust and goes to throw himself on the couch, but I hold my hand up.

"Ah, I wouldn't. She was a squirter." He pauses, his mouth dropping open as he glances between me and the couch, looking interested at first but then shuddering before sitting in the chair on the other side of my desk. I walk past him, giving him a kiss on the cheek, and he scrunches up his face as he pushes me away.

"Ew, don't, you smell like cunt again and that's just not right."

A genuine smile crosses my face for the first time tonight, and a laugh escapes as I slip into the bathroom attached to the office and clean myself up. "What's so important that you unlocked my door and barged in? Anyone else, and I would have shot them," I call through the door, feeling curious because if the door's locked, he'd normally have been happy to wait.

A frown crosses his face, and he stiffens, putting me on high alert. "It's who's in line waiting to get into the club that's the problem." There's only one person Gio would be worried about me seeing, and I feel my own body stiffen.

"Fuck, really?" I sigh and step out of the bathroom. I suddenly feel like I'm back in high school at the start of my senior year—a year that should have been filled with parties and fun and milestones. Instead, it was full of sadness, grief, and anger.

Then I remember I'm a fucking badass, and if they cause me any grief, I'll just kill them. I've discovered a bullet through the brain can solve most problems. "It's fine, Gio. Let them in. Knowing them, they'll become some of our most valued clientele. They've all got a lot of money to splash around. I'll be fine, I'm not that girl any longer. They will figure that out soon enough."

He stands up and leans over to kiss me on the

cheek before thinking better of it. "Wash the scent of pussy off your face and come join me in the box. We need to show them who the real king and queen of Suncity are. It's about time they worked out who is in charge around here."

One year ago

"Oh my God, Tori. I can't believe your mom and dad trust you to stay home alone when they go out of town for two weeks." My best friend Stacey bounces up and down on my king-sized bed, her excitement sparkling in her cornflower blue eyes. "Mine won't leave me overnight, let alone for that long."

I shrug my shoulders, my long black braid flipping over my back with the movement. "It's not like I'm on my own, Gio's here too and Dad trusts him to look after both of us. Not to mention Penelope had a catering company cook meals and freeze them for us before she left, and the cleaning service is still coming by. Basically, all I have to worry about is buying school supplies for the new semester and having as much fun as possible before it starts."

Stacey squeals in excitement and jumps off the bed, racing over to her overnight bag and pulling out a bottle of vodka. She holds it up in her hands like she's a game show hostess. "Speaking of having fun, I brought party favors." I roll my eyes at her. My parents have a fully stocked bar, and they wouldn't even notice if we took anything, but she says it's more illicit and exciting if she steals it from a liquor store. I have no idea how this girl doesn't have a criminal record.

"Come on. Let's go downstairs and find something to mix it with. I'm not drinking it straight," I tell her before heading out of my bedroom. The rooms in our house are basically soundproof, so the minute I open the door, the sound of my brother's party hits my ears. Music is playing, and voices drift up the stairwell.

My brother is a year older than me and just graduated from high school. He's always been one of the cool kids, so his parties are always really popular. Stacey and I are popular adjacent, but she is determined to upgrade now that we're going to be seniors and ride Gio's coattails, so to speak. Me, I don't care either way. I'd rather have friends who like me for me as opposed to who I am and what I can do for them. My family has money. We live in a nice two-story, six-bedroom house, and Dad owns and runs quite a few businesses in the city we live in, but we live a quiet life. He travels a lot for business, mostly within the States, but sometimes he goes overseas. My stepmom used to stay behind when we were smaller so that our lives weren't disrupted, but now that we're older, she accompanies him everywhere. She's the quintessential Stepford wife, eager to please my father and just as eager to spend his money.

"Tori!" My brother's voice draws my attention to him, and a smile crosses my lips when I find him center stage surrounded by his groupies. His black hair is tousled, and I'm not sure if he did it deliberately or if some bimbo has been running her hands through it. It's probably the latter, since he's such a man whore. His blue eyes sparkle with sadistic mirth. I know that look, it's the one that says Gio is up to no good. He's looking to fuck or fight. I'd put my money on both, I know him well.

His groupies look up when he calls my name. They are all sycophants, competing with one another to establish themselves as my brother's number one, but they fail to realize that position is already filled. There are only nineteen months between the two of us, and we've been thick as thieves for as long as I can remember. Him being a boy and me being a girl has never made a difference. One thing Dad instilled in us from a very young age is that blood is everything. If you can rely on your blood, then you never need anyone else. It may seem lonely, and don't get me wrong, we both have other friends, but he's my ride or die.

"Come do shots with me," he demands, and I head over to where he's sitting. He shoves the guy sitting next to him hard. "Move and let her sit." Stacey drifts up behind me and waits.

The guy who looks like he's two sheets to the wind

stares at Gio in confusion before it switches to anger. "You want me to move for your sister? What the fuck for? It's not like she's sucking your cock or anything."

The group instantly falls silent. The party continues all around us, but the core group here knows that this guy basically volunteered for a beat-down. No one disrespects our family.

"What did you just say?" my brother growls menacingly, and the guy swallows nervously, looking to the group for backup. I smirk as the rest of them avoid his gaze.

"Man, I would get it if the bitch you wanted me to move for was polishing your knob, but dude, I can't believe you're making me move for your kid sister." The guy's whining like a bitch by the end of his sentence, and the people next to him all scramble to move out of the way. I just watch in amusement, pouring Gio, Stacey, and me a shot of black sambuca from the bottle on the table as my brother stands to his full height, the slow movement an intimidation technique that seems to work well. The guy shrinks back before squaring his shoulders and sitting straight again.

Height runs in my family, but for some fucking reason, I didn't get it. I'm five-five, and my brother is almost a full foot taller than me. He towers over the guy who has put his foot in it big time. The scowl on Gio's face is enough to make any sane person piss his pants, but drunk boy still doesn't get it. He laughs nervously.

"Did you just talk smack about my sister? My sister

is worth more than a million bitches who may be sucking my dick."

The guy shrugs his shoulders.

"Apologize!" Gio demands, and the guy looks around the room for support, but no one will meet his eyes. When his gaze meets mine, his eyes flash with fury, but I just salute him with my shot and throw it back, the black licorice flavor burning its way down my throat.

"Don't look at her like it's her fault. This is all on you, asshole," Gio sneers.

The guy stumbles to his feet. "Fuck this," he slurs and pushes his way past the gathered crowd. Gio smiles down at me. "Sorry, little sis, I've got to go take out the trash." He takes his shot and throws it back before following the drunk dude. Oh well, at least he's drunk enough to feel no pain.

The crowd thins as most of them follow my brother, and Stacey quickly jumps into the seat Gio just vacated. "Oh my God. Your brother is so fucking hot." She fans herself, and I screw my nose up. Sometimes Stacey is a bit too much. I would never let her anywhere near my brother. Even though she's my best friend, she drives me nuts with her schemes to become popular. I want my brother to find someone to love him for him, not because of what he can do for them.

"Yeah, well, keep your panties on. He gets plenty of offers and has no need to look at an inexperienced girl like you." The shot has gone to my head, and my internal filter is slipping. I'm also getting a little sick of her constantly drooling over my brother. It makes me think that maybe she's only friends with me because of him. I cringe slightly when her eyes crease with anger, and I quickly pour another shot and slide it toward her. "Here, drink this, then we'll go find something to mix that vodka with."

Shouts from the front of the house register, and Stacey's eyes widen as she's distracted from my comment about my brother. "Should we go make sure everything is okay?" She just wants to learn all the gossip, but I couldn't care less.

"Go if you want, but Gio will take care of things, he always does." I see indecision flit across her face, and I know I've lost her to the drama and Gio as she gets to her feet.

"I'm just going to make sure nothing gets damaged," she says, chewing nervously on her lip.

Rolling my eyes at her bullshit excuse, I just wave her away and watch as she disappears into the crowd. Really, I shouldn't have expected anything less.

I make myself comfortable on the couch and have another shot of the thick black liquid, quietly watching the chaos around me. It's nothing new. Gio has been throwing parties for years. From my vantage point on the couch, I can see quite a lot in our open-plan living area. It's why Gio likes to plant himself here when he has a party. He can keep an eye on everything. There's also a similar spot outside that has a view over the huge backyard. I'm sure the party will gravitate out there as the night wears on and people decide skinny dipping is a good idea.

For the moment, though, there's still a large number of people inside. There's a game of beer pong going on in the kitchen that has people cheering every time someone makes the shot and groaning when they don't. There's a makeshift dance floor that has lots of writhing, grinding bodies on it, and there are people standing around observing much like I'm doing. A flash of red out of the corner of my eye has me groaning in annoyance.

Nikki Steel is the resident mean girl of my year and Miss Popularity. Basically, she's who Stacey wants to be. Personally, I don't see the appeal myself. I mean, don't get me wrong, she's pretty with her long, wavy, brunette hair, but there's this aura of fakeness about her. She always has this calculating glint in her sea green eyes.

She's flanked on either side by the Golding twins. Felicity and Fiona are identical Nordic, blonde, blue-eyed beauties who are part of the mean girl posse. Felicity is a little more standoffish than the other two, more of a silent observer.

They walk up and tower over me. Nikki crosses her arms and raises an eyebrow. "Hey, Tori. Didn't expect to see you here."

I snort in amusement. "Really? Where did you expect me to be?" I ask, not letting her intimidate me.

"Well, I didn't realize you knew Gio."

Seriously? Could this girl get any more self-involved? I'm just about to say exactly that when Gio returns, throwing himself down on the sofa, his arm going behind my back.

"All done. Where were we?"

My eyes drop to his knuckles. One is a little bruised, but he didn't split them. He must have gone easy on the guy. Gio sees where I'm looking, explaining, "Stupid asshole was so drunk he was out after one punch. We left him on the front lawn." He looks up at the girls standing in front of me, blocking us off from the coffee table and our bottle of sambuca. The minute he returned, they all pushed out their boobs and asses in a way that makes me think they look more constipated than sexy. His gaze scans Nikki's body, and she preens for him, causing me to snort once more. She shoots me a look of hatred before simpering.

"I was just asking Tori how she knows you well enough to get an invite to the party."

Gio's mouth drops open comically, and he gapes at me with disbelief. "Is she serious?" he asks incredulously, and I just shrug. He looks back at her and laughs in her face.

Annoyance crosses her features, and she huffs. "Am I missing something?" Neither of the twins have said anything, but Fiona looks just as confused as Nikki. Felicity, however, knows what's going on.

"What's your name, sweetie?" Gio's voice is deceptively seductive.

Nikki flutters her eyelashes, and I see her nipples

pebble in reaction to his purr. "Nikki," she replies breathily.

"Well, Nikki, this is my sister Tori, you stupid bitch. She's the only one here who matters. So fuck off out of our way so we can drink. Go find some other poor sucker to harass. Maybe if you got down on your knees and sucked some dick, you would get the attention you crave."

Oh, snap! Fuck, Gio is in one of *those* kinds of moods today. He can be such an asshole to people.

Nikki reels back like he slapped her in the face, and Fiona's mouth drops open in shock. Felicity doesn't show any reaction, though I see her lips twitch slightly.

"How dare you speak to me that way? Do you know who I am? Do you know who my daddy is?" She stomps her foot and has a tantrum like a toddler. Gio raises an eyebrow at me in question. I'm sure he's probably seen her around school but didn't give enough of a crap to find out.

"Her dad is the mayor," I tell him with a shrug, but Gio doesn't seem impressed at all. Smirking, he ignores the tantrum and shoos her out of the way so we have access to the alcohol again. Nikki has been dismissed.

"You'll pay for this," she growls at me before turning and storming off. Fiona hurries after her, as does Felicity, although she's slower and she throws me a wink over her shoulder as she leaves. Well, that was interesting. I turn back to my brother in annoyance.

"Thanks, asshole. I still have a year in school with her."

He waves me off. "You'll be fine. Stacey's got your back." He pours another round of shots, looking around. "Speaking of, where has the little Klingon gone?" I frown at his insult.

"She went outside to watch the beatdown, but she won't be far now that you're back."

Sure enough, the words have barely left my mouth before she comes racing back toward us, her expression shifting between glee and terror. It's a weird grin that kind of makes her look like Venom—all teeth.

"What did you say to Nikki Steel? She just left the party cursing your name, Tori." She flops down on the other side of Gio, her leg against his. It's a little too close for my liking, but he doesn't seem to care. He's more interested in the bowl of party favors that's in the middle of the table.

My brother always provides a few recreational drugs, such as weed and ecstasy, for his inner circle to use, but none have returned since the altercation, so maybe he told them to leave him alone.

I roll my eyes and sit up to grab my shot. "I didn't do anything, this asshole did, but of course she blames me." The three of us clink our glasses together, and I throw back my—is it my fourth shot? I've lost track, and I'm feeling mellow and relaxed, while Stacey still bounces in excitement.

Gio kisses my head and stands up. "I'm out, T. I'm going to find someone to suck my dick." Eww. I didn't need to know that.

"I'll do it."

Gio and I stare at Stacey in shock. Indecision flashes across her face like she can't believe she said it out loud.

"What the fuck?" I'm pissed now. She's supposed to be here for me, not hitting on my brother. Thankfully he just laughs.

"Would you even know what to do, Stacey?" He pats her on the head and wanders away.

I'm still glaring at her in anger, but she just looks disappointed, and I see calculation in her eyes.

She turns to look at me, and she must be able to read the anger on my face. "Oh, Tori, I'm sorry, the alcohol's gone right to my head. I didn't mean to say that out loud," she apologizes quietly, her cheeks blushing. Yeah, like fuck I believe that.

I stand up and grab the bowl of party favors. I'm not leaving these for just any random person. "Come on, I'm over it all now. Let's go up to my room and smoke a joint."

A smile crosses her face once again, and she grabs hold of the vodka bottle she's been carrying around everywhere. "I'll grab a bottle of juice and a couple of glasses."

"Grab some snacks too," I tell her as we move into the kitchen. I pull open a junk drawer and take out a lighter, and then I open the cupboard below the sink. I know there's an ashtray under here. Dad uses it for his smelly cigars when he and his buddies are playing poker. Grabbing it, I glance at Stacey and see she has everything we need, so I turn and make my way back through the house. Nobody says anything to me, and I'm able to stay mostly invisible. Apart from Nikki and the twins, most of the kids are older, so they leave me and Stacey alone. Plus, they know upsetting me is not worth Gio's wrath.

The noise fades away until we're finally back upstairs in my room. Closing the door, I lock out the rest of the noise and breathe deeply, finally able to relax since we first left the room. I'm really not much of a people person. I prefer my own company, happier reading a book or watching a movie than socializing. I do try, though, for Stacey's sake. She wants it so badly. I think we will probably end up drifting apart this coming year, but for now, I'm going to make the most of it.

Chapter Two

S tacey makes herself at home in my room, throwing the snacks and drink supplies onto my bed before following them down.

"What have you got there?" she asks, gesturing to the favor bowl, and I shrug and drop down onto the bed next to her. Upending it, I take note of the contents.

"Holy shit." Stacey sits upright, her eyes bugging out of her head. "Where does Gio get all of that from?" she questions, pushing a dozen joints to the side and lifting a baggie of pills. Inside are a bunch of multicolored pills all stamped with a butterfly logo. Ecstasy. I guess Stacey has never seen Gio's bowl before. It was probably emptied out by the time we usually joined the party.

I shrug my shoulders in response. "Not sure, he always has something or other to offer." Truthfully, I don't really know where he gets them from, and I choose not to look at it too closely. I didn't think her eyes could get any rounder, but then she holds up a little baggie of white powder.

"What do you think this is?"

I lean back against the many pillows at the head of my bed. "Coke, probably. He doesn't agree with many of the harder drugs. Coke, X, and pot are all okay as far as my brother is concerned. Everything else is just a disaster waiting to happen. He doesn't need friends so hooked on drugs they can't function, nor does he want anyone overdosing in our house. I know what he does get is top quality." Gio's word is law, and if they want to continue to be included in everything he does, then they know to toe the line.

She drops the bag back into the bowl and sets it aside. "It doesn't bother you that he does drugs?" God, Stacey is so oblivious. How she can be my best friend for so many years and not know this shit by now is beyond me. Sometimes it's like she's in her own little world and doesn't pay any attention to anything going on around her. She is a total narcissist, and it's beginning to annoy me a little bit.

I raise an eyebrow at her. "Have you ever seen my brother drunk or high?"

Her brow creases in concentration as she thinks about it. "No, I haven't actually."

"That's because he doesn't indulge in public or with this many people around. Only his inner circle has seen him drunk, but even then, there isn't really anyone he trusts, so he doesn't do it very often."

"So he never drinks or indulges in those?" she asks, pointing to the bowl.

"I didn't say that, I just said you'll never see it—unless you make his inner circle, that is."

"But you have?" she pushes, unable to let it go.

"Well, yeah, of course. He trusts me." I push off the bed and grab the glasses she brought with her. "Let's pour a couple of drinks, and then if you want, we can light one of those joints." Her face lights up, and my distraction does the job. I needed her to stop prying about my brother. It's giving me an uneasy sensation. It's almost like she wants to be friends with me because of him. It's a pity she wasn't there when he dealt with Nikki, it may have changed her mind.

Once we have our drinks, we head out to the two recliners on my balcony. We can hear the music from downstairs, and the pool is now full of people, the party having made its way outside. Stacey eyes the action wistfully like she wants to join them, and if I told her to go, I know she wouldn't hesitate to leave me, but I don't, and she takes a seat next to me instead.

I put the joint between my lips and flick the Zippo lighter, puffing a couple of times before taking a drag of the pungent smoke. I hold it in then blow it out as Stacey looks on, wide-eyed again. Her naivety is really showing tonight, and sometimes I wonder if it's all fake.

"You've done that before," she accuses, and I shrug again.

"Yeah, occasionally Gio and I will sit down together." I take another drag and then pass it to her. She looks a little apprehensive, but that soon gets replaced by determination, and she takes a big drag before a cough explodes out of her lungs. "Take a smaller drag until you get used to it," I suggest once she stops spluttering and coughing.

She rolls her eyes, unhappy with my instruction, but does as I suggest.

The mellow feeling works its way into my limbs as she takes another drag, this time more cautiously. We pass it back and forth until it gets to the end, and I stamp it out in the ashtray, feeling more relaxed than I've felt in a while. We watch as people splash in the pool. One or two girls are now topless as games of chicken take place. Stacey giggles uncontrollably as she observes the action below.

I watch my brother as he sits poolside, surrounded by sycophants. I can't see his eyes, but I know they won't be showing the same joy his smile seems to portray. Party Gio is a persona he cultivates, and in private, he's a very different person. Some of Gio's friends pull off their shirts and jump into the pool, and Stacey leans forward in anticipation for him to join them, but he doesn't. Amusement over her disappointment floods my body, but that quickly turns to guilt. I shouldn't be laughing at her misfortune. I should be helping her find a way to get what she wants, which I probably would if she didn't want my brother.

Stacey watches, her face wreathed with disappointment, as he stands up, pulls the girl who was sitting next to him to her feet, and heads into the pool house, tugging the curtains closed over the glass doors.

"He wasn't wrong, you know?" Her quiet voice has me jumping slightly. I really had been mellowed out and not expecting her to talk. It's not often that I can get quiet around Stacey. I shake myself out of my fog and sit up, determined to pay attention.

"About what?" I ask, a little confused about what she's speaking about.

"Not knowing how to give head." Well, shit, that was not what I was expecting her to say. "I've barely even kissed a boy, but this year, that's going to change." There's a hint of determination in her tone, and my heart sinks. I know she's going to try and drag me into whatever scheme she's planning. "We're seniors now, and it's time to start dating."

I wave a hand at her and lean back again. "Please, all the idiots in our year are the same lame-ass morons they have always been."

"Don't be like that, Tori. Some of them aren't so bad. But to attract their interest, we have to know stuff. We can't be inexperienced. They want girls who know what they are doing."

I can't believe the words that are coming out of her mouth. What kind of medieval bullshit is this? I knew her dad was a misogynistic asshole, but wow. Does she really think that giving a blowjob is a requirement to have a boyfriend? That's really fucking sad. I want someone who is interested in me as a person first rather than me as a cum receptacle.

"And I want to be part of the popular crew. I want to be friends with Nikki and the twins."

Oops, I think I've already fucked that up, but I don't tell her that. "We don't need them, we've got each other," I assure her, but her expression tells me she's not convinced.

She reaches out and grabs my arm. "I know, and we will be best friends forever, but I want more. Please help me with this."

Sighing, the mellow still affecting me, I reluctantly agree. "Okay, what do you need from me?"

"I need experience." What is she talking about? Turning my head, I stare at her in confusion, and then the anger starts to rise.

"So, what, you want me to ask my brother to teach you shit? You want me to pimp him out to you?" There's no way it would ever happen, but I can't believe she has the audacity to ask.

Excitement blooms on her face, and her eyes light up. "Do you think he would?"

I get up and storm back into my room, annoyed as fuck—or annoyed as one can be after smoking a joint. Flopping down on the bed, I watch as she follows me inside. "Fuck no," I snap. Her smile drops, and I instantly feel guilty. Jesus, it's like I have a devil on one shoulder and an angel on the other. I can't commit to a mood one way or the other. "Look, ask me for anything but that, okay? I don't want to see you sad when he says no, and he will say no."

She gives me a shaky smile and climbs onto the bed

next to me. "Well, that wasn't what I was going to ask anyway. Look, you and I both need experience, so what if we give it to each other?"

Say what? I don't even get a chance to ask her what the fuck she's talking about before she leans in and places her lips on mine. I've kissed one or two boys in the past, but they were always wet, sloppy things that left me unwilling to repeat the experience, but Stacey's lips are soft and plump and feel good. She leans back, looking to see if I'm going to stop her, but all the alcohol and smoke are kind of convincing me that this is a good idea. My instincts aren't screaming no either, so that's good enough for me.

She moves closer and swipes her tongue across the seam of my lips, and I open my mouth to let her in. She tastes faintly skunky from the joint, but the sweet taste of juice from her drink quickly covers that as her tongue sweeps into my mouth. Without touching beyond our lips, we lean into the kiss. Her tongue tangles with mine, and a weird feeling starts to tingle in my core. Stacey's kiss is making me feel something that has never happened with another person. A shiver courses down my spine, and my nipples pucker with excitement. Holy fuck, I'm turned on. My mind races with the implications. What does this mean? Am I gay? Is that why I've never really been interested in boys? But then again, I've never really been interested in girls either.

Before I can come to any conclusion, Stacey pulls

away and wipes her mouth, a smile curving her lips. "Was that okay? Do you think guys would like it?"

Dazed by the lust-fueled fog, it takes me a moment to answer, and she must take that to mean I don't think they'll like it, because her smile drops and she grabs my hand. "Will you help me this summer? We only have a week left, and by the end, I want to be a pro at kissing. I won't be a victim of gossip saying that I don't know what I'm doing." Her eyes sparkle with chaotic determination bordering on obsession.

I scrunch up my face at the thought of who would be spreading that kind of gossip and wonder why she would want to be kissing those kinds of people anyway. Once more, she assumes my reaction means I'm going to deny her.

"Please, Tori, please."

Shit, what should I say? I guess it wouldn't hurt to help her out, but what would that mean for our friendship?

"It will be our secret. Nobody needs to know that's how we learned those kinds of things." Her eyes beg me to give in to her, and at this stage, I don't have any good reason to say no.

Climbing off the bed, I put my back to her so she can't see that my nipples are as hard as rocks. I pour us both another drink and hand it to her before I give her an answer. "What's there to practice though? We've kissed, and it seemed pretty good to me, so what else do you need to know, because honestly, I'm not sure what else I can do to help. I don't have the right equipment." I gesture to my nether regions and the lack of a dick.

When I turn back to her, I take a good look. Her coffee brown eyes are glassy and not quite focused, and I realize she's absolutely hammered. She'll have forgotten all about this by morning. Another shiver courses down my spine, and I'm shaken when I realize it's a shiver of disappointment. I really need to examine that when I'm sober, but for now, I'll play along.

"Well, what do guys expect you to know? How to give blowjobs and hand jobs, and it probably wouldn't hurt to not be a virgin," she reasons.

"Whoa, hang on a second. I definitely don't have the right equipment to help you with that." Does she even hear the words coming out of her mouth? As she tosses back the drink I just handed her, I know I've lost her. Her mind is away with the fairies, planning all the things she needs to learn by the end of summer. This makes me a little nervous. Stacey's schemes always end up going haywire, but I hate saying no to her. I'm such a pushover.

Pulling her shoes off her feet, I tuck her into bed, but as I go to leave, she pulls me down again and mumbles, "You're a pretty good kisser, T," and then she plants another kiss on my lips before she rolls over and falls asleep.

Taking my drink, I head back out onto the balcony to watch the rest of my brother's party, keeping an eye on our kingdom while he's off getting his dick wet. One of us always needs to know what's going on to protect our interests, but most of his friends know the deal now, and if they fuck up, they won't be invited back. Pissing off Gio Russo is tantamount to party suicide. If only I was as cool as him, then I could give Stacey exactly what she wants—popularity.

Chapter Three

T he following morning, my head is foggy as I
slowly wake up. I didn't close the curtains over
my patio doors when I came inside after my brother
had rejoined his party, so the light is shining right
through them. Groaning, I roll onto my back and
freeze. Out of the corner of my eye, I see a body lying
next to me. Did someone get into my room last night?
Slowly, I turn to the side, and the mess of honey-
blonde hair has me sighing with relief. Stacey slept in
my bed last night. Usually, she sleeps on the pullout
sofa, but I remember tucking her in while she was
scheming in her head.

Stretching my toes, I climb out of bed, leaving her
to her comatose state as I unlock my door to go see
what condition the house is in. My brother's door is
closed, and I know he's probably got it locked if he's
inside, so I don't even bother looking. None of the
spare bedrooms should be occupied—we lock them—

and people know they are not allowed to be upstairs, but oftentimes someone convinces Gio to open them, so I will check just in case. If there is anyone in them, they get a small reprieve for now.

Once I get downstairs, I survey the remnants of the party. There are a few people asleep on the couches, but it doesn't look like there was any major destruction, although it's nowhere near as clean and organized as it usually is. Sighing, I head into the kitchen to grab some trash bags. I find a couple of giggling girls trying to operate the coffee machine. I clear my throat to get their attention. They whirl around and immediately go into bitch mode, looking me up and down, obviously wondering who the fuck I am. I mean, seriously, I know I'm quiet and not part of the cool group at school. I'm a year behind them, and I prefer my own company to being social, but what the fuck? I'm here every time my brother throws a party. I know these two girls, but they obviously overlooked me, too self-involved to pay attention to anything outside of their own little bubble.

"Who are you?" Bitch One demands.

The second one just looks at me like she's trying to figure out how she knows me. Bitch Two is the one that hooked up with my brother last night in the pool house. "Where did you come from? You weren't asleep in the pool house with us, and you weren't in the living room when we came through before."

I can see her calculating the odds that I came down from upstairs. I don't owe this bitch anything, so I decide to play a game. "Oh, from upstairs." I stretch my arms over my head, my tank top pressing against my ample breasts. "I slept so well."

Their eyes narrow as they think about where and why I might have had an amazing sleep. "Who did you sleep with?" Bitch One demands as the other one eyes me with a calculating glint. She probably thinks she can score brownie points with Gio if she outs me. "You're not supposed to be upstairs. No one is."

I wave them off and move over to the fridge to grab a carton of juice. My mouth is dry from the joint last night. Pulling it out, I move to the cupboard with the glasses. The girls' eyes narrow even further with my familiarity in the kitchen. "Please, we all know the spare rooms are used for hooking up, just like the pool house is. People just wait until Gio's occupied to use them."

That's enough to tip his girl from last night over the edge, and she assumes the worst. "Listen here, you little bitch, Gio is mine, and no two-bit preschooler is going to take my place by his side," she says, looking me up and down. "Are you even old enough to go out to a party?" The girls snicker with amusement, and I roll my eyes.

"Oh, burn. You cut me so deep," I deadpan, clutching my imaginary pearls before turning my back on them. I hear them move, and a hand brushes my hair. With quick reflexes, I turn and grab the hand, twisting the catty bitch's arm until it's bent behind her and she's squealing in pain as she bends over our kitchen counter. She flails her other arm and thrashes her body like a fish on dry land, but I have a good grip, and she can't break free.

"Oh dear, looks like you can suck cock like a Hoover, but you're not really bright," my brother drawls. I look up and see him leaning on the door-frame with his arms crossed, wearing an amused expression on his face.

"Gio!" the bimbo in the arm lock squeals. "Help me with this psycho bitch."

His eyes narrow, and the amused look turns deadly as he steps away from the doorway and stalks across the room. When he gets to us, he grabs the girl's hair and yanks her head, making her look at him. She groans, but I think it's with pleasure, not pain. Ewww.

"How about you don't talk to my sister like that?" he whispers, his tone deadly with intent, and her eyes widen in alarm. "Now get the fuck out of our house before I let her kick your ass a little more."

He nods, and I let go of her arm and step away. The other girl has been watching the entire time, not trying to help her friend at all. Fuck, that's some loyalty for you.

"But, Gio, didn't we have a good time last night?" Bitch Two simpers, cradling her arm carefully. Her hair is messed up, and there's a red mark on her cheek where it was pressed against the counter, but she doesn't let it deter her. I've got to give it to her, she's determined.

"Fuck off. You were mediocre at best. Your head

skills were the best thing about you. You moved around more just then than you did while I was fucking you." He nods to where I held her down.

Her face drops, and she looks like he stabbed her in the heart with a knife.

"Whoop, there it is. Not sure what it says about you, Gio. You always pick the ones who think they can tame you. Now get the fuck out of our house." I wiggle my fingers at them as they both scurry out the back door like rats abandoning a sinking ship. I stick my head out and shout, "Don't even think about doing anything spiteful. We know where you live." They run a little quicker to the pool house to grab their stuff. I don't close the door until I see them leave through the side gate.

When I turn around, Gio has poured us both glasses of juice and he holds his hand up for a high five. "Nice threat." He snorts, and I shrug, slapping his hand.

"What? It works. Luckily, you've cultivated this don't fuck with me persona, and everyone is either scared of you, wants to be you, or wants to do you." I go to the cupboard, pull out a box of cereal, and slide it across the counter, followed by two bowls and spoons. Sitting next to him, I wait for him to finish pouring his and hand it to me before I pour myself a bowl.

"Did you have a good time last night?" Gio asks as he shovels sugary goodness into his mouth. He always likes to check on me after a party. He knows it's not really my scene, but he always tries to make me feel welcome.

I can't help the snort of amusement that comes out of my nose, as well as some milk as I had a mouthful at the time.

"Ewww, gross, Tori." He swipes at the milk that landed on his arm and gets up to get a dish towel, scowling at me.

I get my choking under control as he cleans up my mess. "Sure, don't help me or anything," I grumble as I take a sip of my juice. Standing, I head to the coffee machine. The girls had turned it on but hadn't gotten any further. I'm not sure how since the damn machine is automatic. It grinds the beans, and the water is already in it. Putting my cup underneath the spout, I press the one cup option and let it run, turning back to face Gio with a shrug. "You know it's not my kind of scene, but I think Stacey had a good time and would have preferred to stay down here instead of up in my room. She got drunk and high and passed out."

Gio grunts when I mention Stacey's name. He has never really liked her, but I'm not sure why. It was a miracle he even let her sit next to him on the couch last night. Usually, he does his damnedest to not be anywhere she is. Then again, I don't really like any of his friends either. It will be interesting to see if he makes any new ones when he starts college in a couple of weeks.

"Man, I'm really going to miss you when you move into the dorms," I tell him, feeling a little sad. Dad's spending more and more time traveling for business, so it's going to suck being here alone. I switch out the cups, sticking another one underneath, and press the button for him before grabbing the sugar out of an overhead cabinet.

"Aww, sis, I love you too." He smiles at me, but there's a wicked glint in his eye. "And you won't be alone, you'll have Penelope to keep you company."

The mention of my stepmother's name has me cringing. We can't stand the woman. Our own mother died not long after I was born, and we had an amazing nanny/housekeeper who looked after us for years—or she did until I was thirteen and Dad came home and announced he was getting remarried. He promised us we would always be number one for him, but he was lonely. For his sake, Gio and I tried, but Penelope is a bitch. Luckily we were thirteen and fourteen and already knew how to take care of ourselves, because although she was here when Dad wasn't, she had no interest in cultivating relationships with us. She puts on a good show when Dad's around, but the minute he's gone, we don't see her. She's happy spending his money and lunching with her friends. Cliché Real Housewives stuff. Gio and I confronted him with the truth. His response was, "Things happen for a reason, kids. One day, that reason will become apparent."

What a load of shit. When my seemingly no-nonsense Italian father spouted off that spiritual crap, I asked him if he had a tumor. He just laughed and gave me a kiss, assuring me he was fine.

The less I have to see her, the better, and Gio knows it, the asshole.

"Fuck off," I grumble as Stacey stumbles into the kitchen. Her blonde hair is in disarray, and she's still wearing the outfit from last night.

We both watch as she waves a hand in our general direction before sticking a mug under the machine. Gio quickly finishes his breakfast. I know he's looking to escape as swiftly as possible now that she's here, but I can't help watching her with a newfound appreciation.

Her dress hugs her sexy curves in a way that draws my eyes to her body. The hem sits just below her butt, making her legs look longer and causing me to wonder what they would feel like wrapped around me.

Crap, did I just think that? Am I really having these thoughts about my best friend?

A gasp escapes my mouth, and I run a hand over my face. Fuck, I'm checking her out like Gio checks out a chick he wants to sleep with. Is that kiss from last night enough to trigger a sexual response like this? I've never really felt this way before, neither attracted to either males or females, especially the ones that go to our school. I can appreciate an attractive guy as much as the next girl, but all the kids at school come across as shallow, and I'm not interested enough in anyone to put in any effort to get to know them.

Do I feel this way about Stacey because I know everything there is to know about her? Sure, she and I don't have a lot of the same interests, but I know her better than anyone else except for Gio.

"Tori... Tori, are you okay?" Stacey has spun around, coffee in hand, and she's frowning at me.

I blink once, twice, before responding. "Yeah, I'm good," I assure her, and when a blinding smile crosses her face and my stomach lurches, I know I'm in trouble. I'm attracted to my best friend, and Stacey is completely boy crazy. Last night's drug and alcohol powered kiss was nothing but an experiment, and now I'm going to be left pining over my best friend while she moves on to bigger and better and more male things.

"I'm out," Gio announces, getting up and putting his things in the dishwasher. Stacey's smile dims a little at his announcement, and my stomach lurches again, this time in disappointment. Of course the smile was for him.

"Make sure you clean your party crap up and get all the stragglers up and out of here," I snap, taking my disappointment out on him.

His head tips to the side in question, unsure what to make of my cranky attitude, but he decides to leave it alone, not wanting to stay in the same room as Stacey any longer. "Sure, little sis, don't you worry." He kisses the top of my head and bolts with a quick wave at Stacey. I watch her watch him as he leaves. Her smile drops, and cool calculation slides across her eyes before they return to me. Stacey is starting to make me question her motives with her behavior. Maybe this has been all about Gio from the start. Before I can question her, however, she brightens up again.

"So I woke up a little while ago, and I was thinking about what we talked about last night." She comes around to sit on Gio's vacated stool before grabbing my arm and swinging me to face her, placing her soft hands on my naked thighs just below my sleep shorts. My skin prickles and goosebumps cover them, and I can feel my cheeks flush. I hope she doesn't notice my reaction.

"What about last night?" I'm not sure where she's going with this, but there's no way I want to put my foot in it in case she means something else.

"What did you think of the kiss we had?" she asks straightforwardly, and I feel my eyebrows crinkle into another frown as I try to hide my surprise at the question.

"What about it?"

"Well, was it any good? Do you think a guy would get turned on or off by it?" There's no hesitation or embarrassment in her question, and she obviously can't see my discomfort.

Fuck my life. I thought for sure she would have forgotten about it this morning, that it was the drunken rambling of a girl rejected by my brother, but it seems like there might be more to this.

"Yeah... I mean, I don't have a lot to compare it to, but it was pretty good," I tell her, not wanting to make a big deal out of it in case she doesn't feel the same way. She bounces up and down on the stool.

"Yeah, that's what I thought. It was one of the better ones I've had, so maybe I'm not a bad kisser and it was the guys I've kissed in the past that were bad."

I shrug, not knowing how to respond to that or where she's going with this whole conversation.

"James Walter," she announces with a look of reverence, like she's announcing her soulmate.

I screw up my nose in confusion. "Isn't that Nikki Steel's on-again, off-again boyfriend?" He's also the school quarterback or something. All I know is that girls watch him like a lioness watches a wildebeest calf.

She nods enthusiastically, all signs of her hangover gone. "Yes, but if I can't have Gio Russo, then he's the next boyfriend goal."

"But... Nikki will eat you alive."

"Meh." She brushes me off. "Rumor has it she's stringing him along because she's worried if she puts out, he'll dump her. Gossip also has it that he doesn't care so much, and he secretly wets his wick on the side. I want to be that side girl and be so good for him he'll dump Nikki and announce to everyone that I'm his girlfriend. With James Walter on my arm, I will be the most popular girl in school." I know she's been obsessed with becoming popular, but this is taking it to a whole new level. I can't say I'm surprised, though, as her schemes are often ridiculous and over the top

"Ah, okay. I'm not sure what any of that has to do with me. I mean, I think Gio knows him. I guess I could get him to drop a good word or something."

She waves her hand, dismissing my words. "No,

don't do that. It needs to be a secret, like an illicit affair to make it spicy and exciting. Then when he can't get enough of me, boom! Nikki will be gone, and I will slide into my rightful place. But I need your help. I need to become a sex guru, and you, my friend, are going to be my workout partner."

I'm speechless as I blink at her in confusion. "How the fuck am I going to help you with that?" I finally ask once my brain starts firing again.

She just pats my hand and digs something out of the front of her dress. "With a little creativity and a few of these."

My eyes are drawn to the little baggie she's holding. She must have grabbed some of the ecstasy pills out of the favor bowl from last night, because the pretty little butterfly stamped pills are nestled in the bottom of the plastic bag.

"Please do this for me, Tori, and I'll make sure you ride that popularity wave with me," she begs as she stuffs the bag back into the front of her dress.

Who am I to care about popularity? I really couldn't give a crap. I could be popular with Gio if I wanted it, but I really don't. Stacey knows this, but for the sake of our friendship and to work through a few more of these unexpected feelings, I guess I can give it a go.

"But you're not bisexual, are you?" I ask, and she shrugs.

"I didn't hate what we did last night," she admits,

which reassures me that she's not just using me to get what she wants.

She must see the acceptance in my eyes, because she squeals before jumping up and kissing me on the cheek. "I've got to go, but I'll be back tonight, and we can work on a plan," she promises and, in a whirlwind, disappears before I can respond.

My hand comes up to touch the spot she kissed. An ache in my stomach warns me that I'll probably regret what I just agreed to, but without Stacey, I have no one apart from Gio, and it's not the same. The thought of being friendless is the only thing that is convincing me to go along with her scheme. Well, that and I can't say I'm not curious as to what scheme she's cooking up and what my involvement will be.

Chapter Four

Gio kicked out all the stragglers, and instead of doing the cleaning himself, he hired a crew to come in and take care of it. They did a fabulous job, and the house smells fresh and inviting, not like there was a huge party here last night. I'm waiting for Stacey to return when I decide to give my dad a call. I haven't spoken to him for a couple of days which isn't like him, he always calls to check in on us.

Putting my phone to my ear, I wait to hear his slightly accented voice answer, but instead, it rings and goes to the recording instructing me to leave a message. I hang up without saying anything and frown at my phone. That's unusual, Dad always makes time for us no matter what. Telling myself there's no need to worry just yet, I throw the phone on the coffee table and use the remote to turn on the TV, then I grab my knitting basket that's sitting next to the couch and pull out my latest project. I'm knitting Dad a scarf for winter. He always complains about how cold he gets during meetings or on planes when he travels. He says he must be doing business with penguins. It's a variegated black and gray wool, which is going to look nice against his slightly graying black hair.

I start a new row of stitches and look up at the screen. The picture flicks on to a gruesome scene. It's a news report of a gang-style shooting. I missed most of it, only hearing that authorities are investigating before it goes back to the news anchor. Not wanting to hear any more bad news, I change the channel until I find one of those tattoo shows. I like the ones where all the artists compete against each other to be the best. Perfect. I don't need to pay attention to what's going on and can just appreciate the talent and skills involved. I want to get some tattoos, but Dad says I need to wait. He won't sign off on them while I'm still in school, but once I'm eighteen, I can make my own decisions. He's not anti-tattoo, he has a few of his own, but he thinks that you need to be one hundred percent sure before you make those decisions, and of course they should be meaningful. Each of his has a story, though he doesn't like to talk about some of them. He is very closemouthed about one in particular—a Latin phrase tattooed across his heart—only telling Gio and me that when the time is right, he will tell us its significance.

Gio drops down on the couch next to me, jostling me out of place. "Hey," I complain, but he just ignores me and stays where he is. He rests his head on the armrest and closes his eyes like he's going to take a nap.

"Have you heard from Dad?" I ask him after a moment of silence. The worry I feel is tugging at me.

His eyes open, but he doesn't move. "I spoke to him yesterday. Not for long though, he's got some stuff going on with the business, but he said he still plans to be home when he said he would be."

"Oh, okay. I just tried to call him, and he didn't answer. I was worried, it's not like him."

A funny look crosses his face, and I swear he's hiding something. "Gio, what do you know that I don't?" I growl, and he closes his eyes again.

"Tori, I promised Dad I would let him tell you when he gets back." His eyes open once more, and I flinch. There's a hardness in them that I'd never seen before last summer. "Make sure you enjoy the rest of the summer, because life is about to change, and it's going to be a bitter pill to swallow."

He sounds cold and calculating, and a knot forms in my throat at what he knows and what Dad has to tell me. Something happened to Gio last summer. Dad sent him away for most of it, and when he returned, he was different—not to me, but to everyone else. Something had made him harder, almost dehumanizing him. When I asked him if he was okay, he just told me he was fine. That was when he drifted from the good friends he'd previously had to cultivating all the hangers-on who were basically underlings at his beck and call. I know my brother is no Boy Scout, and I'm pretty sure he's been involved in some shady dealings, but he loves me and his family, and that's all that matters to me. Family first and always is the very creed that Dad has instilled in us from the moment we could comprehend it. The three of us are a team. Sure, Penelope's around, but she's never been a part of Team Russo, and she never will be. She's a pretty ornament for Dad to keep on his arm and not much else.

My mind whirls with everything Gio just told me, and I almost jump out of my skin when the front door bangs open and Stacey comes in carrying a bag over her shoulder, as well as a couple of shopping bags with the logo of a nearby adult shop. Holy crap, what is she up to now?

She comes to a sudden halt when she sees Gio on the couch with me and quickly swings the bags behind her back, but he had his eyes closed and didn't see them.

"Oh, hey, Gio, I didn't expect you to be here," Stacey stammers nervously, and my brother's eyes open slowly.

He turns toward her, his face blank as usual when dealing with her. "Where did you expect me to be? This is my house." There's no warmth in his voice, and Stacey fidgets on the spot, not quite sure how to respond.

Smacking my brother on the leg, I decide to put my best friend out of her misery and get up off the couch, putting down my knitting. "Come on, Stace. Let's leave this grump alone. I don't think he got enough sleep last night. He was too busy banging randos."

He flips me off and closes his eyes again, grabbing a cushion and placing it over his head. It looks like he's settled in for the afternoon.

I lead the way upstairs to my bedroom with Stacey following behind, quiet like a mouse. I'm not sure how she thinks her plan for popularity is going to go if she gets nervous around Gio the minute things get difficult. He's one of the popular people, after all, but I guess he's in a whole category by himself.

By the time we get to my room, she's back to her normal, bubbly, over enthusiastic self. She throws her bags on my bed and turns, grabs both of my hands, and jumps up and down. "I am so excited about this. Thank you so much for helping me."

I must look unsure, because her face drops. "You don't want to help me anymore?" she whispers in a disappointed voice, and guilt stabs my heart.

"It's not that I don't want to help you, Stace, I just don't know how I can." The upset look disappears, and she's smiling again. Deep down, I know she's manipulating me to get her way, which should sting because I'm supposed to be her best friend, but because she's my only one, I'm going to let her get away with it.

"Right, so my thought is that to get James, I'm going to have to wow him with my sexual prowess."

I gag a little internally. It's such a bullshit reason for a guy to like you. They should like what's on the inside as well as the outside, and not for how well you suck their cock. However, I'm pretty sure that has a lot to do with her upbringing, and her chauvinistic father and doormat mother.

"Yes, and that's why I don't know how I can help you. I have no say in who Gio fucks. Trust me, I wish I did, I'm sick of him picking skanks. Anyway, nothing I say to him will convince him to have sex with you." Not that I would do it anyway, but she doesn't need to know that.

"Yeah, yeah, I know. Although he's not picky, he still won't give me a second glance." She sounds bitter and twisted, and the look that flashes across her face is one of anger, but it's only there for a second before she's smiling again. "I'm sure it would be easy enough to lose my virginity to any number of boys, but then there will be rumors flying around about it, and I won't seem so mysterious." She digs around in her bag before pulling out an object. "So that's where you come in." She holds up a strap-on dildo with a huge grin, and I think my brain just about leaks out of my ears.

"What the fuck do you want me to do with that?" I cross my arms, and I'm sure she can hear the disbelief in my voice.

She drops the thing onto her lap and looks at me. "You've never been interested in boys before, and I don't think I've ever seen you on a date," she says with a small frown on her face.

"So? What the fuck does that have to do with anything?"

"Well, aren't you gay?" Now, even she sounds confused.

Oh wow. I sit down on the bed in surprise. "Well, I'm not really sure. I guess I've never thought about it. I mean, ah, yeah. I guess. Maybe."

Fuck, I'm all flustered now that she brought it up. Call me a late bloomer, but she's right, I've never been all that interested in boys, and the few I have kissed were more something that was expected, not something I wanted to do. I mean, sure, there are some women I find attractive, but gay was something I only just started considering. Obviously Stacey had been thinking about it for a while.

"You kissed me last night," she states, and I get defensive.

"No, you kissed me," I correct her"

"Yeah, but you didn't hesitate," she accuses me, and I shrug.

"No, but we'd been smoking and drinking, and you asked me to, so I just went with it. What about you, are you gay?"

"No, I mean the kiss was nice and all, but I really like boys." Now she looks unsure, and we sort of just sit there in awkward silence.

"Well, it's possible to like girls too," I say quietly.

She shrugs, and the lost look disappears. "I don't care, I just know that I want to be good at this stuff before we start school again. Will you help me with this, or should I find someone else? I'm asking you because I trust you to keep it a secret. It would just be between you and me. I won't tell anyone you're into girls until you're ready to tell everyone."

Normally I'm not a weak person, and I have no problems saying no to something that I don't want to do, but Stacey knows just how to manipulate me into doing things her way. I cave every time. I know it's happening subconsciously, I just don't know how to tell her no. It's like she has a superpower—not to mention I'm secretly interested in playing her game.

"Please, Tori, please," she begs, and I hold up my hand.

"We'll start slow. If, at any stage, either one of us wants out, we just have to say so and it will never be mentioned again. I don't want this to ruin our friendship. I still want to be friends at the end of summer, even if it means you go back to school a virgin. You have to promise not to hold it against me."

She squeals and jumps up and down on the bed before throwing herself at me and giving me a big hug. "Awesome! Shall we start now?" she asks, wide-eyed as she pulls away from me.

"Fuck, I need a drink." I run a hand through my long dark hair and stand up. "I'm just going to get us something to drink to ease the nerves a little."

"Oh, don't go, I've got something here," she tells me, pulling a couple of premixed drinks out of another one of her bags. I wonder what else she has in all of them.

"Okay, I'm just going to go check on Gio and see what he's up to this evening." The last thing I want is for my brother to walk in on Stacey and me. That would be fucking awkward. Not to mention I need a bit of space. I need to think without her sexy floral scent convincing me this is a fantastic idea.

My feet sound thunderous on the stairs in the quiet house, but when I get to the lounge room where I had left my brother, he's gone. On the table lies my cell phone. Picking it up, I scroll through my messages. There's still nothing from Dad, but there is one from my brother saying he's gone out for the night and not to expect him back until morning.

I frown at the message. That's been happening more and more often. Last night's party was the first time he had been home for the night in ages. I need to pin him down and grill him about where he's going and what he's doing. I'm worried about him.

I check my phone for missed calls and voice messages as well, hoping Dad returned my call, but there's nothing.

Another pang of worry hits me, a kind of gut feeling that something is wrong and that my life is about to change. I don't know if this is brought on from what I'm about to try with Stacey or some other phantom concern.

I slide the phone into my pocket and head to the game room and Dad's fully stocked bar. Choosing a bottle of whiskey, I quickly pour myself a shot and throw it back before grabbing two fresh glasses and carrying them all upstairs. I know I have some Coke upstairs to mix it with.

When I get back to my room, Stacey has already opened both drinks, so I put the bottle of whiskey down and take the one she offers me. She's also moved most of the bags onto the floor beside the bed, and my TV is on, playing a movie.

She climbs up on my huge bed and pats the covers next to her. "Come on. Let's just relax and not worry about what I asked for now. We've got plenty of time to discuss it before school starts. I just want to watch a movie with my best friend."

A sigh leaves me, and I'm not sure if it's in relief or disappointment, but I gladly climb up on the bed next to her, taking a big sip of my drink. She's propped a bunch of my pillows together, so we lie side by side, our arms brushing as the opening credits begin on the movie.

"Alexa, dim the lights." The room darkens with my command, and we're left with only the light from the TV illuminating the room. The action-packed opening scene has me enthralled, and before I know it, my drink is empty. I feel a little light-headed and like I'm overheating, except we don't have any blankets over us.

"Are you hot?" I ask Stacey, and she looks at me, wide-eyed.

"No. Why don't you take your pants off? It can't be comfortable watching a movie in jeans."

I look at Stacey and realize she's wearing a skirt,

which has risen quite a bit while we've been lying on the bed. "Yeah, okay, good thinking." I jump off the bed, the light-headedness making me sway slightly, and a giggle escapes as I try to pull off my jeans. It's not so easy after a drink. Wow, I must not have eaten enough today if a shot of whiskey and a premixed is affecting me this much.

As I climb back on the bed, Stacey watches me with amusement in her pretty blue eyes.

I blink owlishly at her. "What? What are you laughing at?"

She shakes her head, still smiling, before cupping my cheek and running her thumb across my bottom lip. A small moan leaves my mouth at the feel of her skin on mine. God, what is wrong with me? I lean into her hand before it slowly makes its way down my body.

All thought of the movie vanishes as my focus lasers in on what Stacey is doing and the feel of her hand on my body. A fingertip brushes across the fabric covering my collarbone, and I inhale sharply before it trails down over the curve of my breast until it reaches my nipple. The light touch has my nipples puckering and my core throbbing as a louder moan leaves my lips.

When I tear my eyes away from her finger and look at her face, she's slightly out of focus, but there's still a small smile on her lips. "What's going on, Stacey? What did you do?"

"What I had to," she replies before she leans in and seals her mouth to mine.

Chapter Five

Stacey's tongue slips into my mouth, and my body shudders as her hands roam over my curves. She lies back on the bed, pulling me with her, and brushes my hair from my face as she breaks the kiss. "See, this is what it's like making out with a boy, Tori. It feels good, doesn't it?"

My skin feels tight, like my nerve endings are on fire. Everywhere Stacey touches me feels intense and amazing. I rub my thighs together, trying to ease the sudden ache that's between them. "Did you drug me?" My words sound slurred to my own ears as her mouth moves to my neck and sucks a path downward. My fingers grip the sheets as her head raises and she smirks at me.

"Just an X tablet. I took one too, I thought it might help us relax," she says, her pupils blown in her blue eyes.

"But why? I don't understand?" She rolls her body

on top of mine, and a groan escapes my mouth as she presses her pelvis to mine and grinds slightly. "How is any of this going to help you with boys?"

"Come on, Tori. I've seen the way you look at me, the way you don't have any interest in guys. Don't deny that you lust after me. You want this, I know you do, and what better way for me to get sexual experience? Guys love girl-on-girl action."

I know there's something wrong with her words, but my body isn't cooperating with me. I want to push her off and talk about it some more. It's not that I'm completely opposed to this. She may be right, but taking away my choice and my free will by drugging me is not what friends do.

She rolls off me and sits up, peeling off her top before wriggling out of her skirt, revealing a pretty, pale blue underwear set. She runs her hands across her body.

"When I went home, I watched some girl-on-girl porn, and it was really fucking sexy. The way their bodies moved together..." She trails her fingers over her body as I lick my lips, mesmerized by the motion. "I've always been curious about whether oral sex is all it's cracked up to be. How can it feel any better than just rubbing your clit with your own fingers?"

Her hand dips into her panties, and although I can't see it, I know she's touching herself. I rub my legs together to try and ease the ache between them.

"What do you think? Have you ever wondered?"

My head feels heavy as I shake it back and forth. "Not really," I admit, and she giggles.

"Tori, you're so weird. Do you ever touch yourself? Have you ever had an orgasm before?" She removes her hand from her panties and leans over me, trailing her fingers over my lips.

I can feel and smell her desire all over them, and I can't stop myself from licking my lips. I shudder at the taste. It's a sweet, musky flavor that is strangely addictive.

"Haven't you ever licked your fingers to see what you taste like after you orgasm?" She pushes her two fingers into my mouth, and I suck them, trying to get all of her delicious taste off them. "I like the flavor myself." Stacey's voice is all dreamy as she roughly fucks my mouth with her fingers. "That's it. Oh, you'd make a guy happy, Tori. Your lips are so fucking pretty wrapped around my fingers."

A moan leaves my mouth as she withdraws them, and I chase after her, unable to stop myself. Suddenly, I'm chest to chest with Stacey, and I blink with the abruptness of it all.

"Come on, Tori, you must be burning up. Let's strip that shirt off of you." Stacey peels my top up over my head and quickly flicks my bra open before drawing it down my arms.

There's a smile on her face as she openly admires my breasts. They are large and full, but at the moment, they feel tight, and my nipples ache for something or someone to touch them.

"I've always been so jealous of your breasts." She cups her hands beneath them and pushes them together, running her tongue across the tops. I shudder at the feeling as she tightens her grip, squeezing just this side of painful. "Perfect-sized breasts for a man to fuck with his cock," she growls and squeezes a little tighter, causing me to gasp before she releases them and runs a finger around one of my nipples. "But I guess they'll never get the chance, will they? You being into women and all." She takes my nipple into her mouth and sucks, which shoots a line of fire directly to my pussy, and another loud moan leaves my mouth. "Does it feel good?" she asks as she pulls away, her eyes glazed with what I think is lust.

"Yeah." My head feels foggy, and my tongue feels heavy and slurry as I answer her. How is she so coherent if we both took the same thing?

"Show me?" she demands and reaches behind her back, flicking the clasp of her bra and shimmying the straps down her arms before tossing it away. She sits before me topless. Her breasts are about half the size of mine, but they are round and high and perky. Her nipples are a pretty pink color against the milky white of her skin. She cups them and pinches the tips.

I wrap a hand around her waist and drag her toward me, making her kneel higher so my mouth is in line with her breast. Tentatively sticking out my tongue, I lick around one of her nipples. Her hands thread through my hair and she holds me there. "Oh, that's nice," she mutters as I get bolder and take one into my mouth and suck.

She squirms against me as I lave my tongue around the tight bud, the throbbing in my core making me want to rub against something. I pull back. Her nipple glistens and looks so pretty, so I swap to the other one, wanting to even them up. Her hands slip out of my hair and slide down to my chest, where she tweaks both of my nipples before moving one hand even lower. She slips her hand under the waistband of my panties, her finger fumbling around until she eventually finds my clit. She circles it a couple of times, drawing a gasp from my lips.

"Can you touch me there too?" she asks shyly. I pull away from her nipple and look up at her. Stacey's eyes are heavy with lust, and she's biting her lip. She looks so fucking sexy I can't deny her anything, even though what she's doing doesn't exactly feel the best, like she doesn't quite know what she's doing but is still trying.

I push her backward so she's lying on her back looking up at me. Holding her gaze, I pull her panties down until she's naked before me.

Like me, Stacey is waxed down below. She insisted we get Brazilians last summer, and I liked the result, so I kept up my appointments. It looks like Stacey had too. Stretching out my body next to hers, I roll onto my side, throw my leg over hers, and slide my hand to her naked mound. Sliding past her clit, I dip my fingers between her folds, collecting some of the slick and dragging it back up to her clit before circling it. Her eyes squeeze closed, and a little sigh leaves her mouth. Now I may not have any experience with a partner, but I know how to get myself off, and I use the same technique with her that I've used with myself.

Her thighs clench together, and she fists her hands in the sheets as I continue to play with her clit and suck on one of her nipples. I start to rub my pussy against her thigh in an attempt to relieve the ache within me.

"Oh shit, Tori. That feels so good." Her moans and mewls are sexy as fuck, and before I know it, I've slid down her body and settled between her thighs. Replacing my fingers with the tip of my tongue, I circle her clit before wrapping my lips around the whole thing and sucking.

The groan that leaves Stacey's mouth is low and sexy, and it makes me feel invincible. Her taste on my tongue is exquisite, and I wonder why I have never tried this before. How did I never consider the fact that I might be gay? But now that I've tried this, I don't think there's any going back. I can't get enough of her honey, and I lap it up, plunging my tongue between her folds and thrusting it into her pussy before going back to her clit.

She grabs my hair once more, thrusting against my mouth and covering my face in her cream, and I just about come on the spot.

I slide two fingers into her channel. It's tight and hot, and she tenses, but I keep sucking on her clit, and her body relaxes once more. Sliding them in and out, I scissor them before trying to find that elusive spot on the front wall of her pussy. I must find it, because she shouts out loud.

"Oh my God! Yes, there. Keep going."

Now I'm horny as fuck and need something for myself. I pull away, and she looks up, annoyance flashing across her face.

"What are you doing? I was almost there."

"Well, I was wondering if it feels any good?" I ask, and she nods.

"Yeah, it feels fucking amazing. You're really good at that."

"Will you do it for me?" I ask and she nods slowly.

"Yeah, but can you finish me?"

"I thought we could do it together." I push her shoulders back and kiss her, letting her taste herself on my lips. The kiss is all lips and tongues and teeth, and both of us are panting when I pull away. Climbing on top of her, I slide my body back so my pussy is above her face and quickly go back to work.

She's tentative at first, but it doesn't take her long to get into it. She was right, the feeling is fucking mind-blowing. Before long, I feel my orgasm hovering just out of reach, and I know she is on the cusp as well. Adding another finger, I slam into her cunt, sucking hard on her clit, and I feel her stiffen below me and lose her rhythm as her orgasm explodes through her.

"Fuck, Tori," she gasps as I continue to thrust my fingers in and out of her spasming channel. I don't let her ride it for too long, though, before I'm grinding my own pussy against her face, and she finally presses her fingers inside of me. It's just what I need to send me over the edge, and it's my turn to scream her name.

When I roll off her, we're both panting, and as I wipe my face on the sheets of the bed, I hear her sigh, "Wow."

Lying next to her, I look at the ceiling, trying to get a hold of my mind, but the drug is still rolling through my system. "Yeah, I always thought people were exaggerating when they said oral was amazing. No wonder guys always want blowjobs."

"I wonder if they taste anything like us," she murmurs, and I shrug.

"Who knows? Hopefully, because you tasted pretty good." I close my eyes, relaxed and feeling sated, but Stacey's finger circles my nipple, causing them to snap open again.

"Don't go to sleep, Tori, we're only just getting started."

Chapter Six

My head is pounding and my mind is fuzzy as I struggle to open my eyes. It takes me a couple of tries, and while my eyes are adjusting to the light, I realize my mouth feels like it has cotton shoved in it. Where am I?

I look around, and the familiar view of my bedroom comes into focus. What happened? I try to sit up, but I'm dizzy and disoriented. Taking a deep breath, I close my eyes until the feeling dissipates. Jesus, what did I do last night? It's not like me to get so wasted I can't remember. I don't like being out of control.

The dizziness clears, and I feel like I can focus a little better, so I open my eyes. I push my tangled hair out of my face, and a groan escapes my mouth. Fuck, that hurts. Why is my arm sore? In fact, my whole body aches like the day after doing a new workout routine. I run my hands over my body, trying to figure out what's wrong. Why am I naked? My skin is sensitive to the touch, and it feels tight, but the most noticeable thing that makes a chill wash over my body is my aching pussy. My pulse starts to race, and a sob escapes my mouth before I can stop it. Flashes of memories return to me.

I see Stacey and me sitting on my bed watching a movie, then a flash of our naked bodies, her mouth on mine, mine on her breasts, entangled in the sixty-nine position. Orgasms. Stacey drugged me with ecstasy. More memories become clearer. A blush washes over my cheeks as I remember enjoying what we did. The ecstasy made it easier to admit that I was into it and wanted it.

Struggling, I sit up and look around. My blankets are all pushed off the edge, and I can see a strap-on dildo lying on the floor between my bed and the door. More memories flash through my mind.

Stacey asking me to wear it so she could practice blowjobs and me making her choke on it. Her eyes watering as she moaned around it, gagging. Enjoying the feeling of power as I looked down on her as tears streamed down her face. A shudder runs over my spine. The feeling of dominating her turns me on something fierce, and I rub my legs together. The ache reminds me that more must have happened.

I search my mind, trying to remember. *"Please, Tori. Do this for me, I promise I'll never tell anyone, it will be our secret."* Stacey asked me to take her virginity with the same dildo I choked her on, and I only hesitated for a moment. All those memories come flooding back in.

It started out soft and gentle, since I didn't want to hurt her. I was careful and used plenty of lube on it to help, but Stacey was so wet it slipped in. Then I got to her barrier. I didn't know what to do, but she was begging for it. The little bullet she held against her clit had her squirming and crying for more, so I pulled back and jammed it in. She screamed loudly.

"Fuck, it hurts." More tears ran down her face as I leaned in and kissed her, trying to soothe away the pain, but soon enough, the bullet had her worked up again, and she asked me to move, so I did. And I liked it. The strap-on rubbed against my own clit, causing my core to throb as I thrust it into her repeatedly. Our tits rubbed together, our mouths joining and tongues tangling. I hitched her leg over my hip to get a better angle, and the look on her face as she finally tipped over the edge into orgasm was powerful shit.

Once the pain was gone, she became insatiable, begging me to fuck her again. The second time I had done it doggy style, pulling her hair and slapping her ass as I fucked her hard. Gone was the apprehension. The thrill of the ride, combined with the X in my system, was exhilarating, and there was no stopping my roll. Sweaty and breathing hard, I reveled in my role of dominating her. When I added a finger to her ass, she exploded, screaming in pleasure. I felt so powerful that I orgasmed myself just from the harness banging against my clit and the feeling of being able to do that for her. When I pulled out and removed the dildo, I left her lying there shaking from pleasure while I had gotten a drink and peed. Then, I was feeling on top of the world, but now all I feel is shame.

None of that would explain why my pussy aches though. The strap-on was not double-sided, and I don't remember any other toys. The last thing I recollect is when I returned from the bathroom. Stacey was wearing the dildo and a wicked grin.

Stacey wanted to return the favor, reminding me that not only boys liked experience. I remember us arguing when I told her that's not what I wanted. I'd been happy to do it for her, but I wasn't ready for something like that. I kind of had this old-fashioned idea that I would lose my virginity when I loved someone. Even though what we had done could pretty much count as me losing it, whether we broke my hymen or not, and I wasn't sure what Stacey and I had was love. Somewhere in the back of my mind, I was still aware that Stacey was using me. The last thing I remember was Stacey going to her bag and grabbing something. She returned, leaned in to give me another kiss, and then nothing.

What had she done? Groaning, I roll off my bed and pad to the bathroom needing to pee. Sitting down on the toilet once more emphasizes my aches and pains. Peeing burns, and tears well in my eyes at the discomfort. When I wipe, there's dried blood all over the toilet paper, but I know it's not from my period. I'm not sure how long I sit there staring at it before it all starts to add up in my brain and a feeling of dread settles in my stomach. I bolt off the toilet, lean over the bathroom sink, and vomit. My body heaves as I expel everything that was in my stomach before sliding down the cabinet to the cold floor, a sob leaving my mouth.

Did Stacey rape me?

My body quivers as I rock back and forth, not willing to accept the fact that my best friend, the person I trusted most in the world apart from my dad and brother, took away my choice. Where the fuck is she now? Why would she do this to me?

A knock sounds on my door before the handle rattles. Fuck, Gio!

I run around looking for a shirt to pull over my head. I find that and a pair of panties and crack open the door, not letting him see past my body.

"Yeah?" His eyes widen at my appearance, and he steps back, wrinkling his nose when he gets a whiff of my breath.

"Holy fuck, you look like hell and don't smell any better. What have you been doing? Have you been crying? Are you okay? You've been asleep all day." I can hear the worry in his voice as he scans me up and down and the questions pour out of his mouth.

"Ugh, what time is it?" I ask, ignoring everything else he just said.

"Three-thirty in the afternoon." His frown deepens and turns slightly disapproving.

Fuck, I've lost a whole day.

"Tori?" He sounds exasperated now.

"Uh, yeah, I just drank too much last night."

"Why was the door locked? Is Stacey still here? Are you sure that's all you did?"

"Ah, no, she's not. She must have locked it behind her when she left. Just let me shower and I'll come downstairs," I tell him, trying to sound normal but wanting him to go away.

"Uh, okay." He sounds confused. I've never not let him into my room before, but there's no way he can see it looking like it is. Not only is the strap-on still on the floor, but I also noticed that my sheets have blood-stains on them. "I'll make you a coffee. I thought you wanted to get school supplies today. I wanted to come with you and get a few things for college."

"Shit, I forgot. Yeah, okay, let's do that. Give me half an hour." I shut the door, much to his surprise. Leaning against it, I heave out a sigh and shudder again. I'm not sure how I'm going to make it through shopping without breaking down and telling him everything. If I told him that I think Stacey raped me, he'd kill her—literally. I need proof first before going down that road.

Stepping away from the door, I spy the bowl of party favors from the other night. I grab one of the joints and my phone off the bedside table before heading out onto my balcony and lighting one up. I drag in the skunky smoke before letting it out again. The afternoon sun is hot on my skin and helps warm me up a little.

Opening my message app, I shoot Stacey a text.

Tori: Where are you?

Tori: I need to talk to you.

I take another drag while I wait for her to reply. Her phone is never far from her hand, so it shouldn't take long.

My emotions are all over the place as I take another shaky drag, the pot finally taking effect. I stop shaking, and my body relaxes minutely.

Tori: Stacey, what the fuck? Answer me.

I'm starting to get pissed off now. No matter what I toss around in my mind, I can't come up with any other reason for my condition except that Stacey didn't take my no for an answer, and she somehow knocked me out and raped me with the fucking dildo.

Anger starts to seethe through my body as my hands clench, snapping the joint, and the cherry drops to the floor of the balcony.

Tossing the rest of the joint in the ashtray, I storm back inside. I open my desk drawer and pull out the date rape drug test kit that Gio had given me at the beginning of summer. He said I could never be too careful, and if Stacey and I went to any parties, I should take a strip or two. I had thrown it in my desk and forgotten about it because we never went to any parties apart from Gio's. Pulling out a strip, I head over to the bottle Stacey had given me last night and tip it to the side so I can swipe the strip through the small amount of liquid still left in the bottom. I take a deep breath, knowing that the next few moments could change everything, and pull the strip out. I hold it out and watch as the control line fills in pink. Holding my breath, I wait for the other side to fill in pink as well and tell me what I suspect my friend did is wrong, but nope, that square stays clear, telling me I have a positive result for Rohypnol. I'm not sure how long I stand there staring at the strip. Fucking hell, I thought she slipped us ecstasy, and while I wasn't too upset about that, now I know better. The strip crumbles as I clench my hand into a fist and scream in anger.

How could she do that to me? I did *everything* for her. I followed along with all her stupid schemes, no questions asked, because she was my best friend. I thought I meant as much to her as she meant to me, and now she can't even be bothered to answer me or explain what happened. What was the point? Why would she do something like that? She took away something that I can never get back, and yeah, it might seem stupid in this day and age to believe your virginity is a gift, but call me old-fashioned, because that was how I felt, and she destroyed it for her own selfish needs.

I grit my teeth and straighten my spine as my fury and anger turn cold. Well, Stacey better watch the fuck out. Just because I'm usually quiet and happy to follow along doesn't mean that I'm meek or pathetic. She really fucked with the wrong person, and I'm going to make that bitch pay.

Picking up the dildo, I look around the room. There's a knocked over bottle of lube at the end of the bed mixed with the blankets, so I pick that up also and put both items on the counter in the bathroom. Stripping the bloodstained sheet off my bed, I dump it onto the floor with the blankets. Everything can go in the washer. I take off the shirt I covered myself with when Gio knocked and add it to the pile along with the panties.

Back in the bathroom, I flush the toilet from before and wash the vomit out of the sink. Snapping the lid closed on the lube, I run that under the tap to clean the bottle before pulling the dildo out and washing both it and the harness. I leave them to dry on the counter and turn the faucet on in the shower. While I wait for it to heat up, I think about confronting Stacey and what I'm going to say to her. Through my cold fury, there's still a sliver of doubt, but there's no way we can ever go back to being friends again, even if she says she was doing me a favor. There's no way I'll ever trust her. Maybe I just need to take a deep breath and wait to see what she has to say.

I step into the shower, and it finishes doing what the joint had started. Once I've washed my body and hair and stepped out to dry myself, I feel so much better. Things are also much clearer. I will confront her and hear what she has to say. How I deal with her depends on what she will say, though I can't imagine she has a good reason for doing what she did. Although, in her mind, she might see it that way. Her parents have completely warped the way she looks at the world, hence being in that situation in the first place. But why she would think taking away my choice was the answer, I have no idea. Maybe it's because her parents have made so many decisions for her all her life. Choice is not really a word in their house. Everything we did last night was her attempt to make herself attractive to men. I realize that now in my mostly sober state. In her mind, being good in bed is essential to that, and maybe she felt like I needed those skills too, but I kind of hoped she wanted to explore what we had as well.

I know she wasn't doing it because she wanted our relationship to change. She didn't want to be my girl-friend. She wouldn't have drugged me in the first place if that was the case. No, Stacey selfishly took what she wanted with no fucks left to give about how it might affect anyone else.

Well, Stacey is going to learn that she is not the center of the universe and her actions have conse-quences. She better pray that the price she will pay is not more than she can handle.

Chapter Seven

S hopping with Gio is exhausting. Keeping up the pre-rape Tori act is hard, especially when all I really want to do is burn down the world in my anger. I want to confront her before I say anything to Gio though, mainly because I know Gio's reaction won't be good. If she doesn't wind up dead, she may very well wish she was, and I kind of want to be the one who dishes out the revenge if any is needed.

My emotions are all over the place. Anger and fury are followed by doubt and denial, and then it goes full circle, returning to anger again. I can't concentrate, and I'm sure I don't buy anything I actually need.

At one stage, Gio questions me again. "Seriously, Tori, what the fuck is wrong with you? Are you high? You haven't stopped chewing on your nails the whole time we've been here."

"Just a little. Hair of the dog and all that, right?"

Not wanting to stop and look at him, I keep walking, and he grabs my arm.

"What's gotten into you? I didn't think you liked to indulge like that unless we were at a party. That's not the Tori I know."

I rip my arm away from him. "Like you can talk. You're a much different person from who you were a year ago too. People change," I sneer, hoping to take the focus off me and put it on him. I watch as his eyes shutter and a wall goes up, having the effect I wanted it to.

He shakes his head. "Not overnight they don't."

"You did," I retort, and he sighs deeply before stalking ahead of me. I follow along behind him, relieved he's dropped the subject. But I know Gio, he's like a dog with a bone. He may have dropped it for now, but he will come back to it eventually. I just need to think of what to say to him when he does. Maybe I will have spoken to Stacey by then, but I have a feeling she's ignoring me.

We only have a week until school starts, and I don't want to go back with all this hanging over our heads. Gio is moving into the dorms tomorrow, and I promised him I'd help him move his stuff. Then, it will just be me until Dad and Penelope return.

I need to confront Stacey. If she doesn't call me back, I'll have to go to her house and bang on her door until she fucking answers.

We finish our shopping and return home. Gio is still giving me the silent treatment, and he disappears the moment we get back. I trudge upstairs and place the few things I bought into my school bag, ready for the following Monday. The stress of everything is getting to me, so I pull out the bottle of vodka Stacey left behind and pour myself a big shot. It's all running through my mind over and over again, from the start of the night to when it goes blank, and I remember nothing. I *need* to talk to her. I *need* to know what she did and to hear the truth come out of *her* mouth.

I grab another joint out of the bowl, but the little bag of powder catches my eye. I wonder if coke will stop everything that's running through my mind. I just want to stop thinking about it. My stomach aches from worry, and I've bitten my nails so low they hurt. Shaking my head, I turn my back on the little bag of white powder. I'm stronger than that. I don't need drugs to numb myself to get through this. Gritting my teeth, I look at my cell screen again. Still no response from Stacey. That's it. I can feel my anger flowing through my veins as I clench my fist, trying to control the urge to launch my phone across the room. My head pounds and my body aches from worry and because I've been so tense since I woke up. If she's going to avoid me, then I'm going over to her place. Shoving the phone into the back pocket of my shorts, I hurry downstairs.

"Hey, where are you going?" Gio calls from his room as I go past.

Sighing, I turn around and go back to his open doorway. I had been hoping he wouldn't see me run by. I really don't want to keep lying to him. He's got some boxes on his bed, and I can see he's trying to decide what to take with him and what to leave behind. A pang of sadness whips through me. Fuck, this is it. He is really moving out. I don't know what I'm going to do without him. He must see the sadness in my eyes, because he smiles gently.

"Don't worry, T, it's only for a year. Then you will join me at Suncity College, and we will be together again. If you don't want to live in the dorms, we can get an apartment together."

Gio is going to the college in the next city over, Suncity. It's only a twenty-minute drive from our hometown, but that's twenty minutes more than I would like, especially since I'm used to him being two seconds down the hall.

"I know. I'm just running out for a moment. I need to see Stacey, and she's dodging my calls."

His eyebrows jump in surprise. "Seriously? That's not like her, she's usually hanging around like a bad smell."

"Hey, I know you don't like her, but she's my best friend, or she used to be anyway," I defend automatically.

He seems to latch onto those last muttered words. "Has she done something?" His tone is harsh, and I flinch back.

I think carefully about my answer. I don't want to say anything that will send him off in a Hulk rage. "I'm not sure, to be honest. I want to talk to her before I accuse her of anything."

He turns away and starts muttering. I catch the words "betraying bitch," but I don't question him. He's never liked her, and I don't want his attitude affecting mine.

"I'll be back later," I tell him, but he doesn't respond, so I leave him to finish packing and run downstairs.

Grabbing my keys from the bowl near the door, I head out to the garage. It has space for three cars, and usually, mine has to be parked outside, but with Dad and Penelope away, I can park in his spot. My car beeps as I unlock it and climb in. I've been driving around in Penelope's old car. She had gotten a brand-new one when I turned sixteen and convinced Dad that I should have her old one. She insisted that if he gave me a new car, I wouldn't appreciate it. She smirked at me the entire time when he agreed. I swear I couldn't have hated her more at the time, especially because she insisted that Gio needed a brand-new one when he turned sixteen and had gotten his driver's license. Penelope's opinion of women is similar to Stacey's parents' outlook. In their eyes, we are only second-class citizens to men, and we should be seen but not heard. Most of the time, Dad ignores her, but occasionally when he's distracted by work, he caves to her whims. I want to shake him and tell him to wake up, but Gio says one day Dad will come out of his fog and realize Penelope is a poor substitute for our mom, and then she will be out on her ass.

I wrinkle my nose at the smell inside the car. I have no clue what it is, but from the first moment I got it, it smelled like something died. I've had it detailed three or four times, but still, the smell remains. When I complain, Penelope just points out to Dad how I'm whining over a perfectly good car that drives just fine. I try to cover the stench with as many smelly air freshener trees as I can, but it still lingers.

Backing out of the driveway, I head in the direction of Stacey's house. The town we live in is big enough to have two high schools, but we don't have a college, which is why Gio is going to the one in the closest city. The suburb our house is in is fairly well off, but I have to drive through the upper-class suburb to get to Stacey's place. On the way there, I pass a place everyone around town calls the fortress. It's a huge, dark, ominous mansion surrounded by a wall that has razor wire along the top. Big wooden gates block the entrance, preventing anyone from casually driving in, and there's a manned guard box at the front.

Rumors abound regarding who owns it. Sometimes it's a Hollywood producer who uses it to escape the paparazzi, while others say it's a weird older couple who kidnaps children and then eats them. There's another one that says it's owned by the Mafia. I've never seen the gates open, but as I drive past, they slowly start to move. I don't stop because I don't want to draw attention to myself, but just before I turn the corner, a car pulls out of the gates. Black and nondescript, it has tinted windows very much like my dad's car, but I have to turn the corner before I can see what kind of car it is or who's in it. It would have been fun to tell Gio or Stacey that I saw someone coming from the fortress.

Ten minutes later, I make it to Stacey's house, park in her driveway, and get out. Stacey's family is well off too, but her house is ostentatious and gaudy. There is a lot of Italian marble and gold decor, and it has this air of coldness to it. I try not to come here because I'm fairly certain neither of Stacey's parents like me. Her dad was downright aggressive when I visited in the past, so it's just better if she comes to my place.

When I ring the doorbell, their housekeeper answers. She's a thin woman with a nose like a hooked beak, and her lips are pursed with disapproval. "Hi, Mrs. Smith. Is Stacey here?" The snooty bitch looks down her nose at me over a pair of glasses. *Bitch, please, you're just the help,* I think, but I keep a pleasant smile on my face.

"No, she was invited to go somewhere with a group of friends, and she will be away until the day before school starts." A sly smile crosses her face. "I'm surprised you didn't get invited, Tori." I feel the smile slip from my face. Who the fuck could she have gone somewhere with? She doesn't really have any other friends but me.

"Ah, do you know who the friends were?" I probe, and she grins.

"I believe she said it was Nikki Steel, the mayor's daughter, and a few of her friends." My stomach lurches, and I stumble backward. Without saying goodbye, I hurry to my car. I hear the door close behind me, a faint evil cackle echoing after me.

Getting in my car, I head back home in a daze. What the fuck is Stacey doing with them? I know she had plans to go after Nikki's boyfriend, but I thought she'd wait until school starts. Why would Nikki even invite her? Unless maybe she's trying to get back at me for the way Gio treated her at the party the other night. She knows Stacey's my only friend, and it would certainly be revenge if she managed to put a wedge between the two of us.

My breathing starts to get a little panicky. I need to know what happened last night. I need to know what Stacey did. What if she's there right now telling them everything? My eyes start to sting as tears form.

I have to face the reality of my situation, even if it destroys me. I slowly take a deep breath then let it out as the tears roll down my face.

"My best friend drugged and raped me." The words sound like a shotgun in the silence of my car. My stomach threatens to revolt as I finally admit what happened out loud. There's no going back now that they have been said aloud.

My best friend drugged and raped me and left me to deal with the aftermath all on my own while she lives it up with the popular crowd. But why?

"Fucking why?" I scream, banging my fist against

the steering wheel, the road a blur from the tears that refuse to stop.

My emotions are all over the place. There is sadness and worry, but what comes to the forefront is anger. Now that I've accepted what I've known in the back of my mind, I seethe with fury. I grip the steering wheel, turning my knuckles white as I think about what school's going to be like on Monday if she told everyone. But will she? I mean, she has to implicate herself and admit that she's the one I was having sex with. I'm not sure how that would go over with the popular group. Homophobia is still a very real thing at our school. My hands start to relax a little bit. Stacey wouldn't risk being ostracized. There's no way she's going to tell people about what we did. She's just going to use her newfound skills and seduce James Walter. Then, Nikki Steel will regret inviting her to join their little clique. When that happens and Stacey comes crawling back to me, I have absolutely no plans to forgive her. Eventually, I'll even tell Gio what she did. He will wipe the floor with her. Wouldn't that be the perfect revenge? Wanting to be popular but instead becoming a pariah?

I tear into the driveway and park my car in the garage. Slamming the door behind me, I stride inside, but instead of going up to my room, I head down into the basement. We have a gym set up down here, and I want to make use of the punching bag to get rid of some of my anger, not to mention calming all the thoughts running through my mind.

Since I was very young, Dad put Gio and me in every self-defense class he could find. I am a black belt in several different disciplines, but right now, I just need the mind-numbing repetitive action of smashing my fist against a leather bag. Throwing my keys and cell on the ground near the door, I toe off my shoes and grab some hand wraps out of a cupboard. Quickly wrapping my knuckles, I start to hit the black leather bag hanging from the ceiling. I swing over and over again, trying to rid my mind of everything that happened in the last twenty-four hours.

Twenty-four hours. That's how long it's been since I was betrayed by the one person I thought would be a constant in my life besides Gio, and it is not a small betrayal either. You can't get much lower than drugging and raping someone. I know I should go to the police, but I have no proof. A rape kit isn't going to pick up any DNA evidence from a strap-on dildo. I'm sure there's probably some tearing down there with how sore I am, but who is going to believe me? No, I'm going to deal with this my own way. It might not be today, and it might not even be this week, but one day, Stacey is going to wish she never knew the name Victoria Russo.

Chapter Eight

My body aches again when I wake the next day, but it's from the two hours I spent pounding the sandbag. I had to smoke another joint before bed last night so I could get some rest from all the insidious thoughts running through my mind. I'm now out of weed, and I need to ask Gio for more before he leaves today.

We are moving all his stuff into his dorm room this morning, and then tonight will be his last night at home. He wants to move in and get to know his room-mates, who were assigned by the school, and learn his way around campus before classes start this week.

I run into him on the stairs as I head down for coffee. "Hey, there you are. I was getting worried." He's smiling, but it doesn't quite hide the worry in his eyes. "I didn't see you after you got back from Stacey's yesterday. Did everything go okay?"

I can't stop the sigh that escapes my lips. "No, it didn't, but I'm not ready to talk about it just yet." I see him gearing up to argue, so I put my hand on his arm. "Please, Gio, just let it go for now."

He grits his teeth in annoyance but nods. "Okay, but I won't let this go on forever. I will get it out of you." We've always told each other everything, so I guess it's a shock for me not to tell him this time.

"I'm not sure how you're going to manage that. You won't be here," I say as I push past him and continue to the kitchen. I feel the weight of his stare on my back, but I don't turn to look at him. I'm feeling so fragile that I know it won't take much to push me over the edge.

I make myself a mug of coffee and take a seat at the kitchen counter. I'm not hungry, so I don't bother with a bowl of cereal. I lose track of time, lost in my thoughts, and I'm not sure how much later it is when Gio appears in front of me again with one of his boxes in hand.

"Hey, I'm all packed. You ready to come with me?"

I blink a couple of times, and a wave of guilt swamps me. "Shit, Gio, I'm sorry. I completely spaced."

He shrugs. "No biggie, but still lending a hand to move it all into my dorm would be great."

"Okay, sure, let me just grab my shoes and phone." I climb off the stool, leaving my dirty mug where it is. I'll deal with it when I'm home. "Oh, hey, do you happen to have any more joints lying around? You're not going to be here if I want one, so I'd like to keep a few on hand."

He frowns but nods. "Yeah, in the desk drawer in my room. I left some rolled in there, help yourself."

"Great. Thanks so much." I force a smile on my face and press a kiss to his cheek. "I'll be ready in five minutes."

Leaving him in the kitchen, I run back upstairs, push my feet into my flip-flops, and shove my phone into the back pocket of my shorts. I look at myself in the mirror and grimace at what I see. I have dark circles under my whiskey-colored eyes, and they have a kind of hollow, vacant look which matches how I feel. I guess that's why Gio is so worried. Running my fingers through my black hair, I try to tame the waves as best as I can, but without some product and some extra love, I'm rocking the freshly fucked look, and I don't have the energy or time to fix it. I wish I did, because looking this way when it wasn't deliberate makes me feel icky.

Going to Gio's room, I hesitate in the doorway as I take in how empty it looks. I can't believe he's leaving me for the next year. I know he'll be back on weekends, or I can go and see him, but it's not the same. It almost looks like he's moving out completely. All his books, knick-knacks, and junk he usually has lying around are gone. His bed still has sheets on it because he's coming back to sleep in it tonight, but apart from that, there's nothing.

Sighing, I pull his desk drawer open, looking for

the weed, and I stop suddenly at what I find. There are a bunch of rolled joints, but there's also a big bag of weed and a handgun. When did Gio get a handgun? And why does he have it? I know Dad has taken him to the range and taught him how to shoot, but I thought Dad had them all locked away in a safe that only he knew the combination to. He must have told Gio. A pang of jealousy stabs at me for a moment, but I wave it away. I'm sure if I asked, Dad would teach me and give me the combo too. I bet he probably wanted to, and Penelope convinced him it wasn't something girls did.

Gio shouldn't just leave the gun lying around, especially if he's going to leave it there while he's away. I better remind him to lock it up. Grabbing a handful of the rolled joints, I close the drawer. I'm sure he'll probably take the rest of them with him when he leaves tomorrow. Hopefully he won't notice how many I took. Running back to my room, I place them in a hollowed-out book I have on my bookshelf with the rest of the pills and powder from the other night. I'm not a hundred percent sure, but I have a feeling Penelope goes through my room when I'm not here. It's better to be safe than sorry.

Finally, I run down to the garage. The rumble of Gio's Dodge Hellcat echoes through the space as I climb into the sleek black machine. The smell of leather hits my nose while the seat caresses my body as I put on my seat belt. "God, I love this car." I moan as he eases out of the garage and down the driveway. "Why do you get this, and I get Penelope's leftovers?"

"Because she's a manipulative piece of shit. I can't believe Dad listened to her. He's got to have his reasons, and I'm sure one day he'll tell us, but it's not really fair to you."

Gio drives the car in the direction of the city, and I settle back, trying to look relaxed while I hope he doesn't bring Stacey or my weird mood up during the next twenty minutes. We pass the fortress once more, and there's a guard standing in front of the guard box. He's tall and muscular, and looks just like a guard should look with a shaved head and tight shirt, which does nothing to hide any of his burly form. Intimidation at its finest. Gio lifts a finger to wave as he goes past, and the guard nods back at him.

"Holy shit, did you see that?" I gasp as I shift to watch the guard behind us. As he turns and goes back into the box, I see a gun holstered to his side that had been hidden by his arm.

"Yeah, so what?" Gio doesn't take his eyes off the road, but he sounds amused.

I swing back around. "Well, do you know that guy or were you just being neighborly? I've never seen anyone in front of the fortress before."

"Uh, yeah. He must have heard the car coming and stepped out. I, um, had a flat tire in front of that place once, and he helped me change it."

Gio probably doesn't realize it, but when he lies, he

has a tell. He always tugs on one of his ears when he's not telling the truth, and sure enough, it's happening now, so I know he's lying to me. I'm just not sure why. It makes me a little sad, because we've gone from telling each other everything to both of us blatantly hiding things from one another. I can't imagine what the next year apart is going to do to our relationship. He'll probably replace me with his roommate or someone he meets in his classes, and I will have lost both my best friends.

"Oh, okay." Chewing on my lip, I look out the window as we leave my hometown. There's a stretch of forest between us and the outer suburbs of the city. The college is nestled amongst it on the outskirts, which is why it doesn't take all that long for us to get there. When he pulls into the college entrance, there are cars coming and going and people everywhere.

The scene before me is sensory overload. The first thing I notice is the massive university sign with the school's logo. The entire structure is made from steel and brick, and they have even placed colorful flowers in front to drive home the welcoming feeling. It's definitely an attention grabber. The landscape looks like it's out of a magazine, with perfectly manicured trees and bushes. From what I can see, it's a decent-sized campus based on the number of buildings. What has caught my attention the most, however, is how many people there are. I see students pushing carts full of their belongings, and representatives from the school greeting families as they arrive. There's no other way to describe it than organized chaos.

There are more freshmen than I thought there would be, and they are all doing the same thing as Gio and getting settled in.

The car crawls along as families cross the road in front of us, dragging suitcases and carrying boxes. Gio finds a space just as someone vacates it and quickly pulls in.

"That's my dorm there." He points to a dark brick building about three hundred feet away. I grimace as I remember all the boxes he has stacked on the backseat, and I'm sure the trunk is full too.

"Oh well, I guess it could be worse. It could be hours away." I sigh and open the door, climbing out and popping the seat forward so I can grab the first box. Gio does the same on the other side, and shortly after we're walking the path to his room. People continue to mill about. I see a couple of girls look Gio up and down with appreciation. My brother is going to end up getting so much pussy here. Fuck, I hope his roommate can deal with it. I hope he got someone as outgoing and gregarious as him, and not some studious bookworm who is going to end up pulling his hair out at my brother's antics.

Someone's parent holds the door to the dorm open for us, and I smile my thanks as we slip past. The lobby is filled with a seating area for group gatherings. There's a large screen TV with some people sitting on the sofas in front of it, with a couple more seating areas scattered around.

There's a front desk with a wall of mailboxes to the side, manned by a preppy-looking dude. He's wearing a pink polo shirt with the collar popped and a pair of khaki cargos. His hair is neatly combed, and he shoots us a smile worthy of a toothpaste commercial. I struggle to contain my snort as Gio steps up to it. With his ripped jeans, tight shirt, and tousled hair, he's almost the complete opposite of the guy at the desk. Gio and I set our boxes down, and I groan with relief. I'm not sure what I'm carrying, but it feels like the box is filled with rocks.

"Hi, and welcome to Excelsior Dorm. I'm Greg, and I'm the resident assistant. If you give me your name and dorm number, I'll be able to point you in the right direction." I look around the space again, and sure enough, there's a wall of elevators and nothing else. I'm not sure what kind of people he's dealt with in the past, but if they needed to be shown which way to go, should they really be in college?

"Hey, man. Gio Russo, and I'm in dorm seven-six-nine."

Greg's eyes widen, and he purses his lips. "Oh, on the top floor in one of the executive dorms. Wow, they aren't usually allocated to first years," he remarks, and Gio shrugs.

"I guess I have good connections."

Greg marks off something on a sheet on the desk.

"Okay then, you'll be sharing with two others, and they are both here. Just go to the bank of elevators, hit the seven on the panel, and then swipe this card." He slides a fancy embossed key card over to Gio on top of a packet of information. "This packet has all the maps and details of your meal plan in case you didn't bring the original they sent to you. There's also a pile of pamphlets on the clubs you can join. There's a student services fair being held in the main open space next to the cafeteria today and tomorrow if you want to sign up for anything."

I grab the pile of extracurricular activities and scan the pamphlets. "Oh look, Gio, you could join the Glee Club!" I wave it in front of him, and he snorts and pushes it down. I giggle as I comb through the other options. In front of us, Greg huffs. Oops, maybe he's in the Glee Club.

"Great, thanks," Gio mutters, grabbing the rest of his things and popping them on top of his box before picking it up. I smile at Greg before following his lead, dumping all the pamphlets on my box of rocks and hurrying after Gio who is already halfway to the elevators.

"Wow, bro, thanks for waiting," I grumble as I catch up just as the doors open and a family pours out. The father has his arm around a mother who looks like she's been crying, followed by a boy who looks to be a high school freshman. They are nothing like our family at all.

We step in and the doors slide closed behind us.

"Whoa, luckily we're not that kind of family. It could get messy."

"What kind of family do you mean?" Gio sounds curious as he places his box on the ground, presses the button for the floor, and swipes his card.

"The overemotional, quick to react family."

The elevator starts to move as Gio picks up his box again. "Hmm, you might be surprised," he mutters, and I snort.

"Yeah right, could you imagine Penelope doing that? She might wrinkle her Botox."

His mouth lifts in a grin as he imagines our step-mother showing any kind of emotion.

I lean my box on the rail and roll my shoulders. "What did you pack in this box?" I grumble, and Gio smirks.

"My hand weights."

"God, you're such an ass. You knew exactly what was in here, didn't you?" The doors open as the elevator comes to a stop. We step out into a lavish foyer, and I forget how heavy my box is. "Holy shit, this is like a fancy hotel or something."

Unlike the narrow, beige hall I had expected, this foyer is a wide-open space with another comfy seating area overlooking a large picture window. There are only two doors off this space.

I whistle. "It looks like there are only two rooms up here. Talk about fancy shit. How did you score one of these?"

"Dad pulled a few strings. He apparently has an in

with the dean." Gio looks at the numbers next to the two doors and swipes his card through the one on the right. It clicks quietly, and he pushes the handle down and swings it open with his hip while still managing to hold the box in his hand.

I follow quickly behind him, not wanting the door to shut in my face, leaving me stranded outside. I stumble into Gio's back, because he stopped just beyond the threshold, which means he's blocking me from the door and the view. A rumble of voices on the other side of him tells me why. Damn him for being so tall. I can't see over his shoulder. The voice has a low rumbling growl, which is strangely appealing.

"You must be our third. Hey, I'm Xavier, and that's Tristan."

"Hey, come in and put the box down. Do you have much stuff? We can give you a hand, and you'll be done in no time." Unlike the first voice, this one is more cheerful and welcoming, like he's had a bowl of sugar. I wonder if he looks like the Labrador he sounds like.

"Hey, I'm Giovanni, but my friends call me Gio."

"Are we going to be your friends then?" the rumbly voice asks, and I see Gio stiffen up in front of me.

"Well, I guess that remains to be seen, doesn't it?" Gio blows off the guy's intimidation tactics like it was nothing.

"Cut it out, X. You know it will be better for all of us if we're friends. It makes living together for the next year easier for sure." Tristan scolds his friend with a familiarity that comes from knowing each other for a long time.

"Can you decide if you're going to fuck or fight now? Because this box is getting fucking heavy." I push my brother forward, and when he moves, the two guys aren't quick enough to hide their surprise.

Chapter Nine

"Well, I vote for fuck if you're offering," the cheerful voice comments. I carry my box over to a nearby coffee table and lower it gently before groaning and straightening up. Stretching backwards to ease the ache in my back, I finally get a look at Gio's new roommates.

I look at the one who just said that. Let me tell you, Lab boy looks nothing like a Labrador, and he looks nothing like a boy. He's as tall as Gio is and filled out enough for me to know that he works out. He has tousled black hair and blue eyes that sparkle with amusement. His smile is white enough to rival Greg's downstairs, but his holds a hint of mischief as opposed to Greg's insincerity. He's wearing ripped jeans and a black shirt, but his feet are bare. I'm not sure why that takes me by surprise, but there's something comfortable about it.

I turn my attention to the other roommate, Mr. Rumbly. Now he looks exactly like he sounds. Similar in build to Tristan, Xavier is also wearing jeans and a T-shirt, but his arms are covered in tattoos, and he has piercings through his eyebrow and lip. He has dark brown hair and icy blue eyes, and he looks like he hasn't shaved for a few days, but then he may leave it like that deliberately.

"Who's your friend, Gio?" he asks with an arched eyebrow. I roll my eyes at the obvious cockiness that oozes out of these men. They project man whore status like the boys at my school and my brother. I had no reason to be worried, though maybe the elevator tech should oil the cables because there's going to be a revolving door of women through this apartment.

"This is my sister, Tori," Gio answers, introducing us, and I give them an awkward wave.

I can still feel their eyes on me, and it's uncomfortable as fuck, but I refuse to show them that's how I feel.

Gio clears his throat, and the guys stop their perusal of me. "Can you show me my room so we can grab the rest of my shit?" He sounds amused.

"Yeah, it's just this way." Xavier and Tristan both show Gio the way, and now that my attention isn't on both of them, I take a look around the room. It's a living area with a large couch in front of an extra-large TV, and behind it is a kitchen area with full amenities. There's an island counter separating both areas with four stools at it. Everything looks fancy, and nothing like I thought a college dorm would look like. There's a big picture window too, but I can't see what the view is like from where I'm standing. I bet it's like the lord of the manor overseeing his serfs from the tower high above them. Just what my brother needs, to be put on another pedestal.

I go to pick up my heavy box, but it's not there. How did I miss one of the guys grabbing that? I head in the direction they went, curious as to what the rest of the dorm looks like. There's a corridor with three doors leading off it—two on one side and one on the other. The voices are coming out of the single one.

"You have the one with the single en suite bathroom, and Tristan and I share on the other side," I hear Xavier tell Gio.

"Yup, we've shared before, so it was a no-brainer to share again," Tristan adds before going on. "So, Gio, is your sister single?"

Gio snorts. "Don't even bother, man. Tori will chew you up and spit you out. I'm pretty sure she plays for the same team, but I've never actually asked her, and she's never confirmed it. She's never had a boyfriend and shows no interest in having one." Fuck, my brother can be a real asshole, but it's not usually aimed in my direction—though maybe he doesn't realize what he just did.

I step into the doorway and cross my arms. "That's because with your constant revolving door of skanks, there's no room for me to have one of my own," I drawl, even though I'm shaken on the inside. Gio pretty much echoed what Stacey said, but I also have a better idea of how I feel now. Even though what she did to me was horrific, and I'm still avoiding dealing with it, it did open my eyes to my sexuality. While I still find the men in front of me attractive, smoking hot in fact, I'm not sure if I want them sexually. Actually, I'm not sure if I'll want anyone sexually for a while. Stacey took that away from me.

"But yes, Gio is right. I recently found myself in a situation where I discovered I like to eat pussy. Sorry about that. Shall we get the rest of his shit and then order a pizza or something?"

Fuck, it's all I can do not to laugh when all three of their mouths drop open at my statement. Turning after my epic mic drop, I head toward the front door. Before I can get to it, a hand grabs me. Instinct has me reacting unconsciously, and before I know it, Tristan is flipping over my shoulder, and a loud thump echoes through the room as he lands flat on his back on the floor.

"Holy fuck," he whispers, staring up at me with a look of awe. "Please marry me. It just so happens I like to eat pussy too, so we already have so much in common. I mean, I'm equal opportunity about what I put my mouth on, and dick is on my approved list too, but that doesn't matter."

"Get up, you idiot," Xavier growls as he holds his hand out to his friend.

"What? I've never heard you complain about it. In fact, it's usually, 'Ahh, yes, Tris, that's it,' and more," Tristan teases, and my eyes just about pop out of my head. Oh, so that's what they meant about sharing. They are lovers. Well, I wouldn't have called that. I mean, I know you can't tell by appearances, but I would have pegged Xavier as one hundred percent hetero just from the little interaction we've had.

"Come on, let's get the rest of Gio's things so he can get settled in. Are you staying here tonight, man?" Xavier ignores his friend, and Gio shakes his head.

"No, I thought I'd take Tori out to dinner and have one more night at home."

"I don't want to go out. Can we just stay in?" I ask my brother quickly. I'm still not sure if Stacey has told anyone anything, and I don't want to risk running into anyone. Gio lifts one eyebrow but doesn't argue. He knows I'm more of a homebody than a party animal anyway.

"Sure, why not? Pizza and a swim or the hot tub sounds like a perfect end to the day after moving all my stuff."

"Oh, cool, are you guys from here?" Tristan asks as we head out of the dorm room and down to the car.

"Nope, we're from Banebridge, which is about twenty minutes from here," Gio answers as the elevator glides back down to the ground floor.

"Yeah, we know it. Our guardian just moved there over the summer." Xavier's voice is cold and shows no affection when talking about his guardian.

"Oh really? I'm surprised I haven't seen you around town. Where did you move from?" Gio inquires, and I know he's surprised. He has a network of people who keep him informed about shit, and it seems like they missed a new family moving to town.

Xavier names the same suburb that Stacey lives in. Well, let's just be grateful that Stacey hadn't set eyes on them before now.

"Two of our adopted siblings are still at home and will be attending Banebridge Private," Tristan adds as we get to the car. "Whoa, nice car." He runs his hands over the hood and starts spouting statistics which mean nothing to me.

"Tori goes to that school. You'll have to tell them to keep an eye out for her. I'm sure she wouldn't mind showing them around." Gio pops the trunk but doesn't miss the scowl I give him. "Don't be like that. It will be good for you to make friends other than Stacey."

"I have other friends," I snap at him, grabbing another box, and he grunts as I deliberately elbow him on the way.

"Don't be a bitch. You've got your panties in a wad about something, and I just assumed it's so bad that you will need to broaden your friend circle."

I look to the side and spot Xavier and Tristan not even bothering to hide their interest in our conversation. I sigh. "Yeah, you're probably right. I'll keep an eye out for new people on the first day, okay?" I tell them all, and Tristan beams while Xavier nods his thanks. I don't bother to ask what they look like. It's not often we get new students, so they'll stand out like a sore thumb.

"Hey, why don't you come back with us tonight, and have a swim and some pizza and a few drinks? You can crash at our place if you don't want to go back to yours," Gio offers, and I gape at my brother.

"Who the fuck are you and what have you done with my asshole brother?"

He beams at me despite my sarcasm. "What, Tori? If you can make an effort, so can I. It might be nice to have some new friends as well." My gaze moves to the two in question, who look like they are trying hard not to look like they are listening. I somehow doubt these two are going to be as easy to manipulate as his high school buddies, but maybe that's exactly what he needs —someone to stand up to him and not take his shit. I have a feeling these two are up to the challenge.

"Yeah, I won't say no to pizza and a swim." Tristan takes the box from my hands and winks before heading back to the dorm. Rolling my eyes, I grab another box out of the trunk and hurry after him, leaving Gio and Xavier to grab a couple more. With their help, we should only need to do one, maybe two more trips.

On the last run, Gio asks me to stay back and start unpacking his clothes, and I happily agree. It's not like I haven't folded his laundry before. Heaven forbid Penelope do it, and sometimes it needs to be done on the days the cleaners haven't been by. When they get back, I've shoved all his clothes into drawers and hung shit up in the closet, and I'm sitting on their comfy as hell couch with the extracurricular pamphlets in my hands.

"Hey, Gio, they have a Krav Maga Club. You should join. You need to stay fit, you don't want to get the freshman fifteen," I tease as they join me.

"I'm sure I'll get plenty of cardio." He winks, and I screw up my nose.

"Gross. I hope you two are prepared for the parade of skanks about to come through your dorm." I wave my finger around the room, and the guys chuckle.

"It doesn't bother us," Xavier assures me with the first smile I've seen on his face. "Just because we're in a committed relationship doesn't mean everyone has to be."

Oh wow, I was not expecting that.

"All those poor skanks who are going to be hoping for the dorm hat trick are going to be so disappointed."

"What do you mean?" Tristan looks confused, and I roll my eyes.

"Dude, you're not blind, you're both hot as fuck. You've got to know that women are going to want to fuck you."

"I knew you were interested!" he crows, and I laugh.

"Just because I can appreciate how you look doesn't mean I'm interested in banging you," I point out, and he pouts. "Anyway, I thought Xavier said you were in a committed relationship."

"Oh, we very much are, but that doesn't mean we

don't like to invite an occasional person to play with us," Xavier answers for him, and when I look at him, he's watching me with the same appreciation as Tristan did, and I feel funny.

Is it attraction? It kind of feels like when I first realized I was attracted to Stacey. I'm still trying to process it when Xavier stands up.

"Would it be alright if we invited our guardian's niece? She's a freshman in the female dorms and doesn't know anyone. She's kind of shy, and it would be nice for her to have another friendly face on campus."

"Sure, no problem." Gio quickly gives in to his new friends. "Look, Tori, another potential friend."

I flip him off. Holy shit, he really is trying.

I wipe a pretend tear from my eye, grabbing hold of the distraction with both hands. I can think about my reaction to these guys later. "Oh, my little boy is growing up and making friends. I'm so proud of him." The guys chuckle as Gio flips me off.

"Come on, we said we'd meet her at the fair. I told her to bring a swimsuit." Tristan shoves his phone back into his pocket after sending his message before grabbing the pamphlets from my hand and shuffling through them. "Oh look, Gio, Glee Club. That could be fun, right?" He waggles his eyebrows, and Gio's mouth drops open as he looks between the two of us.

"Did you put him up to that?" he asks, and I shake my head as he grimaces.

"It's kind of scary that you two think alike. I

thought I was getting away from the sarcasm and cutting remarks, yet I may have just swapped one devil for another."

Tristan holds out his fist to me, and I bump it with mine. "So you will now be surrounded by super amazing times two," Tristan tells him, and Gio rolls his eyes.

Gio and Xavier are at the door before either of us can get up.

"Oh, I see how it is. Got a new bro now." Tristan stands up, offering me a hand before waving at Gio and Xavier. "No, it's cool. I have a new friend too." He puts an arm around my shoulders and escorts me after the others. He plays with my hair, brushing my ear with his finger, and a shudder flows down my spine that I can't hide. When my eyes meet his, he's smirking, but he wisely doesn't mention it.

"Oh, this is going to be so much fun." He laughs as the dorm door closes behind us, and I'm not sure if he means rooming with Gio or messing with me.

The extracurricular fair is filled with activity booths with many students milling about. The guys get a lot of looks, from both males and females, and then people look at me, and I can practically see them wondering why I'm with them. Gio joins the

Krav Maga Club, but Xavier also tells him about the gym that's available to students. Apparently, both he and Tristan are on the football team and use the football players' gym, which is exclusive for sports teams' use, but I zone out when they talk sports shit. I'm just not that into it.

We haven't been here all that long when a pretty little pixie of a girl runs up to Tristan and Xavier and throws her arms around them.

"Casey, is everything okay?" Xavier holds the girl at arm's length, and she nods even though her bottom lip wobbles and tears well in her eyes. Oh God, now I just want to wrap her in my arms and make everything all better.

"Yes, I'm okay, it's just a bit much. There are all these new people, and I can already see the girls looking at me judgmentally." She's shorter than my five-five frame, and she has pretty blonde ringlets that frame her chin with a cute pixie nose and pointy chin. She's slight, like a fairy, and she's wearing a flowy tiered skirt, a shirt that says "Orcward" on it with the picture of an orca, and flip-flops with bells. She's like the living embodiment of Tinkerbell. I examine how I feel about her, and unlike Stacey, there's no sexual attraction, only a need to coddle her. I'm now wondering if the Stacey thing was completely drug induced.

"Why isn't she staying in your dorm if it's coed?" I ask at the same time Gio offers, "She can have my room and I'll sleep on the couch."

I turn to look at my brother, and he looks like he's

been hit over the head by a two-by-four, complete with little bluebirds flying around his head. My brother appears completely smitten by the pretty little pixie.

"Gio, Tori, this is our adopted cousin, Casey. Casey, this is our new roommate, Gio, and his sister, Tori." Xavier does the introductions, keeping a wary side-eye on my brother. Casey turns her attention to us, but I might as well not exist. A matching enamored expression crosses her face as she locks eyes with my brother, and it's like something from a movie. I can practically hear a romantic instrumental soundtrack playing as they fall instantly in love with each other. I just wave and say, "Hi," to which she waves back, her eyes not leaving Gio's.

She holds out her hand, and he cups it like it's the most precious thing on earth. "It's a pleasure to meet you, Gio."

"The pleasure is all mine," my smitten brother rumbles back.

"Okay, Romeo and Juliet, knock it off," Tristan grumbles and steps between them, tucking Casey under his arm like he did to me earlier. "Let's keep it PG."

Gio is still staring, so I decide to take control. "How about I message you our address just in case you guys get lost following us back? We don't have room for all of us in the Hellcat, so one of you will have to drive."

Xavier hands me his phone, and I input my

number and then send myself a message so I can text him our address.

"Great, so we'll meet you there, yes?"

They quickly agree, and I grab my brother by the arm, dragging him back to his car.

Chapter Ten

"What in the ever-loving fuck was that?" I ask him when we get in.

He sighs and turns to look at me, his eyes practically filled with cartoon hearts. "I think I'm in love," he whispers reverently. "Dad always told me it would happen. It's just like him and mom. Love at first sight. I didn't believe him, but it's true."

"Yeah, yeah, we'll see. But let me tell you, you better not fuck up, because she's got two big cousins who don't look like they would have any trouble kicking your ass." He doesn't respond and still has this dreamy look on his face, so I smack him on the back of the head to bring his ass back to reality. That works.

"Hey, what the fuck?" He scowls at me, and I wave my hand in the direction of the steering wheel.

"Can we go already? They'll beat us there."

He raises an eyebrow. "It's like that, is it?" he teases, and I shake my head.

"Don't be an ass. Tristan is fun, and he's keeping my mind off my shit at the moment."

"Are you ready to talk about it?" I shake my head and he sighs. "Well, maybe it's a good thing that Xavier and Tristan's siblings are going to your school. It's time to expand your friend network."

I avoid acknowledging what he's saying by latching on to the interesting tidbit in that sentence. "Yeah, what's with that? It was a little strange how they referred to them as their adopted siblings, not just siblings, and instead of using the word parent, they said guardian."

He frowns. "I did catch that, but I didn't want to question it. We've only just met them, and I have to live with them for the next year."

"Well, as soon as you find out, I need to know. I don't want to put my foot in it with their siblings."

"Don't worry, I'll find out the tea," he teases, and I harrumph and stare out the window.

"Oh, and you left your handgun in the drawer with your drugs. You might want to lock that up before our guests get there." I feel Gio's gaze on me, but I don't shift my eyes away from the window. "I'll make up a couple of the guest rooms for them. I'm assuming Tristan and Xavier will share one, but make sure Casey doesn't end up sharing one with you. She's not one of your skanks," I warn him, and he grunts.

"Of course not. I'm going to marry that girl. I wouldn't be so disrespectful."

Well, okay then.

"I need to find out their last name so I can do some research on them. It's unusual that they moved to town and I haven't heard about it. If they are in the same suburb as Stacey, they must be well off, and I'm surprised Dad hasn't heard anything either."

"Why would Dad know?" I ask, turning to look at him, my curiosity getting the better of me.

"Dad likes to keep a finger on all the comings and goings in town. It has to do with his businesses." I try to think about why Dad would need to know because of his businesses, but to my shock, I realize I don't actually know what Dad does. I mean, I know he's a businessman, but I don't know what businesses he owns.

"Gio, what does Dad do? It's only just occurred to me that I don't have a clue what businesses he runs. I'm such a bad fucking daughter. I'm so self-absorbed." Gio chuckles as the guilt sinks deeper into my soul. "Don't laugh, you asshole," I snap at him, and he reaches over and pats my leg.

"Don't stress, Tori. I'm pretty sure that was deliberate on Dad's part. He could have talked about it more, but when we were babies, he decided he wanted to keep us separated from it for as long as possible."

"But why?" I ask, and he shrugs.

"He runs clubs, hotels, and casinos, so it wasn't really anything we could be involved in when we were younger anyway." He makes it sound like it's past tense.

"Have you been to any of Dad's clubs or casinos?"

I ask, the feeling of guilt giving way to curiosity and a small hint of jealousy.

"He owns them all over the state. There's a club here in town, but there are two clubs in Ashton as well as the casino. Everything else is farther away. That's why he is always gone."

"So why would he like to keep an eye on the comings and goings in town if his businesses are statewide?" I'm more confused now than ever.

"Because he likes to know who the high rollers are. People living in that suburb have a little more cash to throw around than in others. He likes to send personal invites to come play at his tables or drink at his clubs." He looks over at me and smiles. "I'm pretty sure Dad wants to tell you more when he gets back. You're the same age I was when he introduced me to the family business. Just be patient, but you better prepare yourself. You may never look at life the same way again," he warns me, and I turn forward to look out the window.

"Don't worry about me. My view of life recently lost its rose-colored lenses. I'm seeing everything in black and white now."

We make it to the house before the others. I wonder if they stopped at their home on the way through. Maybe we should have told them to bring their other siblings as well, the ones who are going to my school. I wonder if they'll be seniors like me or if they are younger.

I change into my swimsuit—it's nothing fancy, since I don't feel overly confident with my body at the moment—and head downstairs to Dad's bar. I've been sober long enough today. Now that I'm no longer busy, all my worries come flooding back in and start scraping away at the raw nerves inside my brain. Where did Stacey go? Is she telling Nikki and her clique what she did to me? Or is she hiding it?

My teeth grind together at the thought of her telling them. I'm sure she will avoid sharing the truth and make it look like I'm the bad person in all of it. It's probably time I told Gio what she did, but I don't want to ruin his first week at college. Maybe I'll tell him at the end of next week. Then, he can help me plan my revenge.

With my mind focused on plotting revenge, I grab a glass and fill it with ice from the little machine Dad has on the bar. Turning around, I scan the shelves of liquor, trying to decide what I feel like drinking. The bottle of Patrón catches my eye, and I pull that one down, followed by a bottle of Gray Goose. Putting both on the counter, I pick up a shot glass and slosh some of the tequila in it before pouring the vodka into my glass with ice. I'm sure we'll have some kind of mixer in the kitchen. Throwing back the shot of tequila, I screw up my face at the very distinctive taste before swallowing it down. I wipe my mouth with the back of my hand before picking up my glass with the vodka and heading into the kitchen. I know relying on drugs and alcohol to get by is not a permanent solution, but it works for now.

Placing the shot glass in the sink, I open the fridge and peruse the contents. An unopened carton of pineapple juice catches my eye, and I grab it to pour into my glass. I hear muffled voices in the backyard, I guess the others must have arrived while I was getting changed. I'm sure Gio took them to the pool and lavished Casey with his attention. I cross my fingers, hoping he doesn't get his assed kicked by her cousins.

The sliding glass door opens as I take a sip of my pineapple and vodka, and in walks a half naked Tristan. I'm lucky I already swallowed, otherwise I just may have choked on it. He changed out of his jeans and shirt, and is now only in a pair of swim trunks. His sleekly muscular chest is on full display, but what draws my eye is the tattoo of a rose over his left pec. It looks like it's sitting in a bed of thorns, and underneath it is a quote. I step closer to him so I can read it. *Only pick flowers that have survived the same storms. They will never judge your broken thorns.* I run a finger across the rose, which looks like it's glistening with dew. His chest hitches slightly, and I recoil backward.

"Fuck, I'm sorry." Shit, I was so entranced by the words etched into his skin I practically felt him up and hadn't even noticed. I whirl around, head back to get my drink, and gulp down a large amount. I'm too embarrassed to face him, but I'm not rude. "Ah, did

Gio get you all drinks?" I ask, but the heat at my back has me stiffening on the spot. Tristan spins me to face him and lifts my chin so that I'm looking him in the eye. His icy blue gaze is sparkling with amusement.

"No, not yet. Let me try what you're drinking." With that, he leans down and covers my lips with his. His tongue delves inside my mouth, and before I can react, he pulls away and looks thoughtful. "Mmm, yum, something with pineapple juice. You know what they say about pineapple juice. I think we should all have one." He winks at me, and I just blink, still blown away by the fact that he tasted me. My hand drifts up to my lips, and I press my fingers against them. That wasn't horrible.

"Tori? Are you okay?" He loses his mischievous grin and looks worried. "I'm sorry. I shouldn't have done that. Xavier says I'm going to get into trouble one day. I'll behave myself from now on, I promise." It's the most serious I've seen him since we met.

Shaking off my shock, I think of a quick comeback to get myself back on even footing with him. I don't want to seem vulnerable to someone I just met. It's too soon for him to see behind the curtain to the truth. I shove the carton of pineapple juice at him. "Here, take this, and I'll grab the vodka, glasses, and ice. I'm sure Xavier will thank me later."

He grabs it, startled by my abrupt action, and it takes his brain a moment to compute what I said because the naughty grin comes back and he winks. "Or maybe it will be me thanking you."

Shaking my head, I go back into the bar. Tristan doesn't walk outside with the juice though, following me instead. When we go through the lounge area to get to the bar, he looks around appreciatively. "This is really nice, Tori. Your mom has great taste."

I stumble and recover quickly, but he doesn't miss it.

"Fuck, did I put my foot in my mouth again?" He groans, and I can't help the snort that escapes me.

"Yup, but it's okay. My mom passed away not long after I was born."

"So, what, it's just you, Gio, and your father?" he probes.

Usually I would be annoyed, but he's got that whole goofy Labrador thing going for him at the moment, so I answer. "Nope, there's Penelope too. She's our stepmom." It's only then that it occurs to me how dangerous Tristan really is. He has this way of worming his way under your skin, and you find yourself opening up when you never have before. I'm going to have to be careful around him, but maybe now I can try to worm some personal info out of him in return.

"What about you? Xavier mentioned something about your guardian. Is that your parent?" I step behind the bar, and in the mirror that sits behind the bottles, I can see Tristan. The change in his expression is nothing short of astounding. Gone is the easy-going flirt, and in his place is something harder and slightly frightening, which reminds me a little of how Gio is sometimes.

By the time I whirl around, that look has been replaced by his affable, mischievous grin. "Wow, Tori, your dad really has a great collection of whiskey," he comments, changing the subject, and between that and the look, I decide to let things go. Maybe he'll feel more comfortable opening up to Gio when they get to know each other a little.

I empty the ice machine into an ice bucket. It will fill back up automatically, and then I'll grab more when we need it. I pass the bucket to Tristan to carry with his juice while I grab four more glasses and pick up the bottle of vodka. "Come on, let's go for a swim."

His body relaxes minutely, but I still see the change in him, and I know I've made the right choice.

Outside, the others are already in the pool, and Gio has connected his phone to the Bluetooth speaker system.

"Woo-hoo, Tori, good thinking. I need a drink." Gio swims over to the edge but wrinkles his nose when he sees the vodka. "Vodka? Really? Why not whiskey?"

I flip him off. "Because I'm picking and I felt like vodka and juice. I'm sure Casey will appreciate vodka and juice more than the whiskey." Gio spins to look at her, raising an eyebrow in question, and she smiles shyly and nods.

"I really like vodka and juice."

"Let me get you one." Gio lifts himself out of the pool, and I watch as Casey tries to hide her interest but doesn't succeed in fooling anyone.

Turning away so she doesn't see my smile, I place

everything down on the outdoor table as Tristan does the same. Pretty soon, we all have a drink in hand. The other four are busy chatting about college courses, so I head inside, leaving them to it. I don't want any of them to see how jealous I am that they are all getting along so well, and that they will be their own little tribe and I will be all on my own. I call in an order for pizza and then head upstairs to raid my stash. The alcohol just isn't cutting it, and I need something else to get me out of my head.

My room is still suffering from the aftermath of what happened, except for the bloody sheets which I put in the washer. Luckily Gio has been too busy to want to come into my room, otherwise he'd find the test strip next to the bottle and the lube and strap-on in my bathroom. There would be no chance of explaining away any of that without having to tell him the truth. Grabbing a joint, I sit out on my balcony in view of the pool party, albeit a much smaller one than the last time. I light it and take a deep drag, holding it until it becomes too much before blowing it out. The pungent smell of weed fills my senses, as does the flavor on my taste buds. I should have brought my drink with me to wash out my mouth. I know there's a couple of unopened premixed drinks in my fridge. Stacey had only actually needed the one to do what she did. I should have thrown them out, but I haven't had a chance to yet. One of them will do for now, so with a sigh, I get to my feet.

When I enter my room, the figure I find there has

me gasping. When my eyes adjust to the bright light, I recognize Xavier with the rape test kit in his hand. I steel myself, waiting for the questions, but he doesn't say anything as he puts them back down next to the bottle.

"Are you okay?" he asks quietly, and I know he doesn't mean right at this very moment. It's his way of wanting to know if I want to talk about it. And yeah, maybe it would be easier to talk to a complete stranger, but I'm still absolutely furious as well as mortified about what happened. How will he or anyone else look at me if they find out I was raped by my female best friend? All my extensive martial arts training was completely overridden because I trusted someone I shouldn't have. No, I've definitely learned my lesson, and trust will be in short supply from here on out. So while it's nice to have a superficial friendship with these new people, I won't be sharing anything of value, anything that could be used against me in the future, so I plaster on a smile.

"Peachy," I tell him before moving to my mini fridge and pulling out the drink I wanted. It's a Long Island iced tea thing, but it's the only option, so I offer him one. He shrugs and nods, so I pass it to him. I go back out onto my balcony and take a seat without waiting for him, once more grabbing my smoke. Inhaling deeply, I hold it in again, waiting for that feeling to wash over me. Just as I breathe out, I feel him join me in the other chair.

"Are you super strict because you're in training or

would you like some?" I ask, offering him the weed, but he shakes his head.

"No, I'm good. I'll stick to this, thanks." He waves his bottle, and I shrug.

"Coolio, all the more for me." I giggle a little. Coolio? What the fuck?

We sit in silence for a little longer. It's comfortable, and I don't feel the need to fill the quietness with words, but then I remember that Tristan kissed me, sort of, and the guilt starts to eat away at my insides.

"Tristan kissed me," I blurt out, unable to stop the words from spilling from my mouth. "I'm so sorry." I can't even look at him, but I feel the weight of his gaze on me.

"Did you like it?" he questions quietly, not giving me the response I thought he would. I mean, I know he said they like to invite people to play, but I assumed they talked about it first, and I'd all but admitted I was gay.

Did I like it? It all happened so quickly, and I was too surprised to really take note of how I felt. I wasn't disgusted. That brief taste was better than any other kiss I've had with the male gender in the past.

"It's okay if you did," he rumbles, and his voice does something to me. Before I can examine exactly what I feel, though, my brother shouts from below.

"Tori, put out the weed and get your ass down here, the pizza's here. Is Xavier with you?"

Sighing, I stand up and stub out the rest of my

joint, saving it for later. Leaving it lying in the ashtray, I grab my drink from the table.

"Come on, let's go." Before I can leave, however, Xavier stands up and crowds in close to me. It's intimate and kind of intimidating, and a rush of excitement flows through me. Holy fuck, I'm a twisted bitch. I've just been raped. You'd think something like this would have me cowering in fear, but instead I'm practically panting. There must be something wrong with the way I'm wired. He leans in close, his mouth brushing across my ear.

"This isn't finished. Think about how you felt so you have a clear answer the next time I ask."

He steps back, and for a big man, he's stealthy as fuck, because I blink and he's gone. Looking at the joint in the ashtray and the drink in my hand, I decide I probably need to keep a clearer head around these guys. I have the feeling they are so much more than they seem.

Releasing the breath I hadn't realized I was holding, I follow him. He may want me to examine how I felt about Tristan's kiss, but now is not the time or place. Maybe later, once everything with Stacey has settled in my mind, I can look a little deeper, but I don't have the mental capacity at the moment to examine my sexuality. That can wait for a later time, and if they aren't willing to be patient with me, then I guess that's their loss. I'm surprised to find I'm slightly disappointed at the thought of them not being patient. Hmm, something to scrutinize later.

Chapter Eleven

The evening was fun, but I really couldn't relax and enjoy myself like I might have previously. Casey seemed lovely. She was a little shy but eventually came out of her shell. Funnily enough, all four of them discovered that they have the same classes and are all business majors. Like Gio, they are also expected to join the family business when they graduate, but when we subtly probed about what that business was, the subject was changed. It wasn't until a couple of days later that I realized none of them had ever admitted what the business was. They all left early the next morning before I was even out of bed, and I was okay with that. Yeah, I was sad that I didn't get to see my brother off, but I wanted to avoid any more confusing interactions with Xavier and Tristan.

I barely get any sleep all week. I toss and turn, consumed with what-ifs and anxiety over what will happen come Monday morning. I spend most of the rest of the week either high or drunk, as it's the only way I can stop my thoughts from consuming me and turning me into a quivering, emotional wreck. Instead, I pass the week drifting through space, watching movies, and eating junk food, comfortably numbed from reality.

Gio is gone, and Dad and Penelope still haven't returned, but I spoke to Dad briefly, so at least that's one less thing for me to worry about.

When Monday morning comes around, I'm feeling queasy and nervous as I park my car in the school parking lot. I came a little earlier than normal because I want to confront Stacey before the bell rings. We've always had lockers near one another, and this year is no different.

Walking across the parking lot and up the front steps of the school, I notice a lot of kids stopping and staring at me. They look from me to the phones in their hands and start laughing.

What the fuck could they be looking at?

As I push through the double doors, I feel my phone vibrate in my pocket, telling me I have an incoming message, and when I reach to pull it out, a hand lands on my arm, stopping me. Looking up, I find my friend Gwen staring at me with horror in her eyes.

"Don't open it, Tori," she warns.

"I can't believe she did this to you." My other friend, Louise, is looking around the crowded locker area, scowling at everyone.

Frowning, I look up and see people laughing and pointing at me. "What the hell is going on?" I try to unlock my phone, but Gwen just holds on tight.

Out of the corner of my eye, I see a couple of students I don't recognize. One is a gorgeous redheaded female. Her long legs are on display under her school uniform, and her top stretches tightly across her breasts. She's almost as tall as the boy standing next to her. He has shaggy blond hair that brushes his jawline and black-rimmed glasses, and he is slightly leaner than Gio. They must be Xavier and Tristan's siblings. Before I can move over to them, though, a voice has me pausing.

"Well, well, well. How the mighty have fallen." Nikki Steel steps up, blocking my view of the pretty couple with a smug as fuck grin on her face. Louise and Gwen move away. I don't blame them for not wanting to be on the receiving end of Nikki's attention. Standing next to her is none other than Stacey, who looks gleeful.

"What the fuck are you talking about?" I ask, and she looks me up and down.

"I always knew you were a freak, but I had no idea you were a lesbian femme domme." She snickers.

My stomach lurches, and the nausea I'd been feeling triples as I look at Stacey. "What is she talking about, Stacey?" I grit my teeth and pray that she hasn't done what I think she's done.

"When Stacey told us what you liked, none of us believed her. You're too mousy and quiet to be a real freak. But then she said she had video evidence. And wow, I can't say how surprised we were when we saw it." She holds up her phone, and the sound of sex fills the now quiet corridor as everyone in the school watches the confrontation.

To my absolute horror, there I am in full, glorious HD. The video is a short clip of me eating Stacey out before it switches to us in the sixty-nine position, then to me drilling her from behind with the strap-on, followed by the final shot of me unconscious while Stacey fucks me with it. Throughout it all, Stacey's face has been blurred out, and there is nothing to incriminate her. It could have been with any girl.

"I've got to say, Tori, I was impressed right up until that last little bit. There was so much potential for a fantastic fuck, but you just kind of lay there like a dead fish and took it." James Walters wraps his arm around Nikki's shoulders, and she snuggles into him as they both laugh loudly.

Over and over, I watch it play, lost in the loop. All around me, the whispers and catcalls repeatedly stab me like a knife to the heart. It's my complete and utter humiliation at the hand of the person I trusted the most.

Nikki and James wander away, followed by the twins, leaving me looking at my former friend with disgust.

"How could you?" I can't stop the sob that escapes me, and Stacey shrugs.

"This is all your fault, you know. Always thinking

you were better than me. You never thought I was good enough for your brother, but I know the truth. He would do anything for you, including fucking me if you asked," she sneers, her real feelings for me finally rearing their ugly head.

Wow. I knew Stacey had lofty delusions, but now it's all so much clearer. She was never my friend in the first place, only using me as a stepping-stone to my brother. "You're wrong, he can't stand you," I throw back at her. "He's been telling me to get rid of the deadweight for ages now."

She shrugs. "Oh well, I got what I wanted. My virginity was taken care of, and James was extremely impressed with my blowjob skills. I can suck cock like a pro now thanks to you. It's only a matter of time before it's me on his arm and not Nikki." She keeps her voice low so no one can hear us.

"I'll tell everyone that it's you in that video," I threaten, and she shrugs.

"No one will believe you because I told them you would say that. I paid good money for someone to doctor that film, so you'll never be able to prove it's me." I want to punch her stupid gloating fucking mouth.

The whispers and laughter hammer at my already shattered heart. Catcalls and ugly remarks from some of James's friends have me hunching my shoulders and curling in on myself while she stands there smirking at me, but then her face changes. It loses all color, and her grin is replaced by a look of fear.

"Tori!" My brother's bellow has everyone scattering, Stacey included. Everyone knows better than to get in the way of Gio Russo. He reaches me and pulls me into his chest, hugging me hard. "I will kill that bitch," he growls, and I start to sob into his chest.

"How did you know?" I ask him, my voice muffled by his shirt.

"I didn't. I was coming up to get you because Dad is back and he needs us. I saw people laughing in groups and stopped to see what they were laughing at."

I shudder. I can't believe my brother saw my complete and utter humiliation. Could things get any worse? "I can't believe you saw that." I sob harder, and he shakes me gently as everyone stares and tries to eavesdrop on our conversation.

"I can't believe you didn't tell me what she did. This is what you were so upset about last week, wasn't it? We could have gone to the cops. We still can." He turns me around and leads me back the way I came, tugging my car keys out of my pocket. He stops by Gwen, who has been waiting patiently off to the side.

"Can one of you bring Tori's car home for her after school?" They quickly agree, but I can't even look them in the eye to thank them.

He hurries me through the now dwindling crowd and helps me into his car. By the time we start moving, he's forgotten the idea of going to the cops and is now muttering about the ways he plans on making Stacey pay. I hear confusing words about knowing she was going to be a problem and Dad should have put a stop to the friendship years ago, but at the moment, all I can see in my head is that video.

It was on everyone's phones. God, I wonder where else it's going to end up. I'm never going to be able to look anyone in the eye again. Oh my God, what if my dad sees it? My tears start to give way to ice-cold fury. It wraps its way around my body and caresses me like a lover. I embrace the anger and revel in the fury pulsing through me. Wiping my face, I turn to Gio.

"No."

"No, what?" He keeps his eyes on the road, but I can see the tightness in his jaw and his white-knuckled grip on the steering wheel.

"Whatever you're going to do to Stacey."

He looks at me incredulously. "You want me to leave her alone? You don't want her to pay for this?"

"Oh no, that bitch will pay dearly, but I will exact my revenge. It will be *me* who will revel in her tears and pleas of mercy. I'm going to make it so that Stacey wishes she was dead. Can you help me with that?"

The grin Gio gives me is nothing short of pure evil. "Sis, you have no idea of the things that I can help you with, but you're about to find out."

I sit up a little straighter as I remember what he told me when he had first drawn me into his arms. "You said Dad was back?"

"Yes, and remember when I told you he wanted to tell you something?" I nod. "Well, prepare yourself, because your world is about to get blown apart."

I snort in anger. "Like that hasn't already just happened."

"Tori, that was nothing compared to what you are about to learn, but I think you're going to be okay. In fact, I think this may be the key to getting your revenge against Stacey."

When he pulls into our driveway, the ice-cold fury that is keeping me from falling apart is still simmering in the back of my mind. Sure, I'd love to rage and throw things and burn the world down, but that's not going to solve anything. No, I need to keep a calm head and figure out what my next move will be. It won't be hard to sabotage Stacey. All I would have to do is tell Nikki Steel about her plans for James, but she's probably prepared for that.

"Focus, Tori." Gio is standing in my open car door. Lost in my own thoughts, I hadn't heard him get out of the car. "Forget Stacey and what she did. It's small potatoes, and we will deal with her. You need all your wits about you for what's to come." I start to ask questions, but he holds up his hand. "Just be patient, young grasshopper, it won't be long."

That brings a watery smile to my lips, but it doesn't stay there.

He helps me out of the car, and we enter the house together. I can hear murmured voices in the lounge, and when we get there, Dad, Penelope, and Uncle Mickey look like they are having a quiet argument. Penelope has her arms crossed and appears to be angry, whereas Dad and Uncle Mickey would look relaxed, like nothing was bothering them, if it weren't for the glasses of amber colored liquid sitting in front of them. It's barely nine in the morning, so it's a little early for the hard stuff, which does nothing to ease my anxiety about the upcoming conversation.

"Vicki." My dad stands with a wide smile, and I feel a genuine one appear on my lips for the first time today.

"Daddy." I cross the room quickly, and he engulfs me in his arms. I breathe in his familiar scent and soak in the love. Dad is as tall as Gio and just as broad. He has a touch of gray to his black hair, but he's still a very handsome man, and I can see what Gio is going to look like in twenty years' time.

"Ah, baby, I missed you."

"I missed you too, Dad." My words are muffled against his chest as I hold him just as tightly.

When he pulls back, he holds me at arm's length, looking at me closely, and frowns at what he finds. "What is this? Who has upset my princess?" he asks as he wipes an escaped tear from my cheek.

"No one, Dad. I'm just so happy to see you."

"Pfft, so what am I? Chopped liver?" The gruff tones of Uncle Mickey have me turning to face him.

"No, just saving the best for last," I joke, and a brilliant grin crosses his face.

"Oh, you are a charmer. Hear that, Stefano? I'm the girl's favorite, just how it should be." He grabs my hand and tugs me over for a hug. When he does, he whispers in my ear, "Tell Uncle Mickey who put that look on your face, and I will break their legs."

I giggle slightly, but when I pull back, I see he's dead serious. Whoa. Uncle Mickey is not a blood relative. He's my dad's best friend and has been in our lives for as long as I can remember. My dad does have a brother, but we aren't as close to Lorenzo as we are to Mickey. Lorenzo lives in a city about two hours away, so we don't see him as often as we see Mickey.

"Thank you, but I will take care of it myself." He studies me closely, and I know he can see the cold fury simmering within me. His eyes brighten with pride as he pats my cheek.

"Ah, my girl, I just know you are going to make this family proud."

Penelope scoffs as we all take a seat on the sofa. "This is unheard of. She is a girl. She will be useless. The only thing she is good for is securing an alliance. Let her be useful by spreading her legs for the family. I hear Mario Maricuso is looking for an alliance. I'm sure he has someone we could marry her to. She will give him a couple of heirs and secure that family's loyalty."

My stomach lurches as I comprehend what she's talking about. Alliances? Loyalty? Heirs?

I look at my father, and he has a relaxed air about him as he sits on the couch, drink in hand. He studies me, but Gio can't hold his tongue any longer.

"Unlike you, Penelope, Tori is more valuable than what she can do by spreading her legs. Not to mention she's gay, so she won't be able to be used for a marriage anyway," he spits out, and I gape at him. Seriously? He had to share that with the room?

"What the fuck, dude?" I growl at him, and he shrugs.

"Sorry, babe, but it's nothing to be ashamed of, and thankfully this family is more open-minded than others." I'm getting the feeling that when Gio uses the word "family" that he doesn't mean blood relatives. My eyes swing to my father and his best friend. Neither of them seems upset by Gio's announcement, but Penelope acts horrified despite the cool calculation I see in her eyes.

"Stefano, did you hear that? You will have to have the gay beaten out of her so that she will be sin free when she goes to her new husband."

"Penny, you're getting hysterical. I think that maybe this is all too much for you. Why don't you go and lie down while we talk business?" Dad doesn't even look at her, missing the scowl she throws in his direction. "You know it isn't your place to be involved in the family business."

Just like that, Dad dismisses her. I'm kind of shocked, because I've never heard him talk to her like that before.

She stands up, her cheeks blazing with embarrassment, and smooths out her dress. "Come, Victoria, let the men talk."

"I think you misunderstood me, Penelope. I asked you to leave. I didn't mention Vicki at all." Dad still doesn't look at her, keeping his eyes on me the whole time. I feel like squirming under his scrutiny, but I refuse to look weak, so I hold my head high. I am not embarrassed about being gay, I just would have preferred to tell him myself.

Penelope glares at me with pure hatred before turning on her heel and flouncing upstairs. We all sit in silence until we hear a door slam. At Dad's nod, Mickey stands up and quickly follows her.

"Come, let us go to my office for this talk. It's soundproof and has been screened for bugs."

Chapter Twelve

D ad stands up and leads us to his office deeper in the house. After entering a combination on a keypad next to the door, he opens it and allows Gio and me to enter before he follows and closes it behind us. The smell of cigar smoke and leather books is strong in here. It's one of my favorite places in the house. Dad always let me play in a corner of the room when he was working in here.

"What about Uncle Mickey?" I ask, taking a seat at one of the chairs in front of Dad's desk. Behind Dad is a wall of shelves that hold all the hardback, leather-bound books that contribute to the smell of the room. The carpet is thick and luxurious, and the office furniture is imported from Italy. Nothing but the best for my father. He would say a comfortable, happy mind was a productive one.

"He is watching Penny while we have this conversation." Dad sits down across from me, and Gio takes the seat by my side. "Vicki, Gio has informed me that you have finally started asking questions about what I do."

That pang of guilt rears its ugly head and kicks me in the ass. "Yeah, I suddenly realized how self-absorbed I am. Can you forgive me?"

Dad gives me a gentle smile and shakes his head. "There is nothing to forgive, my princess. It's that way for a reason. I'm sure you are smart enough to realize after all of Penny's blabbing just then that my business may be more than it seems."

"Well, I can't say I don't have questions." I can't hide my annoyance, and he smirks.

"I'm sure after all of the things that came out of her mouth, you must have plenty, but first, let me explain. Your mother was the love of my life, and I would have promised her the world, but the one thing she asked of me was that if I was to ever involve you in the family business that I would treat you as Gio's equal."

Gio snorts and runs a hand across his chest. "I'm not sure how Mom thought Tori could ever equal such a fine specimen."

Dad and I chuckle as he tries to lighten the mood, but I don't bite because I want to hear what Dad has to say.

"I never had any plans to involve you in this, Tori. Gio was brought in because he will be my successor when I step down, but I wanted a normal life for you away from the Russo family."

"Why do I get the feeling that when you say Russo family you mean so much more than just us?" I ask my dad, and he beams.

"My clever princess. The Russos have been part of the American Mafia, or the *Cosa Nostra,* since its inception here in the States. We are a long-standing family that is proud of its heritage, and we are loyal to our brothers. But unlike other established families, I have also seen the way of the future and the value of modernizing some of our more archaic traditions. Where being gay will get you killed or shunned in many of the other families, we accept it. Same with being female. Like Penny suggested, if we were another family, all you would be good for is marrying for an alliance, but that would be a waste of intelligence and cunning. The Mafia is shortsighted in not using women in their ranks. Women are often more vicious than us men could ever be. Am I right?"

Dad raises an eyebrow at me, and I don't know how, but I get the feeling he is referring to Stacey. That aside, I can't believe what I'm hearing. I can't even begin to form a question before he continues.

"Our main business is money laundering through our various clubs, hotels, and casinos, but we also run guns and drugs—mainly weed, pills, and cocaine. We have stayed away from heroin and meth so as not to draw too much heat or attention our way. The DEA focuses on the families who are heavy into them, and we get to stay under the radar. Meth and heroin addicts run the risk of overdosing, and nobody likes to explain an overdose in one of our venues."

Well, that explains Gio's stash of party favors then.

"We have a chemist in our employment who has developed a type of ecstasy that, at this stage, has had no overdoses. He makes them in pretty pastel-colored pills with a butterfly on them—some metaphor shit about the drug causing a person to transform, even if for only a little while. It is the number one seller in our clubs throughout the state, and we supply most of the West Coast. The East Coast is out of our area and is someone else's responsibility. We run guns from Mexico and distribute them, again, throughout the West Coast." Dad pauses and sighs, looking at a photo of my mother that he has on his desk. It's the only place in the house where there is one. Penelope insisted that the rest get packed away when she moved in. My mom was gorgeous, and Dad tells me I look just like her, but I don't see it.

"Once upon a time, we also used to traffic women, but my father put a stop to that. I'm not saying it doesn't happen, but it is not something that our family is involved in. That was my mother's doing. Theirs, unlike my relationship with your mother, was an arranged marriage, but they fell deeply in love, much as I did with your mother, and that was the one thing she asked of him. We still run whores, but they are not forced to be there. They choose to be in that position, and they are paid handsomely for it. Our whores are high-class escorts who can be seen on the arms of many of the rich and famous. They come away with a lot of very valuable blackmail material, so they are not to be underestimated. We also own all the Kitty Cat Strip Clubs on the West Coast. It's another great way to clean dirty money."

I wait for the feeling of disgust to form when Dad tells me everything he does, but it never comes. All I feel is fascination and the burning need to know more. My moral compass may be more broken than I had ever guessed, and instead of feeling frightened, all I feel is excitement.

He studies me for my reaction. I think he's waiting for me to freak out, but he's going to be waiting for a while or, most likely, forever.

"Tell me more," I implore, and he nods, looking pleased.

"I am the boss of the family, and Gio is my under-boss. Uncle Mickey is my right-hand man, and Lorenzo oversees the escort side of the business."

"And me? What will I be?" I ask, and he loses the smile on his face as his expression becomes hard.

"Well, that has yet to be determined. Gio did not automatically become my underboss. Just like my father tested me, he was thoroughly tested to ensure he has what it takes to lead this family and do what's necessary if threatened."

"Well, test me. I can do this. I need this more than ever," I beg.

He leans back and crosses his arms. "It has come to my attention that we have a possible traitor in the family. A gun buy went wrong when a Cartel gang tried to hijack our shipment. Someone obviously gave them the information. I was supposed to be at the meeting, yet Mickey and I had been held up some-where else and weren't able to attend. None of our members made it out alive. You and Gio are the only people I can trust now, so we will see how you do when we give you a crash course in life, family style. If you are still asking me to be included when we are done, then I will assign you a task. Does this sound fair?"

"Of course. You know I would do anything for this family, Daddy. Family first is our motto, right?"

He nods slowly. "Yes, princess, but blood is blood, and we trust them over everything. You will take a leave of absence from school. You can do your senior year online while learning the ropes. Gio will also be taking a leave of absence from college. If you choose to, you can both go next year together, but for now, I need you."

He looks like he's waiting for me to argue, and before what happened this morning, I might have, but now I grab the life raft he's just thrown me with both hands.

"Absolutely, just tell me what I need to do." I look at Gio, and he appears resigned.

"Got something to say, Gio?" Dad raises an eyebrow, waiting for a response, but Gio just sighs.

"No, Dad. It's just that there's this girl, and I really like my roommates."

Dad holds up a hand. "No distractions. I need you

to get Tori up to speed, and your roommates are just people who could be used against you. As for the girl, unless you want to marry her tomorrow and bring her into the family, for now, she is a liability, as are you to her. Anyone could use her against you. Let's get you both in a position where you can keep loved ones safe through power, and then you can pursue her."

"But, Dad, I think she's the one," Gio says quietly, and Dad's eyes soften.

"Tell her you are going away but you will write to her. Court her the old-fashioned way through letters and words, Gio. Romance is dead with technology, so start writing her letters, it's more romantic. If she is still around in a few years' time, then I will let you court her publicly."

"We're going away?" God, could this solution be any better? I won't have to go to school or live in the same town as Stacey. I know that sounds cowardly, but the next time I face Stacey, I want her on her knees begging for my forgiveness.

Dad stands up, smiling slightly. "Come, we're going for a little drive. I have something to show you."

He leaves his office, and I look at Gio. He stands and offers me his hand. "Come on, I think you'll get a kick out of this."

"Do you know where we're going?" I question, following him out of the room. Dad waits at the bottom of the stairs, and he quietly whistles a particular tune. Not long after, Mickey comes back down and shakes his head, frowning in annoyance.

"Goddamn it, Stefano, why did you make your damn rooms soundproof? I had to go out onto Gio's balcony and climb across to yours. Thankfully that door is not soundproof, but it wasn't easy in these pants. I was just coming back in when you whistled." Mickey is wearing a tight pair of dress pants that wouldn't give him much room to move.

"Did you hear anything of value?" Dad asks, but before Mickey can answer, Penelope appears at the top of the stairs. She changed from the outfit she was in earlier, though I don't know why she bothered. It's still the same style of dress, just a different pattern or label or something.

"I'm going out for lunch at the club with some of the women," she announces. Her gaze moves to me, and a sneer crosses her lips. "At least the one good thing to come out of all this is that we will finally be moving to a place befitting our social status." Her cryptic comment has me wanting to ask more questions, but I keep my lips zipped for now and scowl back at her.

"Have fun." Dad doesn't rise to her bait as he calls back before leading the way out of the house and to his car in the garage. I turn back to look at my stepmother, and the expression of rage on her face is breathtaking. I'm not sure if it was aimed at me or my father, but I have never seen her look like that before. Shaking off the tiny hint of dread I feel, I hurry after the others.

Dad's Mercedes is back in the garage, so when Gwen and Louise return mine, it's back to leaving it outside. Gio and I get into the back, while Mickey and Dad climb in the front. Everyone is completely silent as Mickey pulls out a device and turns it on. He waits a moment, and when it beeps, he nods. "All clear."

Dad backs out of the garage, and soon we are heading across town. "I'm sure you have plenty of questions, but I know one you have wanted an answer to over the years is about Penelope. She is an alliance marriage and a convenience. Nothing more. I will never love another woman like I loved your mother, but I secured an alliance with another family by marrying her. They will forever be in my debt now because it made them a hundred times more legitimate than they were. I am afraid, however, that Penelope may have gotten a little too comfortable. She's been vocal lately and has made it clear she does not approve of how I run things. I'm not old-school enough, not that her approval means anything to me. I think Penelope may be a traitor, but she is not smart enough to be the mastermind behind it."

"How do we deal with traitors, Dad?" I ask, bracing myself for his answer. His eyes meet mine in the rearview mirror, and I see something in them I have never seen before—the same ice-cold fury that I feel about Stacey's betrayal.

"We kill them." He doesn't hesitate to tell me the truth, nor does he do me the disservice of trying to soften the blow, and for that, I am grateful.

Swallowing the lump in my throat, I nod.

"Did you hear anything of importance?" Dad asks Mickey.

"No, she made two phone calls. One was to her friends and was mind-numbingly benign, and the other was to someone else who did all the talking. She said nothing useful."

"Have someone follow her to the country club. Make sure that is where she goes. I want a tail on her at all times. I want to know if she is reporting to her family or if it is another individual altogether."

"I can't see Vincent or Marco being stupid enough to double-cross you after all these years," Mickey scoffs. "He likes his cushy life now, so there's no way he would jeopardize that."

Vincent is Penelope's dad, and Marco is her brother. They are both chauvinistic assholes, and thankfully we don't see them very often. They are more like business associates than family, which I guess makes sense now.

"No, you may be right about that, but it's better to be safe than dead," Dad muses. "There is one more thing I must tell you before I allow you to ask questions. It is about your friend Stacey... or not so much a friend now, but an enemy, no?"

"Yes." I don't elaborate, and I know I don't need to. Somehow, both Dad and Mickey have seen the video, I know it in my gut.

"I'm sorry you had to go through that, and I'm afraid some of that is probably my fault. You see, Stacey's dad is from a rival family. He is the fourth son, and as such, he is not much use to his father. I am pretty sure he encouraged her to be friends with you to have a way to get to me. I have an alliance with his father, but it is an uneasy one. I wanted to put a stop to your friendship with her, but by the time I realized who she was and how she was related, it was too late. She was firmly entrenched in your life, so I swore as long as she didn't hurt you, I would stay out of it, but no more. I'm not sure if she did what she did out of her own misguided ambitions, or if she was put up to it by her father. Either way, she will pay. As will her family."

Fuck, I feel ill at his announcement, and I breathe deeply and slowly to try to control the urge to vomit. Our friendship wasn't even real. No wonder she didn't hesitate to do what she did to me. Though it eases my mind somewhat that maybe my judge of character isn't as fucked up as I thought it was and she's just a damn good actress.

"I want to do it." I lean forward, making eye contact with him through the rearview mirror so he can see that I mean what I say. "Please don't take away my revenge."

"You are not ready," Dad argues, his firm tone leaving no room for argument.

"Not now, but when I am, allow me the satisfaction of watching her beg. She took something away from me that I will never get back. Even now, I'm not sure what was real and what was pretend. I'm so confused, but one thing I am certain of is that Stacey will get what is coming to her." I'm practically begging now.

"Let them sweat for a little while. Gregor will believe that Stacey has succeeded in breaking Tori when she doesn't go back to school. We can spread a rumor that she is attending a boarding school overseas. Then bam! Tori strikes, and they won't know what hit them." Mickey sounds gleeful, and I shoot him a look of gratitude when he turns to wink at me.

"Fine, but their family will be made to pay an extra contribution this month and banned from running their money through the casinos for another month. I won't let them think we have gone soft. We will make it clear that what happened to Tori is unacceptable, and next time, we won't be so lenient. That will also lull them into a false sense of security so they won't be expecting Tori's revenge."

"Thank you," I tell my dad, and I breathe out a sigh of relief. No one will take away what is owed to me, and I plan on collecting tenfold.

The car slows, and I finally take note of where we are. The fortress gates loom before us, and the guard steps out of the guard box.

Holy shit! No fucking way. I can't believe we're here.

"Good morning, Mr. Russo."

"Hey, Frank. You know Gio, but this is my daughter, Tori. She is allowed full access from now on, alright?"

"Sure thing, sir. Nice to meet you, Ms. Russo." He

nods politely before stepping back into the box. Mickey pulls out his phone and opens an app. He enters a code, and the gates slowly start to open.

"Holy shit. I can't believe we're going into the fortress."

Dad snorts. "They are still calling it that?"

I nod enthusiastically. "Yeah, they do. Who lives here?"

He laughs at my enthusiasm. "We do, princess."

Chapter Thirteen

The car pulls through the large, towering gates, which slowly close behind us, and drives down a landscaped driveway. We pass the front door to the fortress, which has a stylized R F decorative emblem on the wall next to it. The black brick is imposing, and the windows are tinted so I can't see anything but the reflection of the car slowly gliding past. Around the side of the house, we enter a garage which slopes downward. I gape as the huge mansion disappears above us, replaced with a concrete ceiling.

It opens out into a wide underground parking area, kind of like the public ones in the city but on one level, and Dad maneuvers our car into one of the parking bays.

"Hey, look at that, Tori. You'll be able to park your car inside instead of out in the driveway," Gio teases, and I flip him off.

We get out, and I look around the room. It looks

just like a parking garage, nothing special, but there is an elevator door on the opposite side of us. Dad, Gio, and Mickey start heading that way, so I hurry after them.

"This is our family home, but as you know, the Mafia rumors follow it. Your mother and I wanted you to have a relatively normal childhood without members of our organization coming and going all the time, so we bought the other place. The two of you will move in here, and we will begin your training, Tori."

"Will Penelope be coming too, or will she stay at the other house?" I ask, remembering what she said before we left. Dad sighs, and I'm already dreading his answer.

"No, it's better if we keep her close. She will be coming here." The elevator doors open, and we step in. The interior is all mirrors and polished metal. The doors close behind us, and instead of pressing one number to take us up, he enters a sequence, and I feel the elevator start to descend. "No one has access to the levels below ground via this elevator except for us, which now includes you, Tori. In fact, most people don't even know there are lower levels, including Penelope. She believes we have warehouses and other locations where we store our product. The only other access to the levels below is through a tunnel which comes out halfway into the forest surrounding Gio's college. Only our most trusted members even know the location of that."

The elevator comes to a stop, and the three men look at me.

"Are you ready for this, Tori? If you say no now, there will be no hard feelings. I will change the combination, and you can go back to your life as it was. Maybe I will send you to Europe for school and you will find a nice man—person to marry, and have a *bambino* or two. You are my princess, so if that is what you ask for, how can I not give it to you?"

I swallow hard and shake my head, determined to be an asset to this family, and by extension of that, get that much closer to my revenge on Stacey.

"*Brava*, I knew you would say yes. Didn't I tell you, Stefano?" Mickey crows, and Dad and Gio roll their eyes.

"You're a real know-it-all, Mickey," Dad mutters as he studies my body language, and I guess he must be pleased with what he sees. "Very well then, for now, watch and learn. Save your questions for when we are not in front of the employees."

The elevator doors open onto another wide-open space. It looks like a military bunker from a TV show, all gray concrete and fluorescent lighting. This one has a couple of trucks in it with a few men standing around talking, and a couple more unloading unmarked crates with forklifts.

The four men standing together catch sight of us and quickly become alert. I don't recognize any of them.

"Mr. Russo, I was hoping to see you while we were

here." One of the men holds out his hand as we approach, and Dad takes it. He looks Italian, with an olive complexion and dark hair, but there's a sadness in his eyes I wasn't expecting from a mafia henchman. "Thank you so much for taking care of my brother's funeral bills and for paying off his wife's house. We are forever in your debt." He kisses the back of my dad's hand, and as he straightens, I see a glimmer of tears in his eyes before they shutter and the emotion is locked down.

"Ah, Tony, I am just sorry that I had to. The loss of Louis and the rest of the men will not get swept under the rug. When we find out who the mole is, we *will* make them pay." There's a fierceness in Dad's voice that I've never heard before, but as I'm discovering, there's a lot I've been kept in the dark about, and I'm excited to explore all of it. He holds himself loosely, but there is an air of coiled violence to him that is ready to explode at a moment's notice. Gone is the easygoing father, and in his place stands the stone-cold, ruthless mafia leader I now know him to be.

Tony nods his head. "Thank you, sir."

"Tony, you know my son Gio, but I'd like to introduce you to my daughter, Victoria. She is learning the day-to-day operations of the organization." Tony's eyes widen minutely, but unless you were looking for it, you would have never noticed. I guess not everyone is up to speed regarding equal opportunities for women in the organization.

"It's a pleasure, Ms. Russo." He nods again

politely, and I smile back, not sure how I should play this. I must ask Gio quietly when I can. When I glance at him, it's all I can do not to snort. Maybe I should be adopting a resting bitch face, which is what Gio is achieving at the moment.

"Tony, could you please run Tori through some of our inventory we have on hand at the moment?" Dad asks, and I watch Tony puff up with importance.

"Of course, Mr. Russo. If you come this way, the boys have just unloaded the latest shipment from Mexico." He leads us over to a set of black crates that are lined up against a wall and cracks one open. In it, piled almost to the top, are various weapons. "We mainly deal with small arms, weapons designed for personal use, which are easily sold on the open market." The box is full of different handguns, shot-guns, automatic rifles, and machine guns. He picks one up and hands it to me. I reach out to take it, but Gio intercepts it. He flips a switch, and the thing holding the bullets drops out. He then pulls something back and looks inside the gun. I guess whatever he sees makes him happy, because he hands it to me minus the bullet thingy. I take it, surprised by its weight despite half of it missing.

"When we're done, I'll start your lessons on learning how to use all of these." Gio nods at the box, and my eyes widen. Whoa, talk about starting my training with guns blazing. Although I'm nervous, my excitement and anticipation far outweigh it.

"All of them?" I squeak, and he grins.

"You never know when you might need to know how to use a machine gun." He winks, and when I turn back to Tony, he's nodding his agreement.

"He's right, better to learn now than to find yourself in a situation where you need to know and you don't." He moves over to another crate and pops it open. This one contains more serious-looking artillery. "Occasionally we will bring in heavy artillery, such as anti-aircraft missiles and launchers, mortars, grenade launchers, and heavy machine guns if we are contracted by a privatized army outfit, but it's too easy for these things to end up in a terrorist's hands, and we don't like to involve ourselves in that, so if we don't know who is contracting us, we won't do business with them."

"This is similar to what was stolen in the raid the other night, when we lost all of our men. Luckily it was only one crate, but where they have gone is anyone's guess. The *Cosa Nostra* refuses to help foreign terrorists, and we actively work against those scum invading our cities. The Mexican Cartel is not as scrupulous about who they sell to. Hopefully when we find the mole, they can tell us where the weapons went and we can retrieve them." Uncle Mickey, who had been quiet up until now, has lost all of his teasing demeanor, and I can see the lethal man he must be to retain his position as Dad's right-hand man.

"Thank you, Tony. While I show Victoria a few more things, please see that a variety of weapons are placed in the booth at the shooting range."

Tony quickly agrees, and we leave him to pick things out as we walk in the direction of several doors that lead out of the garage.

Before we leave, though, I notice something at the other end of the cavernous room. "What's that?" I ask, pointing to what looks like a large set of doors.

"That's the tunnel leading out of here. Everyone here will leave that way. It avoids any suspicion that people coming and going above would cause," Gio explains, throwing an arm over my shoulders. "I've got to say, sis, you're taking this better than I thought you would. It's almost like it was meant to be." He's grinning, and I can't help but grin too.

"I know I should be more shocked than I am, but to be honest, I'm just excited," I tell him. "I think I might be broken beyond repair," I admit quietly, my grin dropping as I look down at my feet.

He squeezes my shoulder. "Don't be like that. Don't let that bitch win. You are going to be a phoenix rising from the ashes, and your flames are going to scorch the earth of everyone who has crossed you. This I am sure of."

Shrugging, I glance back at the huge tunnel doors. A semi could fit through them. "No wonder people always think no one lives here or it's a holiday home. Hardly anyone is ever seen coming or going."

"I mostly hold my business meetings in my hotels when I have been away, but now that we are moving back in, I can start holding some of them here again. However, I don't like to draw too much attention, so we will probably disguise the meetings as parties. Penelope will be thrilled to plan events, and it will keep her busy. There are a couple of hidden rooms upstairs that you will need to know about too, but let's finish this tour first." Dad has reached the door, and he inputs another code into the keypad next to it. "Four of us have the code to this door, you will be the fifth." He opens it, and it leads to a long corridor. Several doors branch off the corridor, but Dad walks past all of them until he gets to a door at the very end.

"So who is the other person with the code? Uncle Lorenzo?" I ask as I keep pace with the men, and Mickey snorts.

"No, Lorenzo has nothing to do with this side of the business. He is more involved in the distribution of drugs, and like I said before, he manages the escorts and blackmail material the women learn."

"Oh, is there a reason why?" I question with surprise. Uncle Lorenzo has always had a slimy feeling about him. He laughs a little too loudly, flirts a little too hard with Penelope, and has always looked down his nose at Gio and me.

Dad sighs. "Did you know that Lorenzo is my older brother?"

"Really? I would have pegged him as a younger, jealous brother." I'm shocked by this revelation.

"He is the product of an affair my father had with a woman before he met my mother, so he is illegitimate. As much as I have tried to modernize things, when my father was alive, it was still fairly traditional, so the fact that Lorenzo was illegitimate meant he was passed over for the boss position. There was no question of him getting that role, it just wasn't going to happen, but Dad still wanted him in the family, so he gave him the escorts and drug distribution. It was right around the time when he stopped sex trafficking. It was Lorenzo's idea for the whores to gather blackmail material. My dad was impressed, so he put him in charge as a way of appeasing his first born."

"But he likes to indulge in the product, both kinds, and he has loose lips when he indulges." Mickey grunts in disapproval. "He is not to be trusted." Gio taps his foot a little impatiently while we talk, and I can't deny I'm not eager to see what's behind the door, but I know having all this information is important.

"Unfortunately, Mickey is right. He knows about this bunker, but he doesn't have the code, nor has he ever been down here before. My father never brought him, and neither have I." Dad turns with his hand on the handle. "If anything ever happens to me and you two are left in charge, be very careful who you trust. Each other and Mickey goes without saying, but bringing anyone into your inner circle will be tricky. All I can say is trust your gut. Mine hasn't let me down yet."

With that loaded statement, Dad pushes the door open. It is a well-lit and well-ventilated laboratory with huge fans in the roof sucking out any possible noxious gasses. There's chemistry equipment scattered throughout the room and techno music playing loudly. I recognize it as something I might have heard before, but I think it's from a movie. In the middle is a man, maybe a little older than Gio, with a mop of curly brown hair. He doesn't see us, his gaze locked on the computer screen in front of him, but he's shaking his ass like it's his money maker, and I can't help the grin that crosses my face. Surprisingly, I hear Gio groan over the music next to me.

"Fucking Sage." Mickey and Dad just look amused as Gio walks over to the man, who shrieks and clutches his chest when he catches sight of Gio. Gio reaches out and presses something on the phone to the side of the man, stopping the music.

"Oh my God, Gio. Warn a guy next time. You scared the shit out of me."

"How many times do we have to tell you, Sage? How are you going to hear an emergency alarm to evacuate if you have your music so damn loud?"

Sage shrugs and grimaces. "Sorry, it helps me work and my plants thrive."

"You're such a fucking hippy," Gio grumbles as the rest of us walk over.

"Hey, Mr. Russo and Mr. Mancini. I wasn't expecting you today. I was just about to run a new batch of pills through the machines, and that new strain of weed is ready to be harvested and the test batch has been fully cured. I'm pretty sure this one is going to be amazing. It's going to give a euphoric high while energizing you at the same time. This will be a huge hit in the clubs. But the latest batch of coke from the Columbians wasn't up to their usual standard, and I hope that's not going to become a regular thing." A smile crosses my lips at his enthusiasm. I wonder if he's been testing his own product. He reminds me a little of Tristan.

A little pang of sadness hits me when I think about Gio's roommates. Poor Gio, he had barely gotten a chance to know them. When I had spoken to him last night, he said how much he liked them and was looking forward to this year. I guess that will change now.

"I'm sure you can handle any problems that come your way, my boy." Dad claps him on the shoulder and then gestures to me. "Sage, I'd like to introduce you to my daughter, Victoria. She is being introduced to the business dealings of the organization. I'm hoping you will be open to letting her shadow you occasionally. Although she doesn't need to know exactly how the drugs are made, I'd like her to get a feel for this part of the operation."

It's like Sage has finally realized there is someone else in the room as he does a double take before holding out a hand. I notice he has a couple of leather bands around his wrist and two rings, one on his thumb and one on his middle finger, as I take it. "Enchanted, *mademoiselle*." He places a kiss on my hand, and a giggle escapes my mouth before I can stop it.

Damn it, Tori. Resting bitch face, activate.

"Cut it out." Gio slaps his hand away, and Sage

winks at me. "As you can see, Sage is our chemist. He's the one who developed the ecstasy formula we use, and he's also in charge of growing a small percentage of our weed crop. Now that it is legalized in a lot of states, we have farms all over the country as well, and we supply legitimate dispensaries, but we also try to create our own strains that are in high demand."

"As for the cocaine that comes in from South America, we cut and repackage it, and then it gets sent out to our distributors. Lorenzo handles our distributors," Dad chimes in, and I am suitably impressed. "It wouldn't hurt for you to try our product. It's always a good idea to know what you are selling. We have all done it and built up a tolerance to it just in case anyone tries to use it against us. It's safer to do it here at the fortress, around people who won't take advantage of you and who have your back, than to do it anywhere else."

I blink at my father in surprise.

"I'm not saying you have to become addicted, but we all indulge occasionally. You just don't want it to rule your life like it does others. Our business associates like their party favors, and some of them get insulted if you won't partake with them.

There are other things that our business associates like to indulge in as well. When I was married to your mother, they would overlook things because they knew it was a love match, but my alliance marriage to Penelope is known not to be, and when one of them requests lap dances during a meeting, well, they expect you to partake in the offerings as well." Dad runs a hand through his hair, looking a little awkward at discussing this with me, and I can't say I don't have similar feelings. I'm not quick enough to hide the horror I feel over learning this about my father, and the other three men in the room laugh at us.

"I think what Dad is trying to say in a very awkward way is that you need to develop a decent poker face. You have the resting bitch face down no problem, so that will work too, but you may find yourself in a situation that calls for you to fake it until you make it, and you have to be willing to do that." Gio eyes me sympathetically, but there's also a hardness in his tone.

"As long as I'm not forced to have sex with anyone, I think I can fake most things." The three people who know about what happened grimace. His comment most likely came from personal experience, and not just what Dad said.

"I'm sure we will figure something out. For now, why doesn't Sage show you his latest crop while I go over a few figures with Gio and Mickey?" That didn't actually sound like a guarantee that I wouldn't have to have sex with someone, which worries me slightly, but I'll let it rest for now.

"Sure can, boss." Sage is quick to jump on the tension breaker and holds out his hand. "Right this way, milady." He bows and flourishes his arm.

Chapter Fourteen

He leads me to another vast, open area much like the one where the guns were kept, but this room has a hydroponic setup. Bright lights shine down over hundreds and hundreds of bushy marijuana plants, and the room is filled with the scent of weed. It's not as pungent as I thought it would be, though, considering the number of plants in here. All the plants are in rows of pots, and all the pots have connected lines leading back to large water reservoirs. There must be fifty plants in each row, and every row is in a different stage of growth.

"Ms. Russo, meet my babies," Sage announces, waving his hand like a game show host.

I wrinkle my nose at that name. "God, that's going to take some getting used to, but if I know Dad, he's going to insist on it regardless. How about when it's just the two of us, you call me Tori?" I offer, and his deep brown eyes light up with delight.

"Deal."

"So do you do all this by yourself?" I wander over to one of the plants and run my finger over a leaf. When I pull away, my finger is sticky, and I grimace.

He chuckles and grabs a rag from a worktable against the side of the room. He hands it to me, and I wipe off the sticky residue. "Mostly, but I have two guys who help me with the plants. They come in a couple times a week, and then when it's harvest time they are here more often.

"You must not have much of a life. Between being here and traveling to and from here, how do you find time for yourself?"

His brow wrinkles as he gives me a funny look. "I don't have to travel because I live here. Didn't your dad tell you?" I can't hide the shock on my face, and he smirks as he leans against his worktable. "I take it he didn't tell you. Yup, I have a big room in the mega mansion, which I guess is going to make us roommates if your dad is planning on moving back in." He looks me up and down. "I knew Mr. Russo had a daughter, but I wasn't expecting one as pretty as you, though I guess I should have—Gio is rather pretty, after all. Maybe you and I could be somewhat more than just roommates. It *does* get awfully lonely down here all by myself." Although his tone is joking, I can see by the look in his eyes that he's serious.

I saunter over to him, not quite able to believe he's hitting on me. I guess he didn't understand what Dad meant when he told him he was introducing me to the business. Sage looks at me like I'm a piece of meat and he's been on a vegetarian diet. I run a finger down his rather well-defined chest. "You know, for a chemist, you're rather muscular."

His chest puffs up under my finger. "There's a well-equipped gym upstairs as well as a pool that I make use of most nights."

My finger slides lower, and I press my chest to his, biting my lip as I peer up at him from under my eyelashes. His breathing increases and his pupils dilate as he stares down at me. My hand brushes against the bulge in his pants, and his breathing hitches slightly before it quickly turns into a high-pitched whine as I grab hold of his package and squeeze.

"Oh fuck, what are you doing?" He tries to push me away, but I hold on tight, which makes it more painful for him.

"Did you offer Gio the same thing, or is it because I'm female and you thought hitting on me was appropriate? Did you not hear my dad tell you I was learning the ropes?"

He quickly nods. "Yes, yes, totally hit on him too, and he shot me down, but at least he wasn't violent about it. Fuck, please stop."

His words have me swiftly releasing his package in surprise. "Oh, okay then." I let go and pat it gently. "Good to hear you're an equal opportunity perv. But I am a taco lover and not into sausage, so I'm afraid you're batting zero with both of the Russo siblings." I step back, and he cups his package, glaring at me.

"Fuck, you could have just said no. I think you've ruined my dick. I'm never going to get to use it again." He moans, and I look around the room awkwardly, not sure what to say. "Fuck, your dad will be proud you've got the viciousness of a mafioso already."

"Uh, sorry. I'm a little touchy. I recently had a bad experience and, well, I may have overreacted." I feel shitty now. I allowed what happened with Stacey to dictate my behavior. I need to stop letting what she did to me affect my actions.

"As an apology, well, do you think you could flash me your tits just so I could see if my dick still works?"

Turning around, I punch him in the gut, and he doubles over, groaning and coughing dramatically. I leave him behind as I head back to the lab.

"Wait, wait, please, Tori. Mr. Russo will kill me if you say anything. I'm sorry."

I roll my eyes but stop, though I don't turn around to look at him. "I doubt he will kill you, you look like you're his cash cow, but if you are worried about that, then maybe you should think before you open your mouth, especially when talking to the boss's daughter."

He groans, and when I turn back to face him, he's standing straight but holding his midsection. A tiny bit of guilt prickles my conscience, but I'm mostly okay with my actions. "What can I say? I might be intelligent, but I never claimed to be socially appropriate. Why do you think Mr. Russo keeps me down here? Come on, I'll show you the rest."

"There's more?" I ask as he walks away from me, his steps not as confident as they were before. I guess I did have a good grip on his meat and two veg. A small smile crosses my lips at the thought of what I had in my hand. I mean, it felt like it might have been fairly impressive if I was into something like that, but I also enjoyed how it felt like I was taking myself back, like I didn't have to be that devastated shell of a person I felt like this morning. In fact, I felt confident for the first time since I woke up the morning the thing with Stacey happened, like I could hold my own against him again if I needed to.

"Yeah, there's the drying room, the curing room, and the storage and packing room."

He leads me to another door, and we step through. I wonder how far this underground complex actually stretches. There's another corridor, and all the rooms are labeled. "The drying room is temperature controlled to dry the harvested plants at the right temperature, then we put them into jars and leave them to cure."

"Cure? I thought once it was dried it was good to go."

He shakes his head vehemently. "I mean it can be, but it's a far less superior product than the stuff we produce. By leaving it to cure, you end up with a product that's smoother with a better taste."

He bypasses the drying and curing room and reaches the one labeled "Storage." He opens it and reaches in, turning on a light. Gesturing, he allows me to enter and then follows behind me. The room is packed with shelf after shelf of labeled mason jars filled with buds. He goes over to one shelf that contains a few unlabeled jars. "This is my new strain. I haven't named it yet, but you have inspired me. I will call it Mafia Princess. It will grab you by the balls and have no mercy."

There's a teasing lilt in his voice, but I don't miss the admiration in his eyes. I guess someone doesn't mind a little bit of rough treatment. I mean, he's cute with his unruly curly hair and dimples, but am I attracted to that or the fact that he's being a sassy shit? It's similar to what I felt with Tristan and Xavier, so maybe I'm just starving for any kind of friendship, though I didn't feel the same way about Casey. Fuck, I'm so confused. I need to concentrate on what Dad wants me to learn and worry about my sexual interests once I get my head on straight.

"Tori?" I must have been lost in my head, because he's frowning at me.

"Sorry, what were you saying?"

"Do you want to take some with you?" He shakes the glass jar when I look confused, and I quickly nod. I just realized I'm not going to have to rely on Gio for my weed anymore, especially now that my new supplier happens to live in my house and the product is in the basement. A grin spreads across my face. "Sage, I think you and I are going to be great friends."

He looks a little wary at my announcement. "Sure, but you have to promise you're going to keep your hands to yourself, unless you're going to be gentler with my junk." He tucks a jar under his arm, and we head back through the grow room to the lab. "Do you know how to roll a joint?" he asks before we get back to my family, and I shake my head. "I'll give you a lesson this evening if you want," he offers, and I shrug.

"I'm not sure if we'll move in today or if it will be a few days."

"That's okay, I'll show you whenever you have a free moment."

"Ah, there you are. These projections are excellent, Sage my boy. You really are an asset to our organization." Dad claps him on the shoulder when we return, and he beams with joy.

"Thanks, Mr. Russo."

"Did you show her the safe room and tell her about our safety protocols?" Uncle Mickey asks, and Sage grimaces.

"No, we didn't get that far. I got distracted."

"You hit on her, didn't you?" Gio asks, and Sage nods, not losing the grimace. "And what did she do?"

"She almost ripped my nuts off," Sage mutters, and Dad and Uncle Mickey howl with laughter.

"Sage, if you need some companionship, I can send one of Lorenzo's girls to visit you," Dad offers, and Sage scowls.

"Why can't I go out and find someone myself?" He has a very childish yet somewhat feminine pout to his lips as he surprisingly back talks my dad. He's brave, or maybe it's born from a familiarity that I don't quite understand yet. I remember what he said about hitting on Gio too, so maybe he would prefer a male whore. Do we have male whores? I'll have to ask Gio. It would be narrow-minded not to. Rich influential women need sex too. "Nobody knows I'm your chemist. It would be safe enough."

Dad and Mickey exchange a glance and then look at me thoughtfully. "I have a solution which might solve all our problems, but let's get Vicki up to speed before we put it into play."

I cross my arms and glare at the two of them. "No, if I'm involved, I want to know what you two are thinking now."

Dad glares at me, and I realize I just made a huge mistake. I defied him in front of an employee. Fuck.

"Oh shit, sis," I hear Gio whisper next to me, but I stand my ground, and Mickey chuckles.

"Well, the girl's got sass. I think she's going to do just fine."

"Yes, well, that sass might be okay with us, but there are people who will not take it well. I want her fully armed and proficient before we release her to the public." They talk about me like I'm not even in the room, and I tap my foot with agitation.

"You are lucky you sassed me in front of Sage. Anyone else, and I would have had to kill them so word wouldn't spread."

I see Sage gulp and glare at me, but I still won't apologize. Dad sighs.

"While I am more progressive and don't care that

you are gay, many in the organization will. Having a man on your arm when you attend functions will go a long way in easing some of the hostility that will come your way. You will still get it because you are a woman and the boss's daughter, but if they think you have a man by your side, they will assume he is pulling your strings. It will lull them into underestimating you."

"So you want Sage to be my arm candy?" I ask, not sure if what I'm hearing is right.

"Yes, and then if you are both discrete, you can do whatever you wish in private."

"So because the Mafia is filled with sexist, misogynistic men, I'm going to have to pretend to be straight to be taken seriously." I cross my arms, fuming at what he's saying. How can the world still be like that in this day and age? Women have been successful in businesses everywhere. Hell, the Queen of England has been running a country for over fifty years.

"Yes. There are other options, but this would probably be the best for now."

"What options? I want to know." The look Dad gives me tells me to drop it, and I sigh, letting go of my anger. It's not Dad's fault, and I really shouldn't take my annoyance out on him.

"Okay, fine, I can pretend in public."

They look at Sage, and he shudders.

"Fine, but she's got to promise to keep her hands off my manhood. I may have to be affectionate with her in public, and my ability to have children one day depends on her behaving."

I grimace but nod my agreement when they look at me.

"Good, now that that's settled, let's get Vicki to the shooting range for a lesson. Gio, we will leave it to you while the two of us go upstairs and make arrangements to move back in." Gone is the serious mafia boss, and in his place is the dad I know and love. "When you're done, come up, and you can pick your room." He claps Mickey on the back. "It's going to be so good to be back in the house."

We tell Sage goodbye, and he doesn't meet my eyes when we leave. I'm not sure if it's because I manhandled his junk or because he just agreed to be my side piece. I'm pretty sure that was sprung on him as well as me. It's not like Dad was aware of my sexual orientation before today. He probably came up with the plan on the fly.

Gio throws an arm around my shoulders. "Way to go, sis, you've already alienated one of our employees. One of the most important ones too."

"Did he hit on you also?" I ask, curious if he was telling me the truth.

Gio grimaces. "Yeah, not long after I met him. I came by when Dad was away. I was stressed for some reason, and he offered to suck my cock to release the tension."

I snort at the look on Gio's face. "You might have enjoyed it," I tease, and he shudders.

"I have no problem with homosexual relationships at all. I mean, I've been living with Tristan and Xavier for the last week, but I know I am one hundred percent hetero."

Not wanting to talk about them, I change the subject. "What did Dad mean about safety protocols?" I question, remembering something he said earlier.

"If, for some reason, we are invaded, the whole area down here can go into lockdown. There are reinforced steel doors that drop down over all the normal doors, making it harder for people to get at the product, and there is a safe room to protect any personnel down here, but it's mostly for Sage. He can activate all the doors once he gets into the safe room. There is another escape tunnel that leads in the opposite direction and actually comes out in the gardener's shed in the back-yard of our old house, behind the pool house. Again, that's info that only four of us know. Five now including you."

Oh wow, okay. That's kind of a relief to know. "What is Sage's deal? Where did Dad find him?"

"Sage popped up on Dad's radar when he was caught dealing his own homemade drugs in one of our clubs. Instead of killing him, Dad basically adopted him. Sage was seventeen and living in a crappy foster home who had discovered he had a talent for chemistry. They forced him to make meth for them. He had subpar supplies to work with, and his product caused a couple of overdoses in the club. That's how Dad knew to look for him. When he had seen his living situation, he took care of the foster parents and moved him in here. He finished his schooling online while honing his skills. Dad and Sage are close now. He is impressed with Sage's work ethic and dedication. Dad and Uncle Mickey have both asked him to call them by their first names, but in public, he refers to them as Mr. Russo and Mr. Mancini. He didn't know who you were, so that's probably why he did it earlier. You'll see when we move in."

"You're not jealous?" I ask, and Gio shakes his head.

"No. Dad told me about the things his foster parents used to do to him. I have no reason whatsoever to be jealous of Sage. I'm only thankful Dad was able to get him out of that situation. We've become friends over the past year. I like the guy, and he isn't a kiss-ass like all the kids from school."

I'm silent as I contemplate Gio's words. Maybe Sage and I have more in common than I thought. Maybe he will be the friend I need. Maybe we will bond over mutual horrible stories, though one sexual assault doesn't compare to years of sexual abuse, but perhaps we can still be of some comfort to one another. It's something to think about anyway.

"Come on. Let me show you how to kill things." The light in Gio's eyes is somewhat psychotic, but it calls to something within me, something that I hadn't realized I had, and I feel a grin cross my lips.

"Lead the way."

Chapter Fifteen

Opposite of the lab is the gun range, which is somewhat of a surprise. There are two areas. One section has four narrow ranges where you shoot targets from a stationary position. The second one is a walk-through thing that has targets jumping out at you, dropping down from the ceiling, and flinging up from the floor. There are things like boxes and barrels positioned all over to hide behind.

Gio spends the next couple of hours running through guns with me—pistols, rifles, semiautomatic, and automatic. He teaches me how to take one apart and put it back together, how to clean them, and how to load the magazines. Then he hands me a pair of earmuffs and safety glasses, and I spend the next hour shooting targets in our underground shooting range.

Turns out if I pretend the target is Stacey's face, I can hit the bullseye nine times out of ten.

"Holy fuck, Tori. You're like a gun prodigy." Gio

gapes at me as the targets I had been shooting come forward on the tracks.

"Yeah, I don't know, but I really like the feeling of the gun in my hand. Don't get me wrong, it was scary as fuck the first couple of times, but knowing all the shit you showed me first helped, and it was just a matter of getting used to the sound and the way the gun kicks when I fire it. Now it just feels familiar and comforting. I can't wait to get over to the other side and run through the course."

He looks at me shrewdly. "How are you going to feel, though, when you're aiming it at a real person and it's their life or yours? Or what if you have to kill someone and they are begging you to spare their life?"

My heart pounds with the thought, but I know deep down that I wouldn't hesitate to pull the trigger. I don't know if I want to admit it out loud just yet. I don't want Gio to look at me any differently than he already does. Not to mention I feel guilty that I seem so bloodthirsty and a little shocked that I would be okay with ending someone's life.

"Before I answer, can you answer a question for me first?" I hedge, and he nods.

"Have *you* killed someone?" That cold look that has been his constant companion for the last twelve months appears in his eyes, and I'm assuming I now know the reason for it.

"Yes." He doesn't elaborate or give excuses. "I did what I had to do."

"And so will I," I state, and I'm pretty sure my

expression matches his. Both of us have been broken, and both of us are making the most of the present. The important part is that we have each other's back entirely now that I've been brought into the loop.

"Well, I think it's safe to say you know how to handle a gun, but make sure you practice often. You have access to the range, so make use of it when Dad doesn't have you doing other things. Let's head upstairs so you can see the rest of the complex. It's pretty fucking impressive."

I hesitate, not wanting to leave all the weapons, but Gio waves his hand. "Tony will still be around. I'll get him to clean all this up. Oh, except this one." He grabs the Glock 9mm and passes it to me. "You seem to like this one the most. We'll get you a holster, but from now on, you don't go anywhere without it. I would suggest having a spare in your car and another in your bedside table just in case." My eyes almost pop out of my head, and he shrugs. "That's the reality of life going forward, sis. We have enemies, and they don't like to play nice."

Swallowing, I take the gun from him. "Are you carrying?" He turns and lifts the back of his shirt. Tucked into his jeans is a pistol in a holster that's attached to his belt. I can't believe I've never noticed before, or maybe he doesn't wear it at home. That would make more sense. He turns back around.

"It's much easier when I'm wearing a suit because I can wear a holster underneath the jacket. It's fucking uncomfortable sitting in the car with that thing in my pants. Speaking of, you are going to need a whole new wardrobe."

"What's wrong with what I'm wearing?" I look down at the ripped jeans and T-shirt I had put on for the first day of school. Shit, was that only this morning? So much has happened since then. I desperately want to look at my social media to know what people are saying, but I never want to see that video again. Which reminds me, I need to search my room for a hidden camera, or maybe it doesn't matter because we're moving anyway.

"Nothing if you're an average teenager, but you're not anymore, Tori. Sure, when I'm hanging with my friends from school or when I'm going to be going to classes I can dress normally, but when I'm dealing with family business, I dress befitting my status. I have a wardrobe full of designer suits here," he tells me as we approach the elevator to go back upstairs. "You're going to need the same. Dad will probably get Penelope to take you shopping."

I shudder at the thought as we step into the elevator, and he presses in the number sequence. "Fuck, I think I'd rather shoot myself in the foot." I wave my gun around, and he ducks before pushing my hand down.

"Fucking hell, Tori, that's still loaded," he growls, and I gulp, lowering my hand.

"Sorry?"

He shakes his head, and the elevator stops moving, opening up to a large, glamorous foyer. "Just shove it into your waistband for now so you don't accidentally shoot me or yourself. You're good with the gun, but it's not second nature yet."

I gingerly shove it into the waistband of my jeans near my lower back and follow him out, looking around with amazement. "Holy shit." I hear the awe in my voice echo through the marble floored entryway.

"Yeah, it's a real riot. This place has a ballroom, indoor theater, game room, formal dining room, indoor and outdoor pools, conference rooms, not to mention a couple of secret rooms, and like twenty bedrooms and just as many bathrooms."

"Wow, why so many?" I gape as he leads me through the house.

"When the house was built three generations ago, many of the trusted family members would live together. Now, not so much. It will just be you, me, Dad, Penelope, and Sage. Mickey and Carla have a room here that they use, but Carla mostly stays in the city because that's where her job is."

I love Aunt Carla. She's that fun aunt who is always there when you need her. She was the one I turned to when I got my period or needed help with my homework or was having a fight with one of my friends, not Penelope.

We get to a door, and Gio knocks and waits.

"Enter," my dad calls, and we step into a large room that is obviously his office. There's a big wooden desk in the middle of the room with chairs facing it on the other side—Mickey is sprawled in one. Dad has a laptop on the desk, and behind him are shelves filled with books. It looks so much like his office at home I'm a little stunned. It also smells of cigars and paper. "Ah, there you both are. How did shooting go?" He raises an eyebrow and waves us to the two extra chairs.

"I think we should change Tori's name to G.I. Jane. That girl was able to hit everything, including the moving targets," he grumbles, but there's a look of pride in his eyes.

Dad and Mickey beam at me. "*Bellissima*. This is excellent to hear. It sounds like we have all had excellent days. I have arranged for the staff to move back in full time. The staff quarters have been aired out and are ready for them."

"Staff?" I ask, a little confused.

"Yes, my princess. There's a butler, cook, and a couple of housekeeping staff. The butler and cook are married and have been with us for years, and both girls who are going to be doing the housekeeping are from within the family. They know the importance of discretion and have each signed an NDA. They will alternate days because both are at college. If it is too much for just the two of them, I will hire a couple more. It is good for them to earn a little money while they are studying, no?"

Dad looks down at some notes on his desk. "Ah, yes, tomorrow you and Penelope will go into the city to outfit you for your new station. I will send one of the boys with you as an escort. Then I thought maybe we could meet you for dinner, and I could show you our hotel and casino for the first time. We will stay the night in the city to allow the movers to pack up the house, and by the time we return, we will be moved in here."

"Wow, you've been busy, Dad." Gio sounds impressed, but I'm just pissy.

"You want me to go shopping with Penelope? Can't I just go on my own?" I beg, and he frowns before sighing.

"No, princess, I need to keep Penelope busy for now. Count this as your first assignment. If she takes a call, listen in and see if you can pick up anything suspicious."

I sigh but nod, feeling a little excited that he wants me to spy on Penelope. "Okay, but do I get to pick the clothes?"

Again, he sighs. "Penelope will steer you in the right direction. She knows what is acceptable in our world, so please listen to her."

I sigh and catch Uncle Mickey laughing quietly at me, so I flip him off. He chuckles out loud then winks.

"Gio, show Tori around. Tori, the house is furnished, so the movers will only be packing up your personal things." I think about the strap-on and the rest of the sex toys Stacy left behind.

"No!" I shout, leaping to my feet. Dad startles and his eyes widen in surprise. Quieter, I continue, "I mean I don't really want strange men pawing through my underwear and things. I'll grab some boxes and pack it all up tonight. Then it will be ready for them to move when they grab the rest of our things."

I watch Dad think it over, and he must not like the idea of his men in my underwear drawer either. "Yes, good thinking. I'll have boxes delivered to the house. You can do it as soon as Gio gives you the tour."

I breathe out a sigh of relief and move to the closed door. Gio follows behind, and once we're well clear of the office and their hearing, he grabs my arm and jerks me to a stop.

"What was that about?" he asks, and I shove him away.

"Stop it. Don't I get to have some privacy as well?"

He shakes his head. "What are you hiding?" he all but growls, but I can see the concern in his eyes.

"Fine, but don't say I didn't warn you. The sex toys Stacey bought are all still in my room."

He pales a little at the reminder and shoves a frustrated hand through his hair. "I'm going to kill that bitch," he spits, and I push his chest.

"Get in line."

"Fine, but I want to be there to see it," he demands, and I shrug.

"Sure, why not, we'll make a party of it."

"Just wait until you learn torture techniques. We could always use her as your test dummy," he says over his shoulder as he walks away.

Torture techniques? "Did you say torture?" I hurry after him, not paying attention to my surroundings.

"Yup, you also get to do defensive driving, and they tie you up a lot and smack you around as well so you can learn to withstand anything our enemy might do to you and how to get out of the situation. You've got so much fun to look forward to." Gio's tone is sarcastic, and a pit of worry develops in my stomach.

Fuck, am I going to be able to cope with all of that? Or will I fall apart at the first sign of pain?

Gio looks back at me and notices I'm biting my lip. "Don't worry, you learned to take a punch through our training. Why do you think Dad sent us to so many self-defense classes? You are already conditioned to handle a lot of pain and get back up and keep fighting."

I stop dead in my tracks. Holy shit. That's why he had our instructors beat on us regularly. I used to cry when it first happened, but by the time I was done with all my classes, I was laughing in their faces and telling them they hit like pussies. That would just make them angrier and hit harder.

"I haven't trained for a couple of months," I tell Gio as we start moving again. This time we head up a grand staircase and onto a landing. The landing splits into two wings.

He points to the right. "Dad, Penelope, Mickey, and Carla have that wing. Sage is in this one, and so am I. I'm assuming you want to be near us?"

I quickly nod, and he turns left.

"Don't worry, there's a gym with a boxing ring. We will get Castiel and Lorn to start training you again. It wouldn't hurt to work on your endurance through swimming or the treadmill either. You never know when you're going to have to run away."

I wait for his laugh, but instead he looks dead serious. Okay then, I guess I need to get used to working out again.

"Once you leave the house, Tori, you're always going to have to be on alert. When it becomes known that you are being inducted into the family, people *will* be gunning for you. They will see you as an easy target because you're female *and* because you're the daughter of the boss. Don't be an easy target. Let them underestimate you and then wipe the floor with them. Do you understand? Equip yourself with everything you need to be taken seriously. If that means Penelope has to teach you how to dress, then you need to pay attention." It's like a switch has been flipped. Gio goes from concerned brother to the underboss he's being groomed to be in a blink. His demeanor is nononsense, and his confidence is bordering on suffocating. I have never seen this side of him before, but I can see why Dad trusts him to be his right-hand man.

I nod my understanding but huff at the fact that he wants me to pay attention to Penelope. "Knowing her, she will take great pleasure in dressing me in the wrong clothes."

"Not if Dad asks her not to," Gio points out.

"Yeah, somehow I don't think that's going to matter to her."

We pass a couple of closed doors, but Gio stops

before we go much farther. "Back there is a lounge and a library. The next floor up contains the entertainment rooms. The theater, game room, gym, indoor pool, bar, and bowling alley are on the next floor and can only be accessed through the elevator. Downstairs are the kitchen, conference rooms, ballroom, and a couple of living and dining areas. The rest of this floor is all suites with en suite bathrooms. There is a safe room on each floor and in both wings. Each of them have escape shoots to the same tunnel that leads from the escape room in the underground. Penelope doesn't know about those, so unless we need to use them, she doesn't need to know," he warns.

"Okay," I agree.

"Familiarize yourself with the layout of the place and all the safe rooms, and I'll show you the secret conference room as well when we go back downstairs. The likelihood that we will be invaded is slim, but you need to know where to go in case of an emergency. Most of the living areas all have weapon caches too, and I will show you how to access them as well. But first, pick a room. This is me, and that's Sage." He points to a room farther down the hall.

"Are the rooms soundproof like they are at home?" I ask, and he shakes his head.

"No, that's why I picked one away from Sage. He likes to play his music loud," he cautions, and I grunt.

"I'll take his loud music over the moans of pleasure or knocking beds coming from yours." I move farther down the hall and open the door across from Sage's room. There are four bedrooms between his and Gio's, so that's probably far enough away.

Pushing open the door, I step into a large, beautifully decorated room. It's all in deep greens and copper with dark, sumptuous carpeting and window coverings. There's a big wooden bed with a curtain on a raised platform. The curtains are pulled back, and the pillows are piled high.

"Oh my God. This is freaking beautiful!" I squeal as I run across the room and up the steps to the bed, throwing myself across it. "Are they all like this?" I ask Gio, who is standing in the doorway looking amused.

"They are all beautiful. Some are similar, but mine and Sage's are more modern than this. How did I know you were going to pick this one? I can't believe it was the first door you opened."

I roll around on the bed that I swear could fit five people and giggle. "It's like someone found my Pinterest page and designed it exactly for me."

Gio isn't quick enough to hide his smirk, and I sit up straight.

"Did you do this?" I ask him, and he shrugs.

"I don't know what you're talking about. Come on, I'll show you how to access the safe room in this wing."

I jump off the bed and quickly stick my head through my bathroom door, doing a little dance when I discover it has a huge shower with side jets and a tub built into the floor. It's decorated in green, silver, and black. I can't wait to test them both out.

Sighing, I leave my gorgeous room behind and throw my arm around my wonderful brother, smacking a kiss on his cheek.

"Has anyone told you how awesome you are today?" I ask him, and his chest puffs up with pride. "Come on, lead the way. Show me how to avoid being captured in our house, then I need to see the rest of everything."

Chapter Sixteen

The safe room is off the library and a little bit cliché. You have to pull a book to access it. *The Godfather* is a little obvious, if you ask me, but hey, at least it's easy to remember. It's a self-contained room with a bed, couch, and TV, with a little kitchenette that has a microwave and fridge. There's also a bathroom through a door in the back. It's not much, but it will keep someone safe until whoever is threatening them can be taken care of.

Once done, he leads me back downstairs. He shows me a large conference room that could easily sit twenty people at the huge, wooden table, but he then goes over to a wall and presses a finger into a marble bust. I think it might be a philosopher, but seeing his eye disappear gives me the heebie-jeebies, so I don't pay close attention to it. The wall next to it slides away.

"Holy shit. I couldn't even tell this was here," I tell him, waving my hand in the now empty space. There are a few steps leading down, and they are lit by LED lights in the steps.

He starts to descend. "This space sits between this floor and the garage below the house, and it's soundproof. It's where Dad holds his meetings. No weapons or any outside electronic devices are allowed into these meetings, and each family head can only bring one guard with them. There is a field to interrupt electronics too, so that no listening devices can be brought in."

I follow him down, and we have a quick look around. There's a large conference table with sixteen black leather chairs surrounding it, with a larger one at the head of the table. I guess that's Dad's spot. Off to the side is a little area that looks to contain glasses and bottles of whiskey and scotch. Apart from that, there's not much to see. I guess it's what gets talked about that is the exciting part.

Next, he shows me the safe room on this floor and all the caches of weapons. There are guns hidden in walls, drawers, and special cabinets built into furniture. There's even one in the floor where if you hit it with your heel just right, it slides away, revealing a terrorist's delight.

He then shows me all the things on the top floor, and I can't wait to use the swimming pool. The damn thing is designed to look like Hugh Hefner's grotto at the Playboy Mansion and has a cave with hot tub jets inside and seating areas. It's also long enough to get in a decent lap before having to turn again. In an alcove nearby, there's a glassed off sauna and another hot tub.

The bowling alley just about blows my mind. It's set up 50s style, and there's a snack bar, a jukebox, and a beverage bar. Flashing neon lights and pulsing music all start with a press of the button. Four lanes means that we could almost have a mafia league. Gio laughs when I point that out to him.

"I'll suggest it to Dad."

We are finally done looking around the house, and Dad and Mickey meet us at the elevator to go down to the parking garage.

"Perfect timing." Dad pulls me into a hug, and my gun pinches my skin, causing me to grimace. He pulls away and looks down.

"We'll make sure to get you a holster for that. Now I have something for you, and then I'm afraid I have to head into the city. I have some things to attend to at the casino. We will stay there tonight and see you tomorrow evening when you arrive. You can either stay here when you finish packing, or you can stay back at the other place. See what Penny has to say when you get there," he suggests, and I grimace. I was hoping she wouldn't even be home.

The elevator doors open, and we step out into the garage. Dad's car is not the only one inside, and a quiet whistle escapes my lips when I take in the other one that's there. A dark, shimmery green Dodge Charger Hellcat is sitting in a spot next to Dad's car. I walk over to it and run my hand over the pretty glitter finish.

"Holy smokes, that's nice." I can't help admiring the glossy paintwork and the sexy vehicle. When I turn around to look at the three men, they are beaming at me.

"I picked the color," Mickey says with glee, and Dad and Gio both smack him on the back of the head.

"Good choice, Uncle Mickey, it's really nice. Whose is it?"

Gio rolls his eyes as Dad tosses me a set of keys, which I scramble to catch before they hit the nice paint work.

"Yours of course. I couldn't have you driving around in that POS any longer. I only did it because I needed Penny to think that I paid attention when she talked to me. Sorry you had to suffer for a little while." Dad grimaces and awkwardly runs a hand through his dark hair.

"It's alright, Dad. I'm beginning to understand that dynamic, and this totally makes up for it." I'm grinning ear to ear as I lift the handle and slide into the driver's seat. I run my hands across the leather steering wheel as Gio slides into the passenger seat, and then I press the button to start the engine. It rumbles to life, and I swear my core pulses almost as much as it did when Stacey was licking my clit. Fuck, I don't want to think about her and that.

Dad knocks on my window, so I press the button to roll it down. "Be careful, have fun, and we will see you tomorrow." He leans in and kisses my cheek.

"Thanks, Daddy," I whisper, and I hug him around the neck through the window.

"Anything for my princess." He taps the hood, and Mickey waves as they both climb into his car.

Strapping in, I look at my brother as I put my hands on the steering wheel. "Ready?" I ask as he hurries to strap in too.

"Sure, just take it easy until we get past the gates. They don't open so fast," he warns as I put the car into gear and take my foot off the brake.

I've driven Gio's car before, so I'm familiar with how it handles, and I follow his advice as we head up the ramp and exit the garage. The doors are still open from Dad and Mickey leaving, and I wave to Frank as we exit before putting my foot down and heading back to our home, laughing like a loon.

There are boxes waiting on the kitchen table when we get home, and Penelope is nowhere to be seen, thankfully.

"Look, sis, I need to defer my enrollment, and I need to break the news to the guys. At least Casey can have my room now." Poor Gio, he looks completely bummed about it, so I give him a quick hug.

"Go. I'll be alright. I'm just going to sit here and have a look at how far that video has gotten over social media, and then I'm going to pack up all my things to move into the other house. I don't think I want to stay here another moment. I have no clue how she got that all on video, but I'm not sleeping in that room knowing there's probably a camera in there." I feel sick thinking about it, but I need to know what everyone is saying.

Gio leans against the counter and frowns. "Well, that's going to be harder than you think. Dad had one of our tech guys look into it, but by the time he got a chance, the footage had already been removed."

"What do you mean?" A sliver of hope works its way into my heart.

"It's gone, erased. And every time someone tries to put it back up, it's immediately removed. The tech guy says it's really clever. Someone built a program that searches for it and deletes it. He said it's pretty hard-core tech."

"Who the fuck would have done that?" I'm surprised, but I don't want to look a gift horse in the mouth. I wish I knew who it was, I'd send them a fucking gift basket, or a lifetime supply of weed. Ha! Sage would freak out, that would be fun.

Gio shrugs but pulls his car key out of his pocket. "Not sure, but I'm not complaining. I'll see you at the fortress later, alright? I'll grab some takeout on the way home since the chef doesn't start until tomorrow."

"Okay." I wave as he leaves and pull my phone out of my pocket. Even if the video isn't online, I'm sure people are still talking about it. I pull up the school's internal social board and start scrolling through.

I read comment after comment. Most of them are disgusting and degrading, but occasionally one or two will mention that it looks like I'm unconscious at the end and how the video should be shown to the police. Sexual assault is no joke. One anonymous poster said how hot the beginning of the video was and how she wishes my face was buried in her pussy. Well, that's kind of... sweet? Oh well, I guess it's all out there now. As embarrassing as it was for the whole school to see it, I'm not actually ashamed of any of it until the very end. I couldn't even watch it, so I still have no clue what Stacey did to me. I think it's better that I don't know.

As much as I'd like to have a drink while I'm packing, I have to drive back to the fortress, so I'll hold off for now. Grabbing an empty box in each hand, I trudge upstairs to begin packing, but when I get to my room, I'm reluctant to step into it. What if Stacey is on the other end, watching me? Or worse, she's got friends around and they are all watching me, laughing about the fact that I'm packing up? It's a good thing that I never came home and threw myself on the bed in tears. Now that would have really given them a show. Thank God for Gio, and thank God for the fact that I hadn't bothered with makeup this morning, otherwise I would have been walking around looking like a clown all day with it smeared across my face.

Taking a deep breath, I blow it out and step into

my room. I'm not going to search for the camera. I don't want to give them the satisfaction of knowing they are bothering me, but I will ask Dad to have one of his tech guys sweep my belongings so I don't end up with it in my new room—I didn't think about it before. I put my keys and phone down on my desk, and I slowly pull the gun out of my waistband, placing it with them. Hopefully if someone is on the other end of a camera, I just made them piss their pants at the sight of that.

Placing the boxes on my bed, I start emptying my bedside drawers into them. I shoved all the sex toys Stacey had left behind in one of them, so they all go in, as does my phone charger and my e-reader. I should throw the toys out, but for some reason, I keep them. Maybe it's because it's the only proof of what happened—at least it was prior to the video being released—or maybe I want to keep them to prove I'm not afraid of future sexual encounters.

All that's left are the rest of the drugs from Gio's party—a few pills and a couple of bags of white powder—my lighter, and the ashtray I use when I smoke outside. I probably should have put them with the rest of my drugs in my book, but I can't claim I was thinking straight last week. Going over to the bookcase, I pull out my hollowed-out book, grab one of my joints, and throw the rest of the drugs in there before placing it on the desk with my phone and keys. I'll take that over with me this evening.

Picking up my lighter and ashtray, I head out onto

the balcony and light up. I don't feel guilty about indulging anymore, nor do I care if Penelope catches me *or* if Stacey is watching. I smile as I think about how things are going to change now that I know about everything. Penelope better not get too comfortable pushing me around.

As I sit and smoke, my mind drifts just a little bit as I think back to the beginning of the day. It doesn't seem as dramatic now through the fog of weed, but I will be forever grateful to Louise and Gwen for giving me a heads-up. They could have chosen to say nothing, so I just hope that it doesn't bring the wrath of Stacey down on them. My mind drifts to the two new students who I assume I'm not going to be able to help out. They were an attractive pair, so I'm guessing they will get swallowed up into Nikki's crew. I just hope they are both strong enough to survive the backstabbing and cattiness that will come with being at the top of the social ladder.

My mind drifts to Gio and the love of his life. I hope he takes Dad's advice and writes to her or keeps in contact and she wasn't a candle in the wind. Even though he's still young, he's been a man whore for a long time. It would be nice to see him in a relationship, a *committed* relationship. At least then I might have a chance at remembering her name. I also liked her, which is very different from how I usually feel about the skanks he hangs out with.

"Victoria!" Penelope screeches, and I groan. Fuck, with my room facing the back of the house, I hadn't heard her come home. "Whose car is parked in my spot, and why is your car parked in your father's spot?"

A grin crosses my lips as I wait where I am. She can fucking come to me. I hear the door to my bedroom slam open, the hinges whining with the force, and within moments, Penelope is stepping out onto the balcony. She starts to say something but sniffs, and her face turns red.

"Drugs? You would do drugs in *my* home?" she shrieks, but I just keep puffing away. In fact, I turn my head and blow the smoke in her direction before holding out the joint.

"Want a toke?" I ask, and she screeches again, this time slapping it out of my hand before squashing it out under the toe of her designer shoe.

"Well, shit, what a waste of perfectly rolled weed." I stand up slowly, not willing to have her look down on me, but that backfires because the bitch is taller than me in her heels.

"You are a disgrace—a whore and a disgrace if what I hear is true." My hand twitches with the need to hit her, but I need to practice not reacting to shit, so I keep my resting bitch face in place.

"I guess it takes one to know one, doesn't it, Penny? I mean, that's essentially what you are for your family, isn't it? A way of buying their way up the social ladder?"

She flinches like I've stabbed her with a knife but quickly recovers. "Why don't you ask your dad about my whorish ways? He certainly never complains."

"I guess he has needs, so why not make use of the cum receptacle at home?" Her hand lashes across my cheek. It stings, but it's hardly worth getting upset about.

"Oh, ouch." My sarcasm can't be missed, and as I watch the fury flash in her eyes, I decide I want to stoke the fire even more. "My car is in the garage because I'm assuming that's where the girls left it when they returned it for me. As for the one in your spot, that's my little gift from Dad."

Her cheeks flush even redder in her anger. *Burn, baby, burn.* I smile as I push past her and step back into my room. I've got a nice little buzz going on, so I decide to finish packing before heading over to the new place. But first, I'm going to fuck with my stepmother a little more. I move over to my desk as she follows me inside.

"Don't think you're going to get away with this. Your father will come to his senses. Imagine a female *capo*, and a lesbian one at that. Your grandfather would be rolling over in his grave. Mark my words, you will not succeed, and when you don't, I will ensure he marries you to a man who will make you scream, and not in a good way." She pauses in her rant when she notices the gun in my hand that I tap against my leg. Her eyes widen, and she pales slightly, but then she straightens her spine. I've got to give it to her, she has some brass balls.

"Okay then. Why don't you just run along now. And Penny, when I do succeed, I will make sure that you will be taken care of as well." I wink and aim my gun at her. "Pew, pew."

She screams and ducks, and I snort, unable to hold back my laughter.

"You bitch!" she screams and runs away as I set my gun back down. Oh my God, that was so much fun. I shake my head as I go into the closet and grab a handful of underwear before returning to shove them in a box. I really am twisted, and I think that maybe it's not all Stacey's fault.

Chapter Seventeen

"Who the fuck are you?" The sound of Penelope finally cracking is music to my ears when she finds Sage, Gio, and me eating takeout and playing video games in one of the lounges downstairs after she arrives at the house later that night. It's even sweeter when Gio explains who Sage is and that he lives with us. She stomps her feet and tears at her hair, messing up her perfectly coiffed do.

"Over my dead body!" she screams, and both Gio and I pull out our guns and place them on the coffee table in front of us.

"That can be arranged," Gio says calmly, not taking his eyes off the TV screen. Gio has never put up with Penelope's shit, but she's never really given him any. It must be because he is male. Sage and I are racing around a track in Mario Kart, trash talking one another while Gio waits for his turn to play the winner. I didn't bother telling him about my run-in with her earlier. It's a common occurrence for me.

"We will *not* have a dirty, low-life drug dealer—"

Sage doesn't look up from the screen as he interrupts her. "I prefer to think of myself as an entrepreneur, thank you very much, and I don't deal the product, *I make it*. I'm higher up the food chain."

Gio and I snicker, and I take my eyes off the screen to watch her reaction. It's priceless. Penelope just gapes at us, looking like one of those largemouth bass.

"Your father will hear of this," she threatens, and I roll my eyes as Gio turns to look at her.

"Who do you think set Sage up here in the first place? Don't be daft, Penelope. Know your place." He turns back around, and she screeches again before storming off.

"Well, that was fun." Sage chucks his controller at Gio when I beat him over the finish line. "What does your dad see in her?"

"Alliance," Gio answers at the same time I say, "A warm hole." The boys both grimace, and I shrug.

"I'm going to bed. I have to go shopping with that woman tomorrow, and I need all the sleep I can get so I don't shoot her in the face." I pick up my gun and slide it into the back of my jeans, the action getting easier now. "And possibly some good weed first thing before we head out."

"Oh, hey, that new strain will be perfect for you to try. It will make you feel good and energize you, which you'll probably need. If you want, I'll show you how to roll them and then you won't have to rely on us," Sage offers, and Gio nods.

"That works well, because I need to go into the club to check on something, and I promised Xavier and Tristan I would grab a couple of drinks with them at the dorm when I was done."

"Did you tell them about all this?" I wave my hand around, but he knows what I mean.

"No, of course not, but I had to give them a reason as to why I was postponing school. I told them we had family issues and that I wouldn't be able to concentrate on my classes."

"Oh my God." I sit up straight. "They didn't see the video, did they? I think their siblings were there. What if they sent it to them?"

Gio doesn't meet my eyes as he slowly shakes his head. "No, I don't think so. They didn't say anything about it."

"What video?" Sage asks and nudges me in the side. "Are you into a little home porn, Tori? I would never have pegged you as kinky," he jokes, and I stand up and leave the room.

There's no way I want to tell him about it. He'll never look at me the same again, and I feel sick that the other two might have seen it. Gio is lying to me, even if he wasn't tugging on his ear.

I make my way up the staircase, praying that I won't run into Penelope. I would probably shoot her if she even looked at me.

Going to my room, I close and lock the door, not

caring about Sage or Gio or anyone. I drop my gun on my bedside table and leave a trail of clothes strewn across the floor as I strip and turn on the shower. I don't even take the time to appreciate my new bathroom as I step under the scalding hot water, grab the sponge and soap, and start scrubbing my skin, trying to wash away the stain of what she did. I'd been holding it together all day, but Sage's comment, which I'm pretty sure he hadn't meant maliciously, just tipped me right over the edge. Like a crack in a dam, the walls I built so high come tumbling down, and my scream filled with pain and sadness and anger echoes through the large room. Tears that I just can't stop overflow from my eyes, and my scream turns into sobs as I collapse onto the floor and curl into myself.

I was raped by my best friend, and she recorded it and showed it to the world. What the fuck kind of monster is she? What kind of person does that? She might as well have shoved a knife into my chest, it would have been more honest than doing what she did.

I'm not sure how long I sit under the stream of water, but by the time I stand up, I'm all cried out and lightheaded. I feel like I have purged all the emotions that might interfere with my training, but the one thing I held onto was the need for revenge. Right here and now, I make the decision that I will be the best motherfucking mafia princess the West Coast has ever seen, and heaven help those who cross the Russo family, because they just gained themselves a member who has a few anger issues with zero remorse. I can't wait for someone to underestimate or disrespect me so I can prove them all wrong and show Dad I have what it takes to keep up with the men.

My phone beeps in my ear, waking me the next morning, and I groan, not wanting to get out of bed. This bed was made by angels, and I'm sure it's filled with feathers from their wings. It is the most comfortable thing I have ever slept on, and the thought of getting up and actually moving makes me burrow my head under my covers.

"No, go away!" I shout as I hear my phone beep again. I stick my head out and throw the phone across the room just as the door opens and Sage bursts in, splintering the lock in his wake.

The only thing he's wearing is a tight pair of leopard print boxer briefs that leave nothing to the imagination. He brandishes a gun as my phone bounces off his chest and onto the ground.

Well now, this is awkward. I sit up and push my unruly hair out of my face as he lowers his gun to the side.

"Are you okay? I heard you scream and thought someone was in here."

I barely hear his words as I take in the sight before

me. Sage's boxers do nothing to impede the spectacular muscles his body is rocking. His abs, Adonis belt, and pecs all scream, "Look at me!" His golden skin is free of tattoos, but I can see the pale hint of cigarette burn scars scattered across his torso. He's lean and sculpted, and my eyes drag a little lower to see if I can check out what I had in my hand yesterday. Call it professional curiosity. I mean, if he's going to pretend to be my arm candy, I think I deserve to know if he could satisfy me —if I was that way inclined.

The sound of snapping fingers has me looking up and trying to hide the guilt and disappointment on my face. I hadn't quite made it to where I wanted to look.

"No, no, no." He waggles a finger at me. "No free pass to check out the goodies." He holds his gun and hand in front of his package, and I see him think before a mischievous grin crosses his face. "Unless you're offering me a look. I mean, it's only fair, isn't it? Tit for tat or tit for dick, as the case may be."

I scoff and roll my eyes. "Yeah, that's not going to happen."

He tuts. "Well, that's a shame. It would have made my morning spectacular. Why were you shouting?"

"My phone woke me up, and I don't want to leave the bed of angels." I groan, flopping back and starfishing.

He chuckles and moves over to me after bending down and picking up my phone, still holding his gun in front of his dick. "Yeah, the beds are magic, aren't they?"

He hands me my phone and leans against the bedpost, checking out the green velvet curtains that are tied back. I open my messages. There's one from Gio telling me to get up, because Penelope will be leaving in half an hour, warning me not to miss her because Dad will be pissed.

"Fuck." I scramble out of bed and run into my walk-in closet.

I hear Sage call out, "Aww, that was too fast. I couldn't see anything."

I mentally flip him the bird as I quickly pull off the tank I had been sleeping in and pull on a bra, shirt, and a pair of denim shorts. Running my fingers through my mane of curls, I decide to put them up in a bun and call it a day. I grab a pair of socks and my favorite purple Converse, and then hurry back to the little sitting area, sit on the small sofa, and pull them on my feet.

"Wow, now that was impressive." He must have run back and grabbed some clothes from his room, because he's wearing a pair of sweats, but he's still naked from the waist up. "Here, I rolled these for you last night after you went to bed. Do you want to share one now before you leave?" He holds out his hand with ten joints in it, and I quickly grab them.

"Thank you, God."

"No need to call me God. Sage will do."

Ignoring him, I set them on my bedside table and look around for my lighter, but I must have left it on the balcony at the other place after my run-in with

Penelope. A clicking sound has me turning back to Sage.

"Is this what you need?" he asks, and I sigh.

"Yes, thank you."

"Come on." He moves over to the large drapes and pushes them aside, exposing a set of double doors before turning the handle. It opens onto a good-sized balcony.

I walk over to the edge, and I can see out over the back of the property. A huge swimming pool, tennis court, and croquet field are surrounded by well-groomed hedges and manicured lawns. There is also a large outdoor dining area complete with a firepit and grill. It's really cool. The firepit is built into the swimming pool with a walkway to get out to it and surrounded by a comfy seating area.

"Wow, this is nice." I lean against the wall and breathe in the early morning air.

A click sounds, and the fresh morning air takes on the pungent smell of weed. I turn back to see Sage blowing out a thick plume of smoke before offering it to me. I take it and wrap my lips around the roach, breathing in a deep lungful.

"How are you this morning, apart from your early morning wakeup call?" he inquires, and when my eyes meet his, all the playfulness is gone, and it's replaced with what I think is concern.

"Gio told you what happened?" I ask him flatly, and he shrugs.

"A little. He didn't go into details, just that your best friend betrayed you."

I snort. The weed is working already, as I feel slightly amused at how much he downplayed it. "Yup, if you can call drugging me, fooling around but not being happy about me saying I didn't want to go any further so she raped me once I was unconscious, filming it, and showing it to the entire student body betrayal, then yeah, I guess she did." The words spew out of my mouth, and I look down at the joint in my hand. "Huh, this shit is almost like a truth serum. I clearly wasn't planning on saying all that."

I look up at him, and he's gaping at me with his mouth wide open. Shrugging, I take another deep draw and then pass it back to him. He still hasn't said anything, so I stand up and brush the imaginary dirt off me just so I don't have to look at him again.

"Alright, thanks for that, I better get going so the wicked bitch doesn't have something to complain to Dad about." I take a step, but before I can go any farther, he drops the joint on the table and wraps his arms around me, pulling me in for a hug.

"I'm so sorry that happened to you, and by your best friend no less." His words are but a whisper in my ear, and I shudder.

I'm not sure if it's from what he just said or the fact that I'm now pressed up against all that golden, muscly skin and feeling slightly turned on. God, my head is fucked up. I kind of want to stick my tongue out and lick the pec I'm pressed against.

"Did you just lick me?" He sounds incredulous.

Oh fuck, did I? "Um, no?"

He pulls back and looks me in the eye, a smirk on his face.

"Fuck, that is some really good weed." I pull away and hurry into my bedroom, his chuckles echoing behind me.

Without saying goodbye, I tuck my phone into my pocket and grab my gun, shoving it into the waistband of my pants and pulling my T-shirt over the top. I picked one that was long enough to conceal it. I need to get Penelope to take me to a sporting goods store so I can get a holster. I wonder if I need a license for it. Probably not, considering all our other illegal activities, but I'll ask Gio tonight.

"Tori," Sage calls as I hurry out of my bedroom door, but I don't turn around. I can't face him after doing that. What is wrong with me? I'm a badass mafia princess, I don't go around licking men's bodies. They should be licking mine.

I stop. Do I want that? I mean, I guess I kind of do. Huh. Nope, not thinking about it now. I don't have time for flings, because that's all it will ever be. There is no way I'll ever trust anyone again. Not after what Stacey did.

Chapter Eighteen

When I get to the bottom of the stairs, Penelope is in the hallway in a straight cut dress with some kind of floral pattern on it, and it goes to just above her knees. Seriously, the woman is probably in her thirties, and she dresses like she's in her fifties. I can't believe Dad wants me to take fashion advice from her. Her arms are crossed, and she's tapping her toe. When she looks me up and down, I can tell by the expression on her face she is not impressed.

"Well, it's about time. I have better things to do than spend the day with you. Hurry up, let's go."

Instead of going to the elevator and going down to the garage, she walks out the front door, her heels clicking on the tiles. Rolling my eyes, I follow after her. In front of the steps to the house is a limo. Long, sleek, and black, it has an air of classy elegance.

A man wearing a uniform jumps out and runs around to open the back door for Penelope. "Good morning, Mrs. Russo," he says as he opens the door for her. She ignores him and climbs in, and he turns to me with a smile. "Good morning, Ms. Russo." He must be the escort Dad said he'd send with us, because when he turned, I could see a gun holster inside his suit jacket. I return his smile and climb in behind Penelope, looking around the luxurious vehicle. It smells like leather and expensive cologne.

"Wow, this is nice." I run my hand over the leather interior while Penelope sniffs but ignores me. I guess that's for the best. I don't think either of us have anything to say to each other, at least not anything nice. The pretend air of civility we've always maintained for Dad's sake is definitely gone and the gloves are off.

There are two bench seats—one at the very back of the limo facing forward, and one that runs the length of the vehicle. Penelope and I sit as far apart as possible, and both of us take out our phones. There's a bar area across from me, so I also pull out my gun and place it on there so it's not uncomfortable to sit. Out of the corner of my eye, I see Penelope purse her lips in disapproval, but she can kiss my ass. Dad told me to keep it on me wherever I go.

As the limo moves smoothly down the driveway and out the gates, I pull up the internet on my phone and use good old Google to do some research on mafia families, and more specifically, the ones on the West Coast. I asked Gio their names on the drive from the fortress to the house yesterday. I know the info probably isn't correct, but at least I'll get a heads-up. As I start to scroll through the pages, I decide I'm probably going to need to make a document with all the key players and their photos. I don't want to be caught unaware.

The trip to the city doesn't take long, but I breathe a sigh of relief as the limo pulls up in front of an exclusive boutique. Scrambling, I open the door before the driver can even make it around to our side. The atmosphere in there was frigid and oppressive, and there is no way I will be riding back to town with the wicked bitch of the west. Gio will have his car, and hopefully tomorrow morning I can get a lift back home with him.

Penelope pushes past me and stalks to the door of the boutique, which is opened by an actual doorman.

"Good morning, Mrs. Russo. It is a pleasure to see you this morning. We have taken out a selection of our latest line for you to look over." A woman, maybe the same age as Penelope, bustles over, followed by a salesgirl holding a tray with two champagne glasses on it.

Penelope takes one without acknowledging either of them and stalks over to a lounge and sits down. "Victoria, go with the women, change into the first outfit, and come back out here." She takes a dainty sip of her glass and leans back, settling in.

I smile gratefully at both ladies and take the other glass before downing it in one gulp. My morning buzz is not going to be enough to get through this disaster. Putting the empty glass on the tray, I whisper to the girl out of the side of my mouth, "Keep them coming, and you better each have one yourself, we're all going to need it."

The two women hide their smirks and show me to a luxurious fitting room. There's a rack of clothes, and the older woman whose name tag identifies her as June hands me the first outfit. "If you just pop this on, we can see if anything needs to be altered. Our designer, Francois, will be down in a moment, and Sarah will get you another glass of champagne while you change."

After thanking her, I step into one of the booths and hang the garment on the hook before stripping to my underwear. Dad always taught Gio and me that using good manners and kindness with people in the service industry will go a long way in making the overall experience of whatever you are doing enjoyable. We tip well and are never rude to anyone, because we never know what they can do to our food or whatever. Penelope has never adopted that habit. She's a raving bitch to everyone she thinks is below her.

I shudder when I finally have a good look at the outfit. "You can't be fucking serious," I mutter, eyeing myself in the mirror. She picked an outfit that makes me look like a granny. The pastel pink skirt and top are bulky and square-shaped. The hem of the skirt sits below my knee, but instead of a cute pencil skirt, it's pleated and full. The top is a blouse with no darts in it, so it's not shaped to my body, and it has pearl buttons all the way down the front.

"Well, come on then, Victoria, I don't have all

day," I hear Penelope call from where she's lounging like the Queen of England.

I walk back to the viewing area, step up onto the platform, and do a twirl. When I face Penelope, there is an evil glint in her eye and a smirk on her mouth. "Oh yes, I'm sure that's exactly what your dad was thinking." She lifts the phone in her hand, and I can tell by the sound she just took a picture of me. "I'll send a photo to him to approve it."

"Fuck off. Like hell that was what he was thinking." The disgusted tone has us both looking at the door. Standing there, looking professional and hot, is Aunt Carla and two men in suits.

She's wearing a pair of tailored black pants with a fitted jacket and a black blouse underneath. Her hair is tied back in a sleek ponytail, and her makeup is on point. Unlike my stepmother who looks like she should be dining at a fancy country club, Carla looks stylish and badass.

"She looks like she's about to have tea with the Queen of England. No, scratch that, she looks like the fucking Queen of England who is a ninety-something-year-old woman. Are you blind as well as stupid, Penelope? Or just a vicious bitch?" My aunt stalks forward just as a man rushes out the front.

"I am so sorry. I was on a phone call when you arrived," he apologizes, but then he comes to a screeching halt, throwing his hand over his mouth and gasping. "What in the world are you wearing? Why are you wearing something from our matriarch line?" He looks at both salesgirls who stare down at the ground.

"It's what Mrs. Russo asked us to pull out," Sarah, the younger girl, stammers quietly.

"I fucking bet it was." My aunt sounds disgusted. "Go take all that off. Francois, you know what we need, get to it."

He hurries away, and Penelope loses the smirk and gets to her feet. "Carla," she sneers, trying to look down on her, but Aunt Carla is wearing kick-ass heels with her pantsuit, and she's slightly taller than my stepmother, "what are you doing here?"

"When Mickey told me my favorite niece would be in the city and shopping with *you*, of all people, I just knew that I would have to interfere. Run along now, Penelope, nobody wants you here. Go and do whatever it is you do these days."

"Well, unlike you, I don't spend my days with lowlife strippers and whores," she snaps back.

"I'd rather associate with strippers and whores, who are trying to make an honest living, than you. You're nothing but a waste of space. But did you forget that managing the Kitty Cat Clubs is not the only thing I do? I'm the pit boss of the Lucky Diamond Casino, which is way more important than any role you'll ever hold." She stops, putting a finger to her cheek in a parody of thinking. "Or has Stefano finally decided to trust you with something?"

I can practically see the steam pouring out of my stepmother's ears, but she maintains her expression of disdain. "Don't be ridiculous. I am perfectly happy as I am. Women have no place in business, and I have no idea why he would trust *you* or *her*" —she turns to look at me— "with anything so important. Maybe I should have him examined by a doctor for competency."

The fury turns to calculation, and she picks up her little clutch and pulls out her phone as she walks to the door.

"If you don't want my knowledge and input, I'm not staying, I have better things to do with my time. I'm sure you can find your way to the hotel somehow, Victoria. Don't be late for dinner. Your father would be very disappointed." Carla huffs as Penelope walks out the door and nods at one of the men who came in with her.

"Follow her." He nods and slides out behind Penelope, leaving the other to stand unobtrusively by the entrance. "Well, now that the trash has finally been taken out, give me a hug." She envelops me in a wave of perfume, and it feels so nice to have her arms around me. I shudder as she whispers in my ear.

"You just give me the signal, and Stacey will be feeding the fishes." Uncle Mickey must have told her what happened, but I refuse to break down in public, so I take a deep breath, and when she pulls away, I have my resting bitch face on.

"Thanks, I appreciate the offer, but I will make sure she gets what's coming to her."

She studies me closely and must be happy with

whatever she sees. "Excellent. Let's get you outfitted, and then I have another shop I want to take you to. After that, you can come with me while I check in at the Kitty Cat Club here in town."

It doesn't take Francois long to load me up with a whole heap of tailored pants and jackets, a few pencil skirts—Carla said skirts can be impractical and are harder to run in, but she still insisted I need a few— and a few dresses as well as some club wear. The other fabulous things she makes me buy are all the shoes. They are not too high to be impractical, but I love how they make me feel. I leave one of the outfits on, and I put my old clothes in one of the bags. Carla beams when she sees me.

"Aww, look at that, we could be twins." She's not wrong. She has long black hair, but unlike mine, hers is dead straight, and where she's dressed in all black, I chose to wear a red top under my black suit. When I look at us side by side in the mirror, however, I feel a pang of sadness. She could pass as my older sister. I never got to know my mom, and Carla has been the only maternal figure I've ever known.

The bags get piled into the back of another limo like the one we were in this morning. Penelope took that one when she left, so I pile all my purchases into

Carla's. On the way to our next stop, she talks to me about hair and makeup.

"Get used to wearing it and doing your hair. Appearance is very important, and you will need to do all these things to be taken even partly seriously. I hope you're prepared to hurt a few people, because if you cower and let them intimidate you, you might as well get out now. There's a reason your father had you train all your life. Use it, because men will get grabby and take liberties, and you need to put them in their place immediately. Trust me, it was no picnic to get to where I am now, but I persevered, and with Mickey and your father's support, I am respected and feared."

"It's fine, Aunt Carla. A recent revelation has made me open my eyes to the world and how untrustworthy people are in general. I've decided that no one will ever take advantage of me again. I have no issue with using my fists or my shiny new gun to solve my problems." I squirm and pull my gun out again, huffing. "Do you carry a gun?" I look at her closely, and even in her tailored jacket, I can't see if she's carrying one.

She chuckles and slides her jacket off her shoulders. Underneath, she's wearing this lacy corset type top that sits just under her bra. It looks lovely, but when she turns, I see that the back of the corset has two pockets, and she has a gun slipped into both holsters. Her jacket also has a slit cut in the middle of the back so she can reach behind her and grab her guns with no problem.

"Oh, that's really nice." She slips her jacket back on and smiles.

"That's actually where we're headed now. You need a range of options to go with different outfits, and unlike your stepmother who carries that ridiculous purse, I believe having both hands free at all times is a good idea, so I have pockets built into all my jackets so I can just slip my phone and ID in there, along with lipstick or a credit card."

Aunt Carla gives me a whole heap of practical advice I had never thought about from a female's perspective, and when we stop, she loads me up with different holsters and corsets in every color. She also throws in spare magazines, pepper spray, brass knuckles, and a small pocketknife. While the man is ringing everything up, she leans forward and reaches into the top of her bra, pulling out the same pocketknife she added to my pile. The man doesn't even blink at our haul or the fact that she's flashing her knife around. Aunt Carla says he's on the family payroll.

"If you wear padded bras, no one will ever see it tucked in there, and you never know when you might need it." She hands it to me, and I slip it into my bra. It feels a little weird, but I'm sure once I get used to it, I won't even notice it.

Again, everything is bagged up and put into the limo. We stop and have a quick lunch at a nearby taco truck before going on to the next destination. Carla's bodyguard—or errand boy—is quiet and unobtrusive the whole time.

"The Kitty Cat Club used to be Lorenzo's jurisdiction as well, but he's been slacking, and the manager at the one I'm going to visit is skimming from the take and making the girls do things they are not being paid to do. Just because they are stripping doesn't make them whores. I found out because one of the girls came to me. It's hard in a traditional male organization, and a misogynistic one at that, so having a woman at the top of the food chain has made it so the women who do work for us feel like they have someone to advocate for them. Because of this and the fact that your dad insists that they are treated fairly, we don't have a high turnover, and most of them stay clean and sober and are reliable."

The limo pulls up to the front of the Kitty Cat Club, which has a big sign over the top. The neon lights are on, even though it's the afternoon, and the stylized sexy woman with a cat tail and ears is winking at everyone that goes past.

"Okay, let's go. Your uncle wouldn't let me get rid of the manager, so I do surprise inspections in the hope that I will be able to catch him unaware. Fingers crossed today's the day." Her grin is evil, and I can see the bloodlust in her eyes. I recognize the look because it's what I see in my eyes every time I think about Stacey. "Be alert. I'm pretty sure the security is loyal to us, but there may be one or two who are in his pocket. My informant said he makes the girls blow them to keep their loyalty."

"Why hasn't Dad done anything about this?" I ask as we step out into the afternoon sun.

Carla grimaces. "Lorenzo is a touchy subject for your dad. He feels guilty that he is the boss and not Lorenzo just because of birth status. But between you and me, Lorenzo hasn't got the head for business, and he is a lot less ethical than your dad. I know it sounds weird. We run guns and drugs and girls, not to mention launder money, so what's so ethical about that? But there are lines your dad won't cross, such as sex trafficking. Lorenzo wouldn't blink an eye at doing something like that. He is also all for having the whores and strippers hooked on our drugs so they are easily manipulated, but your dad won't have that either.

"All the whores and strippers go through rigorous drug and STI testing. Addicted whores and strippers lead to loose lips and sloppy performances. The occasional recreational use is fine, but if we find track marks, or if any of them test positive regularly, they are out. They get sent to rehab, but they are done with us because we don't want them relapsing. They also know to keep their mouths closed about any business transactions that may have occurred when working for us, otherwise they will find themselves floating face down in a dirty puddle, dying of a suspected overdose. We know how to make it look like an accident."

"That's good enough motivation to keep quiet, I guess. I never liked Lorenzo, he makes me feel icky," I tell her, and she laughs.

"I think he makes a lot of people feel that way.

Okay, let's go. Hopefully nobody has alerted him that we're here."

I probably should feel something more than interest from a business point of view, like maybe somewhat horrified that we're willing to go to those lengths, but I'm really not. Not anymore. I've made peace with what our business does.

Chapter Nineteen

Despite it being late afternoon, there are a few people occupying the tables surrounding the stage. "Bad Girlfriend" by Theory of a Deadman plays loudly as a girl does a routine on the pole. She's in a bra and thong with sparkly heels, and she does some impressive move that has her upside down and doing the splits before she slides down the pole and, with feline-like grace, crawls across the stage before kneeling and stripping off her bra. She shakes her perky tits, runs her hands through her hair, and then keeps crawling across the stage, allowing the patrons to tuck bills into her black thong. She's sensual in a way I never thought a stripper would be. I thought it would all be fake, but she's hot as fuck. I hope she makes plenty of money, because she's good at what she does, but I have other things to concentrate on now.

"Come on, this way." Carla leads me toward a door at the side of the stage. When the security guard at the door sees us coming, he reaches for his earpiece. Carla whips out her gun and points it at him. "Uh-uh, I wouldn't do that if I were you." I look around the room, and apart from the bartender who is paying no attention to us, I can't see any other security.

Carla holds out her hand, and he pulls out the earpiece and drops it into her palm. "Good boy. Go sit at the bar. Tori, if he follows us, shoot him."

He slides by me, bumping my shoulder and muttering something under his breath on the way past. Carla quickly shakes her head, so I turn and grab him by his hair, kicking a shoe into the back of his knee, and he goes down. Pulling my gun, I hold it against his temple and walk around to the front of him so he can see me when I talk to him.

"Oh, I'm sorry, what was that? I didn't quite hear you. I'm pretty sure I heard you say, 'Yes, ma'am,' to my aunt? And I'm also pretty sure you must have tripped when you went past me, and what you meant to say was, 'Sorry, Ms. Russo.'" I watch as he pales when he hears my name, and a sense of satisfaction washes over me.

He stammers before getting himself together. "Sorry, Ms. Russo, I didn't know who you were," he says, trying to excuse his behavior, but I shake my head.

"Not good enough. I suggest you think very carefully about whether or not you want to continue working here while we go speak to your boss. I'm hoping when we return, you have an attitude adjustment."

I pull my gun away from his head, and there's a red mark there because I had been pushing fairly hard. My hand is steady as I tuck it into the holster I put on under my jacket, but as I turn and walk away, I breathe out a sigh and shake out my hand. The adrenaline is still running through my body. I'm lucky I didn't accidentally shoot him in my nervousness.

We walk through the door, and Carla grabs my arm, stopping us. "You did good. It gets easier. One day, it will be second nature, but you need to establish your dominance and who you actually are from the get-go. Don't let anyone use the excuse they didn't know who you were. As a woman, respect needs to be demanded and taken in this organization."

I nod and wet my lips, wiping my sweaty palms on my pants. "Okay, let's go."

We walk up a set of stairs, and when we get to an office door that says, "Manager," Carla doesn't bother knocking and just walks in. What we walk into is certainly an eye-opener. There's a naked girl tied up with two men spit roasting her. Tears leak from her eyes as the man in front holds her head, choking her on his cock. Her ass is red where the man fucking it has been smacking it with each thrust.

"Fuck off, Izzy, if you don't want to be next, that is." The man fucking her ass doesn't even turn to look as he speaks, but the man at the girl's head does.

"Oh fuck." He quickly pulls his dick out of the girl's mouth and tucks it back into his pants. The girl sobs, and it doesn't sound like pleasure as the man stammers, "Mrs. Mancini, we weren't expecting you today."

"No shit, Joe," my aunt drawls dryly. The man in the girl's ass stops and turns, looking over his shoulder. "Ah, Eddie Kodet! I'm pretty sure I warned you about what would happen if you were caught with the merchandise again."

He pulls out and shoves the poor girl. Because her arms are bound, she lands hard on the floor. "What's it to you, bitch? Lorenzo and I have an arrangement."

Joe gapes in disbelief at Ed, who doesn't care about being naked and just goes around to the other side of the desk and lights up a cigarette. His dick is still hard and glistening with the woman's juices.

"Tori, untie Misty and help her up." My aunt ignores the naked man. "Joseph, if you value your life and your job, you will go and get Candy from the stage and send her in here before joining Bill at the bar. I will deal with the two of you after."

Joe doesn't even have to be told twice, not looking at his naked boss for approval as he hurries out of the room. Ed sits down at his desk and eyes me up and down. "Did you bring me a new girl? Well, let's see how well she can suck my cock before I give her a chance."

I gag loudly enough for him to hear, and he loses his smirk as a look of fury crosses his face. I ignore him, knowing Carla is about to blow a gasket, and hurry over to untie Misty. "Are you okay?" I ask the poor girl as I try to rub feeling back into her arms. She has mascara and lipstick smeared all over her face, and her bleached blonde hair is in disarray.

She shakes her head. "No. Ed told me if I didn't do it, I was out. I have a baby at home, and I need this job. He said I only had to suck Joe's dick. He's handsome and he's always been nice to me, so it was no hardship, but then Ed grabbed me and tied me up and fucked me. I said *no*, but he wouldn't listen."

The ice-cold fury I felt when I realized what Stacey did to me washes over me in an instant. I help Misty to her feet just as the door opens behind us and the stripper from the stage walks in, still only in her thong. She's sexy as fuck with a banging body. Her red hair hangs over one shoulder, covering one breast, and the other one is uncovered, but not even that can distract me at the moment. I reach for my gun, but Carla puts her hand over mine.

"Not yet. Patience, my dear," she says quietly.

"Hi, Carla. You wanted to see me?" She catches sight of Misty next to me, and her smile drops. "Fuck you, Ed, you fucking cunt." She hurries over, puts her arm around the tearful girl, and leads her out of the room. "I'll take care of her, I promise."

"Thank you, Candy," my aunt replies, her gaze remaining on the scum in front of us.

"Well, Ed, not only did you break my rules, but you also just told Stephano's daughter to suck your cock."

"Isn't that all she's good for?" he asks, shrugging, not showing any concern at all.

Carla pulls out her phone. After tapping at her screen, she puts it to her ear. "Mickey, I have a candidate for Tori's interrogation training." Ed's face blanches, and his dick finally starts to wilt. "I know it's a little earlier than we planned, but it's not every day the perfect candidate lands in your lap. Could you send someone to pick him up? Oh, and we need a new manager for the Kitty Cat Club too. I'll leave Phil here for today, but it needs to happen ASAP."

He must be talking, because she listens for a moment before saying, "Okay," and hanging up.

"Today's your lucky day, Ed. I was just planning to put a bullet in your brain, but you get to breathe for another twenty-four hours—maybe even a little longer depending on how well Tori's interrogation lesson goes tomorrow. Though I'm pretty sure by the time they are done with you, you'll be begging for a bullet."

He scrambles out of his chair and runs around the room, gathering his clothes while we watch.

When he's finally dressed, Carla looks at me. "Can you guard him while I go get Phil? He's watching the other two at the bar for me. Don't let him leave. Oh, and Tori, we need him alive for your training, so behave yourself."

"Sure," I agree, and she leaves. I wander over to the double mirror that looks out over the stage. I can see the whole club from here.

"I didn't know Mr. Russo had a daughter. I thought he only had a son, Giovanni," Ed says from behind me. He must not realize that I can see his reflection in the glass in front of me, and I watch as he edges to the door. He must think he's clever by trying to distract me with the lame conversation.

"I'm sure there's a lot you don't know about Mr. Russo," I muse quietly as I watch him reach for the door handle. I'm surprised he didn't try to come for me. He's smarter than he seems. I spin, and he freezes with his hand on the handle. "Going somewhere?" I ask him, and he sneers, puffing up his body to try and intimidate me, but I've seen him naked, and that's so not going to work.

"No fucking bitch, regardless of being the boss's daughter, is going to stop *me* from leaving."

"Okay, good luck," I say calmly, waving my hand in the direction of the exit. He gapes in surprise before smirking and all but wrenching open the door and hurrying out.

Reaching behind me, I pull out my gun. I follow, take aim, and pull the trigger. The noise is deafening in the corridor, and I wince, not having done that without earmuffs on before. Although my ears are ringing, I don't miss Ed's scream as my bullet explodes his kneecap and he goes tumbling down the stairs, ass over tit, banging his head against the wall as he goes. Oops. Snickering, I hurry after him, dodging the blood trail on the way down.

When I get to the bottom, he's rolling around in agony on the floor, holding his leg, and my aunt and Phil are standing over him. When she sees me, she raises an eyebrow in question.

"He tried to leave," I tell her, shrugging, my voice coming out louder than I expected. Tucking my gun back into the holster, I grab my ears, trying to ease the ringing.

She rolls her eyes. "Jesus, Annie Oakley. You could have just called down to us and we would have stopped him. Now we're going to have to have someone clean up that mess." She waves at the pool of blood under his knee.

"I didn't know if there was another exit," I reason, not wanting to tell her that I really wanted to put a bullet through the rapist's dick so I compromised with his knee. His screams have died down to groans of agony that are still music to my ears.

Leaning down, I pat his shoulder as he whimpers and moans. "Jesus, Ed, you sound like a girl. Grow a set of balls, man." When his eyes meet mine, I see anger in them, and I smirk. "See you tomorrow, *Eddie*." Standing up, I deliberately kick him in the dick before stepping over him. Phil, who hasn't shown emotion all day, smirks momentarily before leaning against the wall without saying a word.

"They shouldn't take too long to come and get him," Aunt Carla begins. "Mickey said he'd send someone right away. Once done, get this mess cleaned up and send the girls home for the night. Make sure Misty is seen by a doctor and give her a few days off. Put a closed for the night sign on the door and then take the rest of the night off. We're all having dinner and staying at the Lucky Diamond tonight, so we won't be going anywhere else. I'll see you in the morning."

"Sure thing. Nice to meet you, Ms. Russo," he says, and I look at Carla with mock shock on my face.

"He speaks."

He smirks, and she laughs. "Come on, let's go scare the crap out of Joe and Bill, and then I can show you another part of your legacy."

I follow behind her, still pulling on one of my ears, trying to get the ringing to stop. You would think that I would be having some existential crisis about shooting a man, but I'm surprised at how easy it was. Yeah, the fact that he was a rapist scumbag helped, so there's no remorse or guilt either. I don't think I'll look too closely at that. If I do, there's a good chance I'll climb into my bed, pull up the pillows, and not come back out. Psychopath was not really what I was trying to achieve with my life, but it looks like it's going to be a good fit.

The Lucky Diamond Hotel and Casino is classy as fuck, and once I'm introduced to the staff, I'm treated with respect and admiration despite my young age.

Dinner is being held in Aces High, one of the hotel restaurants that seems to have an international menu

—if the meals on some of the tables we pass are anything to go by. Carla and I are the last to arrive after she gave me a tour of the facilities. I'm in awe of the operation, but my favorite part was the security room. I could see everything that was going on down on the floor, it was fascinating. That was our last stop. Before that we were on the casino floor, watching the action going on at the various tables. The sounds of the slots were dizzying, ringing as people put in coin after coin, trying to win big.

She took me into the cage and introduced me to a few of the cashiers on duty, then explained about the various vaults that the casino's money is stored in. Thank God Carla manages all of those, because that was mind-boggling and information overload. She then showed me the swimming pool, recreation area, and spa before showing me some of the hotel rooms. I was ready for dinner once we were done. My feet were killing me in my new heels, and I just wanted to get off them, even for a moment.

Once the hostess shows us to the table, I see a few people I don't recognize, but all the men stand except for Uncle Lorenzo. Lorenzo looks furious, and he scowls at the both of us after we've been greeted by the rest of the family and I'm introduced to the others around the table.

"My princess, don't you look lovely. Carla, you have done a marvelous job with my girl. You are to be commended, she looks perfect," Dad praises as he holds me at arm's length, admiring my outfit.

"Ah, it was easy, she's gorgeous," my aunt replies as she gives Mickey a kiss on the cheek.

"What the fuck did you do to my manager?" Lorenzo demands as Carla takes a seat next to her husband.

"I didn't do anything." Carla smirks, and everyone looks at me.

I sit down between Dad and Gio, shake out my napkin, and place it on my lap before reaching for a glass of water. I slowly toe off my shoes, hoping the relief I feel doesn't show on my face, and suppress the shudder that wants to roll through me.

Lorenzo gets impatient and growls at me. "Tori?" He thinks he's intimidating, but I just think he's pathetic. If he allows his managers to take liberties like that, I worry about what the whores under his control are going through.

"He was trying to get away," I tell him, looking him dead in the eye.

"So you shot him?" he spits out, and Dad raises his eyebrows in surprise.

I look at Mickey, and he's smirking. I guess he hasn't told Dad what happened. "I don't like rapists," I tell my dad's brother, and he flinches at whatever he sees in my eyes. Dad and Gio stiffen up on either side of me.

"You can't rape strippers and whores," he retorts, so I reach around and flip up my jacket, going for my gun, but a hand on mine has me breaking my stare down with him and looking at my dad, whose hand stopped mine. He shakes his head, and I release the grip, reaching for the steak knife at my place setting and running a finger along the serrated edge. I want to put it into his dick, but I think blood would be frowned on at the table, and he's too far away. Lorenzo grins at me smugly, and I grind my teeth before putting down the knife and picking up my glass of wine, emptying it in one go.

"You know my rules," Dad tells Lorenzo. "If you can't follow them, then maybe I need to find someone else to run your branch and you can take a silent role in the organization." Dad says it calmly while reaching for his own glass of wine, but I see Lorenzo flinch again for a second time, and I'm thinking there was more to Dad's statement than what was on the surface.

"Come now, no business talk." Uncle Mickey changes the subject with a jovial smile on his face, not quite meeting his eyes. "This is a celebration."

"What exactly are we celebrating?" my stepmother asks, and I hear a slight slur to her words, so I'm guessing that cocktail in her hand is not her first.

"Why, Tori taking her rightful place, of course."

She scowls at his reply, as does Lorenzo, but everyone else raises their glass when Mickey does.

"To the mafia princess," he jokes, and everyone chimes in. Dad squeezes my knee in affection and looks pleased as the server comes to take our orders.

Chapter Twenty

Dinner is a rowdy affair, but Lorenzo, when he's not flirting outrageously with Penelope, shoots death glares in my and Carla's direction all night. I thought Dad would call the two of them out, but I can see he genuinely doesn't care. Nobody looked at him with pity, instead they threw disapproving glances at Penelope all night. They know who butters their bread. I'm thankful when it finally comes to an end and I'm allowed to retire to my bed.

The top floor of the hotel is reserved for the owner and his friends, and I have a suite to myself. I strip off all my clothes and run a bubble bath. Settling down, I scroll through my social media, unable to not check in on what my ex-best friend is posting.

It's only been one day since the incident in school, but it feels like a lifetime. My life has changed so much in the last twenty-four hours I can't even relate to the things that are appearing on my feed from all my school "friends."

Stacey's "Loving my life and being on top" post almost has me throwing my phone across the room. There are photos with Nicki, Fiona, and Felicity, as well as a whole group of students that I recognize as the popular kids who hang out with Nikki and a lot of the football team. My finger hovers over the unfriend button, but then I decide that because Stacey can't help but update her feed every couple of hours, it's a good way of keeping track of her. Silly of her, really, but it shows that she truly doesn't expect me to retaliate or be a threat. When I'm finally ready to deal with her, I'll be able to find her.

As I scroll through my feed, I find post after disgusting suggestive post from random people who have seen the video. Changing it from public to private and unfriending all the perverts goes a long way in making me feel a little more in control.

The water pours off my body as I step from the bath and wrap myself in one of the fluffy robes the room offers. There was a complimentary bottle of champagne sitting in a bucket of ice when I entered the room—I guess they don't care that I'm only eighteen, perks of being the boss's daughter, I suppose—so I pop the cork and pour myself a glass before I shove the key card in one pocket and my Glock in the other. I take the elevator up to a private garden on the roof, which is only accessible with certain cards, and take a seat on the daybed to look at the stars.

It's relatively peaceful up here. Even the echo of the traffic below is a dull background noise. It's a little bit chilly, but my robe does enough to keep the wind off. My ears finally stopped ringing just before dinner, and everyone at the table, except Penelope and Lorenzo, had a good laugh when Carla told them all about my little problem. One of the others assured me it's normal and that it happened to everyone occasionally. One of the other guys chuckled and said, "At least you hit him. There's nothing worse than having to duck from a bullet pinging off a surface in enclosed spaces." Again, the table had a laugh, and everyone told a story about other kinds of mishaps. There was even a guy called One Ear Ernie. Apparently he was in a shoot-out with a rival mob, and one of his guys was behind him and his bullet grazed Ernie's ear on the way past. The top part of the shell is missing from the mishap.

Note to self: never stand in front of anyone during a shoot-out.

I stay up here long enough to polish off the bottle of champagne. A little unsteady on my feet, I get back into the elevator and head to my room. I know that my slumber will be nightmare free and my mind will be able to shut down now that it has an alcohol buzz. I'm hoping one day, maybe after I get my revenge on Stacey, I will no longer wake up in cold sweats with phantom aches from something I can't even remember.

"The thing about interrogation is that you need to decide what you want to achieve," Gio informs me as he pulls his car up to a nondescript building in the warehouse district. We get out, and he leads us through a door on the side of the building. There's a guard located inside who nods at us as we go past him and head down a set of stairs. At the end of the staircase, Gio puts a code into a keypad and the heavy door swings open, allowing us entrance. We step inside the room where there's a table and a few chairs, but apart from that, it's barren and empty. The only other noticeable thing about the space is the viewing window that looks into another room. That one is a little more interesting.

That room is covered in white tile with bright lights, and there's a chair with straps to secure someone to it. Next to the chair are some chains, which hang from a hook, and in the chair is Eddie, who has a black eye and looks decidedly more rumpled compared to yesterday. He also appears like he may have been crying. Next to him, just out of reach, is a table with all sorts of instruments on it.

Gio gestures for me to sit in the room, and we watch Ed from this side. "More often than not, the anticipation is enough to get them to crack. With normal interrogations, we could walk in there and the person would beg to tell us everything we want to know. Then there are the ones who are going to require a little more encouragement. Ed here is just being punished, and sometimes that's all that will be needed as well."

I watch Gio, and I'm amazed at what I see. He has so many masks, but I'm not sure if this is one or if he normally wears one with me and this is how he is now. I imagine this kind of life will change your very being. I know from experience how something can rock your foundations and practically rewrite your existence. He takes out a smoke and puts it in his mouth, lighting it. He takes a puff and then passes it to me.

"The other thing you need to consider is whether they need to be killed or spared. Sometimes if we're going to kill them anyway, torture is redundant. No one can withstand pain past a certain point, and if we inflict a body with too much pain, it just shuts down, and then they are useless to us anyway. Most of the time if we're going to kill them, we will inject them with sodium pentothal. It's a truth serum of sorts. It decreases both higher cortical function in the brain and inhibition, which tends to make subjects verbose and cooperative. We've used it quite effectively. We then put a bullet in their brain once we're done. Minimal fuss and a lot less tears."

He looks to see if I'm still following along, and I swallow the lump in my throat and nod for him to continue.

"Then there are the subjects we can't kill. Whether we need to send a message back to whoever they work for, or if they have information we need and haven't done anything that deserves a bullet, we have to work a fine line between roughing them up enough to send a message or encouraging them to find a new line of work and not going so far that they are useless to us. Again, I can often go in there and sharpen a few knives and test the electric probes and a few other dramatic things, and they will cave before a drop of blood is drawn. I'll still need to beat the crap out of them, though, so nobody thinks I've gone soft." He sighs and runs a hand through his hair. "And then there are the assholes who think they are tough and I can't beat them. They are the ones who we actually have to do things with. Today, I'm going to show you the best kind of techniques to get what we need." He stands up.

There is a bundle of nerves in my stomach that are more like pterodactyls than butterflies, and I wonder if I'm going to be able to do this. Shooting him yesterday was easy, since it was from a distance and it wasn't so in the face. This, right here, is up close and personal. Am I going to be able to deal with all that entails emotionally and physically?

"Remember that man in there is a rapist, and what we are going to do to him is no worse than what he did to Misty yesterday, okay? What he did to her was just another kind of torture, and Ed is never going to see the light of day again. If you need to show emotions or vomit, it's fine this time, but after today, if at any stage it gets to be too much, just walk out. Walk out and catch your breath, but whatever you do, don't give them the satisfaction of seeing you break. You ready?" he asks, and I take a deep breath and blow it out.

There's a tingle in my stomach, but I don't know if it's from nerves or excitement, and if I look at it too closely, I might have to admit once and for all that I'm not right in the head. Who gets excited about learning torture techniques?

He steps up and puts his hands on my shoulders. Gone is the stone-cold killer, my loving brother has returned. "Tori, you don't have to do this. Dad gave you an out. You can move to the other side of the country and change your name and live your life however you want to. We will have to be sneaky about how we see one another, but you will be far away from all the illegal activities, plotting, and scheming, and your life will be safe and, most importantly, under your control."

Biting my lip and staring at my feet, I take a moment to really think about it. When Dad said it before, there was no question about me wanting to stay. Blood over everything, but can I really see myself doing this? I look back at my life more closely. I've never really had any super close friends except for Stacey, and that's because she forced me to be her friend in the first place. I now know this for the lie it was. I knew Gwen and Louise from school, but we didn't hang out when we weren't at school. I've always been closer with Gio and would rather hang out with him and Dad on the weekends or go to my self-defense classes than have normal teenage experiences.

I would look at the popular groups and watch interactions between other friends and wonder why I couldn't make the same connections. Then again, I also didn't want to bother myself with all the ridiculous trite social posing that would occur. I was always much happier with my own company. No, it's nice being treated like an adult, and I can't deny that I got a rush out of being underestimated and then shooting Ed in the leg. Learning about all of Dad's illegal activities didn't faze me at all whatsoever, and I am eager and excited to learn more.

Gio is smiling when I finally stop thinking about it and meet his eyes to give him my decision. "I wouldn't want to be anywhere else."

He gives me a kiss on the cheek. "I knew you'd feel that way, but I felt like I still had to remind you of the offer."

"Come on, let's go deal with the scumbag rapist. When I spoke to Carla this morning, she told me that poor Misty was all torn up and would need some time off to recover. Joe just about shit his pants yesterday when we questioned him, but Ed threatened his life, said he'd tell Lorenzo that it was him messing with the girls. Apparently, Ed might be a little bit bent and needs another guy in the room to get off. Bill said he made all the security guards join in," I tell him as we get to the door. "Maybe we should have brought Sage in to help with the torment, especially if he's as far in the closet as I think he is."

Gio snorts. "I could just imagine Sage here. I'm pretty sure he'd be hysterical before the first drop of blood even hit the floor."

I think back to how he'd been yesterday morning just before I ruined it and licked him. It was almost like he had known what I was talking about and could relate. Gio did say that Dad rescued him from his foster parents, so maybe he's had the same kind of experiences.

"You know, I think Sage would surprise you." I make sure I have my resting bitch face in place before pushing the door open and walking in.

The bright lights make me blink, and when Ed comes into focus, he is smirking at me, but I can tell by the way he's gritting his teeth and sweat shines on his skin that he's in pain.

"Ha, they sent you to torture me? What are you going to do, bore me to death?"

I feel Gio step in behind me, and I watch in amusement as his smirk drops, his face pales, and his fingers tighten on the armrests he's tied to. "I was going to introduce you to my brother, Eddie, but I get the feeling you know who he is."

"The Grim Reaper," he whispers before trying to struggle out of his restraints.

My eyes jump to Gio. "The Grim Reaper?" I ask, and he shrugs.

"I've developed a reputation."

"Aww, man, I want a nickname," I tell him as I wander over to the tray of equipment and start playing with the shiny instruments.

"You've got one. You're Mafia Princess," he jokes, and Ed's eyes widen as he watches us banter.

"What do you think, Eddie? I think Mafia Princess is rather lame." I pick up a pair of pliers. "What about the Tooth Fairy?" I ask as I turn and show him the pliers. "I could keep a souvenir from each of my clients." I look at Gio again. "Is that what we call them? Clients?"

He shrugs and leans against the wall. "I call them victims, but you can call them whatever you want."

"So what do you think? Do you want to be the first of my clictims?" He looks confused. "You know, victims and clients combined."

Gio snickers, but Ed just gapes.

"What the fuck are you talking about, bitch?" he spits, and I can't take the name calling anymore. I punch him in the face. There's a cracking sound, and his nose starts to spurt blood as I shake out my hand.

"Fuck. You've got a hard head, Eddie boy," I complain.

Gio pushes off of the wall and looks at my hand, running his fingers across my knuckles. "It doesn't look like you've broken anything. Thankfully you know how to throw a punch." He turns and picks up a pair of knuckle dusters. "But if you're going to beat on someone, make sure you use these. It will save your hands in the long run."

"Good thinking. So how do you use these?" I ask him, waving the pliers.

He rolls his eyes. "Trust you to pick them. You need to use them in conjunction with this." He holds up a weird-looking contraption. "This jacks open his jaw, otherwise he could bite your hand off as soon as you put it into his mouth. Teeth also take a bit of wiggling before they come out. It's a bit of a process."

"So not the Tooth Fairy then." I throw the pliers back on the tray in disappointment.

"Oh, now don't be like that. You can use the pliers to pull out his fingernails." He picks them up along with a blowtorch. He turns it on, and the sound of the blowtorch is loud in the otherwise quiet room. Ed whimpers as Gio holds the end of the pliers inside the blue flame.

When they are good and hot, he hands them to me. "Just slide it under the nail, grip, and yank. It's going to take a bit of force, so make sure you pull nice and hard."

I feel a little queasy as he hands them to me, and I hesitate for a moment. Can I do this? Am I ready to go all the way? Am I ready to finally embrace my family's legacy?

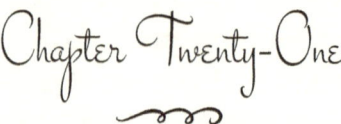

Chapter Twenty-One

Gio must see the indecision in my eyes. "Ed, did you rape all of the strippers?" he asks without looking away from me.

"I didn't rape them, they were paying their dues. Junky bitches were asking for it. All except that bitch, Candy. I hadn't had a chance to drug her yet."

A switch flips inside my brain when he talks about drugging them. I march up to him and don't even hesitate as I slide the pliers under his middle fingernail. He starts to scream as the hot metal touches his flesh, and he screams even harder as I yank, but the nail doesn't budge.

"What the fuck?" I look to Gio for help.

"Slide the pliers farther under. You've got to separate it from the skin."

I do as he says and push the pliers deeper, and this time when I pull with all my might, I manage to tear out his fingernail.

Ed's scream cuts off and his head lolls back as he passes out. The nail bed is bleeding, and I watch in fascination as the bright red blood drips to the floor. It looks so pretty against the pristine white tiles.

"Yup, that's what I was talking about as far as them being useless if the pain is too much." Gio goes over to a nearby sink and fills a bucket with water. He then comes back and tosses it over Ed who comes to, spluttering and whimpering.

"You need to practice, so let's keep going. I personally like the hammer." Gio heads to the table, puts the bucket down, and picks up a good-sized ball-peen hammer. "You can target specific areas nicely with this one, and it's not as heavy as others." He passes it to me, and I hold it in my hand, feeling the weight.

"Okay, I can work with this. So, knees?" I ask him, walking over to Ed who spits at me. It misses, but I don't wait for Gio's advice before I haul my arm back and slam the hammer into his good knee. His scream echoes through the room, and I grin as tears roll down his cheeks much like Misty's did when he was violating her. He doesn't pass out this time, and I look at Gio with my eyebrows raised.

"Oh yeah, I like this one. Where else? Fingers?" I go to his other hand, and the asshole is still defiant despite his tears.

"You are nothing. Your daddy is letting you play the game, but one day, he won't be there to protect you."

I slam the hammer down once, twice, three times,

and just like that, three fingers are crushed, and he vomits. I jump out of the way, and thankfully it only lands on him.

I wrinkle my nose. "Gross."

Gio laughs and pats me on the shoulder. "Good job dodging. I wasn't fast enough my first time, and he got my feet."

Ed has passed out again, his vomit making the room smell, so I grab the bucket and fill it up once more. "I can see why there are drains in the floor now."

I dump the water over him, and it wakes him and cleans him a little at the same time. That's efficient.

"Okay, this is fun. What's next?"

Gio shrugs. "You can get as creative as you like. I like to use this." He holds up a sharp pokey thing. "But stick to fleshy parts. If you go for the stomach, it's likely you will hit a vital organ and he might die before you can get the information you need." Gio walks over to Ed and shoves it into his thigh before pulling it out and shoving it into his shoulder. "You'll have to work on your upper body strength, poking shit into people isn't easy," he says as Ed passes out once more. I don't bother waking him as I take it from Gio and give it a try. He's right, it's not easy. I really have to put all of my weight behind it to get it into his shoulder.

Stepping back, I look Ed over. He's a fucking mess, but I feel nothing except satisfaction. "This is fucking awesome. I can't believe I can make this fucking scumbag pay. I've got to say, Gio, it gives me all kinds of tingles in my belly."

Gio snorts and rolls his eyes. "Of course it does. You're all kinds of messed up, sis."

"Please, bitch, like you're not?" I fire back, and he nods.

"Touché."

Ed comes to once more, and he grits his teeth against the pain and starts to laugh hysterically. "All of this because I ass raped a fucking stripper. You two have no clue. Things are changing, and there are pieces on the board that you won't see coming. When they do, you're going to wish they had put a bullet in your head. You're on borrowed time, little girl, because one day, you're going to be in the same situation as Misty, and I hope they ruin you."

"What do you mean? What are you talking about?" Gio demands, but it's too late. I'm pretty sure Eddie's mind has fractured, as he continues to laugh hysterically despite the blood pouring out of him in various spots and the obliterated bones in his body.

Reaching behind me, I pull out my gun and shoot him in the head. Brain matter splatters across the wall behind him, and his eyes turn vacant, but the laughing has finally stopped.

"What the fuck, Tori?" Gio screams. "He had information we needed."

"Please, that man wasn't going to give us anything. His mind was gone. We'll have to toss his office and see if we can get anything in there."

"Fuck!" Gio shouts and pulls his gun, unloading a

whole magazine into Ed. His breathing is ragged when he finishes.

"Are you done? Well, that was a little overkill, wasn't it?" I remark, crossing my arms, and he growls at me. "Do you feel better now?" I ask as the pool of blood beneath Ed grows.

He ejects his empty magazine, shoves it into his pocket, and pulls another one out of his inner jacket pocket before slamming it into his gun and then shoving it back into its holster.

"Come on. I'll call cleanup to come deal with this while we go search his office."

"So I'm thinking Azrael," I muse as we exit the room and climb the stairs, leaving the warehouse.

Gio looks at me like I'm crazy. "What the fuck are you talking about?" He unlocks his car and we both climb in.

"You know, the Angel of Death. That would be a wicked nickname. I mean, you already have the Grim Reaper."

He just stares at me as I put my seat belt on before bursting into laughter and giving me a kiss on the cheek. "You really are something. I expected maybe a freak-out, a few tears at least, but nope, you're giving yourself a nickname. You know that's not how it works. Someone else has to do it."

"Yeah, but if I leave it to someone else, I'll end up with something lame, like *Mafia Princess*. Nope, spread it around. I want people to be whispering about Azrael, the Angel of Death, by the end of the day."

Gio rolls his eyes again and starts the car. "As you wish, princess."

Tossing Ed's office and house was a waste of time. We didn't find anything of use, and I finally admitted to Gio that I might have jumped the gun by killing him, but I just couldn't take that gloating laughter and he threatened my family—not to mention all the gross pictures of other women he has violated over the years. He was one sick puppy.

After we finished, I got Misty's address from his records and went to the grocery store. I bought her a whole heap of things. Now, I am on my way to deliver them. Gio loaned me his car because he had something to do at the hotel and didn't need it, so I am going to pick him up after my errand and then we'll drive home together.

My heart rate speeds up when I notice someone following me. I ask my phone to call Gio.

"Did you send someone to guard me?" I ask him when he answers. "I've been tailed by a black sedan since I left the shopping center, and it's not being very subtle about it."

"I didn't, but Dad did. He just wants to make sure you're taken care of, especially after I told him about Ed's threats. I'm sure once he realizes you're capable of taking care of any threat coming your way, he'll remove it."

I sigh but don't bother arguing. I'd be stupid to think I was an expert after two days. "Okay, I just wanted to make sure they are the good guys."

We hang up as I make my way into the suburb Misty lives in.

Her house is in a fairly run-down, low socioeconomic area, but it is the nicest one on the street. It is well kept, if a little bit shabby. I do a couple of trips, carrying the bags and putting them on the porch, before ringing the doorbell.

The door is answered by a pretty redhead with a curvy body under her tight shirt and denim shorts, and I feel my interest perk up at the sight. The girl is gorgeous, and I swear I know her from somewhere.

"You're not Misty," I blurt, and she crosses her arms.

"No, I'm Candy, and I have a few more clothes on than when you last saw me."

"Oh yeah. You're the dancer from yesterday, aren't you? You're really good," I tell her, and her eyebrows jump in surprise.

"Thank you. What do you want?" She's guarding the door like she's the gatekeeper.

"Oh, I just bought these for Misty. She mentioned having a kid, and I didn't want them to go without because of something that shouldn't have happened. Oh, and I just wanted to tell her that Ed has been taken care of. He will never bother her again." I'm pretty sure my bright smile is slightly psychotic, because Candy stares at me warily.

"She's asleep. Her pain medication knocks her out. I'm here to look after Sally while she rests," Candy replies, and I nod.

"Okay, good. Let us know if you need time off to help her. Of course you'll both be paid to compensate you for your time," I reassure her, and she drops her arms, sighing.

"What's to stop this from happening again, Ms. Russo?" She sounds weary and slightly defeated. "I managed to avoid him, but he got everyone else. What's to say the next manager won't do the same? None of us are whores. If we wanted to do that, we could."

"Because I'm taking over the strip clubs." I make the snap decision and hope Dad won't yell too much. Aunt Carla won't care, she'll just be happy that the women are being watched over. "It makes more sense for a woman to be in charge of them anyway."

She looks skeptical, and I know not to push it.

"I'll just be heading off, but I'll see you around. Please let Misty know how sorry the Russo family is for what happened to her."

I turn and walk back to my car. When I hop in, Candy is still watching me carefully. Hopefully one day she'll understand that I won't let something like this happen to them ever again.

Once Gio and I finally make it home to the fortress, I quickly strip out of my work wear and pull on a pair of yoga pants and a sports bra. I head to the gym for a workout on the treadmill and weight machines before swimming some laps and putting in some time in the underground range. I pop my head in to see Sage, but he's busy harvesting his plants with the help of a couple of others, so I don't interrupt him.

Neither Dad nor Penelope are home in the evening, but I do get to meet the married butler and cook.

Benedict and Suzette are friendly and welcoming, and when dinner is served, instead of eating in the formal dining room, Sage, Gio, and I sit at the kitchen island and get to know them a little better. Benedict is British and Suzette is French. They met and started working together when my mother and father lived in this house before we were born, and they have been together ever since. They tell us wonderful stories about my mom and dad, which is nice but also kind of bittersweet because they are stories we have never heard before. My mom was feisty, and Dad was completely besotted with her.

After dinner, once Ben and Suzie, who requested us to use their nicknames, have retired, we play more

Mario Kart—or Sage and I do while Gio has his nose in his cell, and all he contributes to the conversation are grunts. Finally, he gets up and tells us he's going out. He doesn't invite us, but I don't really want to go anyway. I'm pretty sure he's heading to the club we own in town, and I don't want to risk running into anyone I know. We haven't talked about what we did today, and I'm okay with that. Although Dad trusts Sage, I don't think either of us are there yet. We both need a little more time to get used to him being in our lives on a more permanent basis. It's just been Gio and me for so long that it's weird to have someone added to our dynamic.

That night I toss and turn as pictures of what I did to Ed run through my head. None of it's from guilt. Well, not guilt at what I did, just guilt that I killed him before we could find out what we needed to know. Gio said he would tell Dad about Ed's ramblings, and I was worried there might be some backlash about killing him too quickly, but all Dad said when I spoke to him on the phone was that it happened to all of them. Everyone got a little trigger-happy and regretted it afterward. He said I would learn to think things through before acting. I keep running over things in my head. I know I should have done something different, but I can't change it now.

I start to make plans for the strip clubs. Dad okayed me taking them over. There's one in the city, but our hometown has one too, and I plan on checking out that manager tomorrow. There are two

255

more in our state as well, so I will need to take trips to those and assess their managers also. I'm making it a priority, because I don't doubt that there are people in there doing things they shouldn't be.

Sighing, I throw back my covers. I think I noticed a few bottles of liquor in the library. I'm going to get myself a drink and hope that will calm my mind. I need to stop relying on weed to do it.

When I open my door, I hear shouting in Sage's room. Turning, I hurry back to grab my gun before bursting into his room. There's a light on in his bathroom, and the door is open so I can see that there is no one else in his room, but he's thrashing back and forth on his bed, panting and shouting. Putting my gun down, I go over to him and try to wake him.

"Sage." I put my hand on his arm, and he flings it off, hitting me in the boob. "Fuck." I can't help the curse that leaves my lips, but it's enough to wake him.

"Tori?" He sounds confused.

I rub my boob and sit down on the bed, using my other hand to push his hair back off his face. His curls are all flattened with sweat. "Babe, you were dreaming. I heard you. Are you okay? Do you want to talk about it?" I can see in the dim light that his cheeks are wet.

He shudders and turns his head so he's not looking at me. "Not really." He sighs and rolls away from me.

Making a decision, I slide in behind him and curl my body around his, draping my arm around him and tangling my legs with his. He holds his breath for a moment before putting a hand over the one I have on his chest.

"Thank you," he whispers.

We lie here for a little while. I've never slept with anyone before, and it feels a little weird, but at least my mind is off everything else. Now, it's fully focused on how my body feels wrapped around Sage's. His legs are hairy against my smooth ones, and it's all I can do to stop my thumb from running across his nipple. My breath blows a curl on the nape of his neck with every exhale. Slowly but surely, he relaxes until I feel his deep and even breathing, telling me he's gone to sleep, but now I don't want to leave. I'm cozy and warm, and to be honest, this feels really nice, so I allow myself to relax and enjoy the feeling, even if it's only for a brief moment.

Chapter Twenty-Two

Over the next few months, I learn so many new things they are hard to keep track of, but one thing's for sure—my life's so different than I thought it would be at this stage. I've been keeping up with my studies online. My grades aren't spectacular, but I think they'll be enough to get me into college if I want to, and if not, I'm sure Dad will grease a few palms and I'll be fine.

Turns out he's got a lot of people in his back pocket—businessmen, politicians, and law enforcement officials all with something to hide or some bad habit that Dad takes full advantage of. It was glorious the day I found out that Nikki Steel's dad, Mayor Steel, regularly makes use of our brothels. He likes to be pegged, so it was no surprise that when I suggested we add male whores to our lineup, he instantly jumped aboard. He also likes to be spanked, according to

Charles, his favorite whore. The reason it's such a secret is because Nikki's mom is the one with the fortune and the reason he was able to run for mayor in the first place. And while Dad doesn't have anything on the dean of the college, they did grow up together and he is an associate of the organization, hence Gio's fancy schmancy room.

After shadowing Gio for six months and learning everything I could about our business, Dad finally let me drop the guard who has been accompanying me everywhere. I took over Aunt Carla's responsibility with the strip clubs and dealt with all the shady managers. I know she tried, but with her responsibilities with the casino, it was just too much, and they slipped through the cracks. By making women and former strippers managers, we no longer have any problems.

Sage also got a crash course on being a mobster, and now he carries a gun and has triple the responsibilities. Not only is he the chemist, but he's my arm candy and bodyguard. While I conduct business during the day, he stays home and cooks his chemicals, but when we have to attend anything at night, he's right by my side.

After that night in his bed, our relationship changed. He eventually told me what he had been through with his foster family, and I talked some more about what happened between Stacey and me, and how confused I am about my sexuality. It built a tentative trust, and although we still banter with pithy insults and sleazy remarks, we've grown close. I hesitate to call him my best friend, because of what happened with the last one, but I guess he's the closest thing I have apart from Gio. Sure, there's plenty of sexual tension there, but I refuse to do anything about it. Denial is not just a river in Egypt, but something I hold onto with both hands like it's a life preserver.

Though some days I really would like to put a bullet in his knee like I did to Ed.

When Dad told Gio to include Sage in the mafia bootcamp, I had no clue that I would be stuck being his partner in just about everything, but it turns out we both have our strengths and weaknesses. Sage is bright as fuck and remembers everything and everyone, but he failed miserably at interrogation. He threw up the first time I pulled someone's fingernails out and plain passed out when I broke someone's kneecap with my trusty hammer. Gio and I made the decision then and there not to ever let him in the room while torture is going on.

Funnily enough, though, he didn't hesitate to put a bullet in someone's brain. It helped that the first people we offered him were his foster parents. When Dad said he'd taken care of them, I thought he'd killed them. Instead, he told them he "wanted" Sage and paid them off. I'm not actually sure why he didn't end them. I think deep down he was saving them for Sage. They lived happily on the money Dad gave them, but just recently, it had run out, and they were back to fostering children. It was time for them to be dealt with properly, and Dad decided that Sage needed to be the one who dealt with them.

After all, it was Sage they put through so much. He was the one they sold to their skeevy friends when they didn't have enough money for drugs. Then, when he was old enough and his foster parents figured out how smart he was in chemistry, they would hold a gun to his head and threaten to kill him if he didn't make meth. He told me he had been a late bloomer physically, so up until he was seventeen, his foster father had been able to dominate him and beat him into submission. It was only after that when they used a gun instead to keep him compliant. Making and selling drugs also got them to lay off him as long as all of the profits went back to them. He had a good system worked out until he fucked up and tried to sell his meth in my dad's club and it brought Sage to his attention. But my dad was smart enough to see the desperation in Sage's eyes, and the rest is history.

Though Dad insisted that he didn't have to continue to make drugs when Sage came to live at the fortress, that he could do whatever he wanted, Sage wanted to pay Dad back for his kindness. Not to mention he's kind of a mad scientist genius and geeked out when Dad bought him all the equipment he requested. Dad made him promise to stay away from meth, and Sage, being the smart man he is, never touched the product himself.

Still, I thought he would hesitate, and he did balk

at the torture part, but after I cut them up a little for him, taking slices of flesh and maybe a pair of testicles, listening to the sounds of their screams and watching as they bled all over the pristine white torture chamber, he'd blown their brains out and then pissed on their corpses.

In the aftermath of that, his emotions were running high, and we had gotten drunk and stoned together. He kissed me, and I kissed him back. It wasn't horrible, but it didn't go any further than a little groping, and the next morning we both pretended it didn't happen. I was okay with that.

Defensive driving, on the other hand, is a whole other situation. While I can now drive like a badass, Sage drives like the Ghost Rider is on his tail and his life is on the line. It just clicked, and today is our last day and a test of his skills.

"Sage, fuck," I scream, grabbing hold of the door handle, trying to keep myself from falling into his lap as the car tears around the racetrack, almost going up on two wheels. He laughs maniacally and swings back the other way, accelerating into the straight before pulling the hand brake and drifting around another corner.

We agreed that he's the better driver when the two of us are in the car together, and after going around the racetrack once, we are supposed to head out into the warehouse district that's been cleared out so we can play evade the bad guys, complete with paintball pistols and pellets. Of course Dad doesn't actually want us to kill any of our own guys and fuck up two of his cars, but it's good to get a feel for how we would react in a real-life situation. A practical exam, if you wish.

I have my paintball pistol in my lap and a couple of spare magazines within reach, and Sage has his pedal to the metal. Sage and I are green and yellow, and the cars in pursuit are different colors.

"For fuck's sake, man, how am I supposed to shoot if I can't even stay upright?" I snap at him as we leave the track and head out onto the road with two blacked out SUVs in pursuit. Before he can even respond, though, he whips the car around another corner, and this time I'm not quick enough—my face ends up in his lap. I'm tangled in my belt and struggling to get up when I feel something harden beneath my face.

"Seriously?" I growl, using both hands to shove off his thighs.

"Well, your breath was all hot and you were thrashing around, and have you looked at yourself? It's practically a permanent state when you're around." He grits his jaw as a couple of thunking sounds hit our car, and I spin around to see one of the cars has gotten closer. "Don't just sit there, shoot back," he demands.

Growling, I unfasten my seat belt and press the button for the sunroof. "If you kill me, I will come back and haunt your ass," I tell him as I stand up, stick my body out of the sunroof, and take aim.

I fire off a few rounds, hitting the cars, but not in any vital spot that might take out the driver. I eject the magazine and slam in another, but then Sage swerves again, and I go tumbling back into the car. This time, however, I end up on top of him with my boobs in his face. I have no idea how the fuck that happened. How did I end up straddling him? He's basically motor-boating my cleavage while trying to see over my shoulder.

"This is fun, isn't it?" He grins and winks as I push against both of his shoulders, trying to get off him. Just as I'm about to swing my leg over, he brakes, and his face connects with my core. "Sorry, there was a cat," he mumbles when I shriek and throw myself to the side. I feel my face heat up, but he doesn't look at me, so I straighten up and take a deep breath. He quickly accelerates, but the cars are much closer now. One of them taps our bumper, and he struggles to stop the car from careening out of control.

"Those fuckers." He's all business now, and once again, I climb out the sunroof. Taking aim, I shoot at the one closest to us. I hit the windshield dead center, and the driver brakes and leaves the chase, knowing if it was a real bullet instead of paint, he'd be dead.

"Okay, I'm done with this shit. I have an idea. Get back in here," he says as a few more paintballs hit the rear of the car. I shimmy back down and sit as he rolls my window down. "Get ready to shoot." He yanks the steering wheel sideways and pulls the hand brake, and we spin, my side coming in line with the car heading directly toward us. Breathing out, I fire and watch with satisfaction as blobs of green paint bloom on their windshield—direct shots that would have taken out both people in the front. They stop, but Sage releases the hand brake and accelerates again, and we leave them in our smoky wake as he burns rubber.

"Yes!" he shouts and holds out a fist for me to bump. Shaking my head, I do so before strapping back in again. "We are such an amazing team," he crows, and I roll my eyes.

"Where are we headed?" I ask him, and he grins.

"Stefano asked me to show you the tunnel entrance to the fortress, so we're going on a road trip." He points the car in the direction of Banebridge, but when he gets to a turnoff into the forest about ten minutes from Suncity, he takes it. We wind through the dense foliage for another few miles before he turns again.

The trip has been quiet up until now, the only sound the quiet music in the background.

"You need to memorize this route. We don't program it into any GPS, and they automatically wipe where we've been once we turn the car off," he tells me as he takes another couple of turns, and then suddenly, he turns onto an off-road track that's blocked off with a boom gate and a no trespassing sign. He presses one of three buttons behind the driver's side visor and the boom gate lifts, allowing us to pass. We drive a little farther and into a cave where he stops. The cave is huge and could easily fit a semi. He then pushes another button on the dash, and the whole floor lowers. We go down a level, and he drives off. As I turn around, I see the floor return to where it was, and we continue down an unlit tunnel with white markings on the walls that reflect when the headlights shine on them.

"Holy shit," I whisper in the tense atmosphere, and I see Sage grin in the dim light.

"Pretty cool, huh?"

"It sure is. I need someone to install that stuff in my car." We drive for another twenty minutes before I see the headlights reflect off the two doors that block the entrance to the underground lair below the fortress. Sage pushes another button, and they slowly open and we drive in, parking where the trucks had been previously.

He turns off the car, and we both just sit there, the adrenaline high gone.

"That was some pretty impressive driving," I say as he pulls a rolled joint out of the cup holder and lights it up.

He inhales deeply before holding it out for me. "It sure fucking was. Your shooting wasn't too shabby either," he replies, blowing out a stream of smoke as I put the joint to my lips.

"Come on. A new shipment should have been delivered last night. Gio asked me to check it over. He had somewhere he had to be today." I pass the rollie back to Sage and we both climb out of the car.

"He's been doing that a lot," Sage comments offhandedly, and I grunt.

"I know, but he's still my brother, and I'm sure he will tell me what he's doing eventually, even if it's starting to piss me off and it makes him look suspicious, like he's doing something he shouldn't. I'm getting sick of covering for him with Dad too."

"Maybe it's a girl," Sage remarks and gets out of the car before I can say anything. I scramble after him.

"Do you know something?" I demand, but he just mimes zipping his lips.

"Asshole. I'll find out eventually, and then I'll kick your ass," I threaten him, and he just grins.

"It's all just foreplay, baby, and you know it."

We walk over to the familiar black crates, and I shove the lid off. No one else seems to be around today. I know these aren't scheduled to leave for a few more days, but I want to make sure the inventory is all there. Sometimes they don't give us everything they are supposed to. Looking down, I see this one is mostly handguns, but there are some military grade grenades inside as well. I pull out my phone to compare the list to what is actually in the box. Out of the corner of my eye, I can see Sage fucking around and looking through the inventory, but I pay him no mind. Scanning through the sheet, I look down and count the grenades. There are supposed to be twenty, but I can only see nineteen. My adrenaline spikes, and I look at what my idiot friend is doing. Sure enough, he has one of them in his hand and he's throwing it up and catching it. Before I can even open my mouth, too stunned to do anything but stutter, in what feels like slow motion, he puts the joint in his mouth and studies it closer.

"What's this?" he mumbles around the cigarette in his mouth, and before I can stop him, he pulls the pin. It clicks, and I watch as comprehension dawns and he looks at me with horror.

"Sage, you fucking idiot. Throw it toward the door and run." Luckily there is a big open space and no trucks in it today, and the car is far enough to the side to be safe. He follows my order, and we run the opposite way. He's slightly behind me when we hear and feel it explode, throwing us off our feet. He catches me as we go to the ground, and I cushion his fall as I land between him and the concrete. A gush of air escapes my lungs, and I groan in pain.

We lie there a moment, trying to catch our breaths as I contemplate all the ways I can kill him. "Fucking get off me, asshole." I demand as I squirm, but once again, something in his groin area starts to harden at my movement. "Are you fucking serious?"

He leans in and nuzzles my neck. "Sorry, baby, but you do feel good, and I feel like we just escaped death. I think we should fuck to reaffirm our lives."

"Sage, the only thing you will be reaffirming if you don't get off me is my foot up your ass." I buck my hips a couple of times, and although his dick continues to harden, he rolls off me. I get to my feet, and luckily there doesn't seem to be too much damage, just a small hole in the concrete. "You are going to tell Dad about that." I point to it and storm away, leaving him chuck-ling on the ground.

"One day, Tori, one day."

I don't respond to his taunts, but I can't help but think about how nice it felt to have him wrapped around me, even if it was for only a moment.

Chapter Twenty-Three

~~~

Since I no longer have a security detail, I scored myself some henchmen like Aunt Carla. Dad said they are assistants, but Dean and Sam have resigned themselves, with long suffering sighs, to being called henchmen, and their lives are much better for it.

The Kitty Cat Club is dark when Sam holds the door open for me and I walk in, my eyes taking a little bit to adjust. I smile when I see Misty on the stage, strutting her stuff to a Katy Perry song. I tried to convince her to choose something edgier, but she refuses, and the patrons seem to like her slightly more innocent air, so I leave her be. She recovered from Ed's rape, and I had all the strippers put into therapy, which is being paid for by the company. When I investigated the other four locations, I discovered much the same arrangement that Ed had here. I took care of that immediately, and although Gio wasn't willing to spread my new nickname, the strippers were more than happy to whisper about Azrael, the Angel of Death. I was so happy I gave them all bonuses.

I installed female managers at all the locations and haven't had a single problem yet.

"Take a load off, boys. I've got a business meeting and won't be needing you for a while," I inform them, heading for the back office. "Have a lap dance on me."

They are good boys and have the resting mafia face mask perfected, but I see them grin at each other like little schoolboys and head to the bar for a drink.

I stop and whisper in one of the waitress's ears. "Lacey, see that my boys are taken care of, yeah?"

She nods eagerly and hurries to one of the private rooms to wait.

They don't know that I know, but Sam and Dean like to have girls together, and I know Lacey has been the meat in their sandwich many a time. As far as I'm concerned, they aren't hurting anyone. They are certainly not forcing any of my girls to service them, and no money exchanges hands, it's purely fun. I also don't expect the girls to do it. If Lacey wasn't interested, I would have shrugged and asked one of the others, but I try to come here when I know she's working, because I know she likes them. Whether she just gives them a lap dance or they take it further, that's none of my business. I have told the boys that no means no, and if they don't like it, I have a bullet with their name on it. They were very quick to agree. It also helps that they both have younger sisters and are way more respectful of women than a lot of the older generation I have come across. The security guards at the club also learned very quickly that I won't tolerate any lewd behavior from them unless the girls initiate it on their own time. Their private lives are just that, private.

Climbing the stairs to the office, I think about how hard it has been to have the older generation take me seriously. Being young and a woman has worked severely against me, but I think most of the men in Dad's organization have accepted me and been impressed with what I have managed to achieve over the past six months. With my ideas, we have increased narcotics sales by twenty percent, as well as increasing the brothel's revenue threefold by adding male escorts. The wealthy women in our area aren't having their needs met by their husbands, and adding a bisexual and homosexual menu has also been effective. As much as the old-school generation doesn't agree with this lifestyle, they can't argue with the money the organization is making.

I open the door to the office and move over to the big glass window overlooking my club. Sighing, I think about the one thing that's not right in my life. Gio is hiding something. He gets secret text messages and goes off for days at a time and tells me I need to mind my own business whenever I ask him. I've tried to have him tailed, and he loses them every time. It's beginning to wear my trust thin. He should know better after everything that happened. I plan on confronting him tonight because I am sick of his secrets.

Speaking of secrets, Stacey hasn't been forgotten. I still monitor her social media, and I'm biding my time, waiting for her to forget about me completely and be secure in her role as number one. Not that she's there yet. I have it from good sources that she's still sleeping with James on the side, and she hasn't managed to get him to dump Nikki. I guess Nikki is still number one because she hasn't let Stacey get too close. I'm pretty sure after what she did to me, Nikki doesn't trust her one bit. I never accused Nikki of being dumb.

Hands touch my shoulders, pressing deep into my muscles, trying to release some of the tension that sits there. "Babe, you're so fucking tense," the husky voice behind me mutters quietly.

"It's been a long day," I murmur as I watch a patron try to touch one of my girls' breasts on stage. Bill jumps in and is quick to dissuade him. Bill and Joe are still bouncers here, but they have been on their best behavior since I showed them images of what I did to Ed.

Two manicured hands wrap around me, and I lean back into the soft chest of my sometimes lover. "How about I get rid of some of that tension for you?" she whispers into my ear before spinning me around and claiming my mouth.

My hands drift up into Candy's red hair as her tongue tangles with mine and our bodies press against one another. I promoted Candy to manager as soon as I realized she had a good head on her shoulders. She's kind and compassionate and can relate to the girls, and it's the best decision I have ever made. I tried to keep things on a professional level, but she was very determined, and in the end, I caved. I'd been curious, and once I explained what had happened with Stacey, she made my first real time special with lights and candles. She had really gone out of her way to romance me before seducing me, which I will forever be grateful for. It was a little awkward without the drugs riding me, but in the end, it had been wonderful.

One thing I was clear on from the start, however, is that there will be no commitment between us. She continues to see other people, and I don't have the emotional capacity to be involved with anyone else. I don't trust, so my situation with Candy suits me perfectly because there are no emotions involved except for respect and affection. Sex for me is nothing but a physical outlet, so emotions have no place in it for me, not to mention being with me isn't exactly safe. She could easily be used against me, which is why I refuse to develop anything other than a genuine affection for her and continue to keep my inner circle extremely small.

She pulls away and drags me over to the office chair and pushes me onto it. I struggle to sit up. "Candy, I can't. I have to meet Gio shortly, we're going out to dinner with the family."

Just then my phone beeps, and when I pull it out, it's a message from Gio saying he's running late. Candy peers over the top and smirks at me when she sees it.

"Perfect." She grabs the phone out of my hand and

tosses it onto the desk. She picks up the remote and presses a button, and the sounds of Nine Inch Nails' "Closer" comes on over the speakers. She steps back and starts to sway back and forth as she undoes the buttons holding her sexy silk blouse together. She shimmies and shakes, and my panties grow damp as she slides it down her arms and tosses it to the side, leaving her in a pair of booty shorts, her heels, and a corset. My eyes widen at the sight of it, and she smirks.

"I thought you might like this. I bought it especially for you." She winds sensually around the pole in the middle of the room. Yes, it's left over from Ed, but she wanted me to leave it there for practice, and now I'm very glad I did. She undulates against it a couple of times as she sings along to the words and pulls her hair out of the ponytail it was tied in.

I feel my breathing speed up in time with my heart rate. This girl knows how to work a crowd, or me, really. I'm pretty fucking basic. She struts over to me and turns, shaking her ass in my face before doing a slut drop.

"Come here," I growl, and she squeals with excitement as I haul her onto my lap and push her hair away to nibble on her neck as my hands massage her breasts.

"I think that was the quickest you've ever broken," she teases, her voice getting breathy as I pull at the laces on her top. I fumble and she giggles, so I lift her and turn her around to face me. She straddles my lap, and I can now easily undo the laces.

"How could I refuse such a prettily wrapped

present?" I make quick work of the corset, and then her breasts are in my face, her perky pink nipples hard with desire. I can't stop myself from leaning forward and tracing them with my tongue. She sighs as I lap at one and then the other, her hands tangling in my hair as she starts to writhe on my lap.

"Oh, Tori, that feels so good," she murmurs softly before pulling my mouth to hers and kissing me. She tries to remove my shirt, but I really don't have time for anything today, so I push her hands away and stand up, carrying her with me to the nearby sofa—this one is new since Ed—and laying her down on it. I settle myself between her legs and peel her booty shorts down. She grumbles as she lifts her butt. "This was supposed to be me relaxing you."

She looks so pretty as she pouts, so I glance up at the clock on the wall. Fuck it, I have time. "Okay, but it's got to be a quickie," I concede, and her smile is enough to make being late worthwhile.

I strip off my jacket, pull my gun out, and place it on the coffee table, then I strip off my corset holster and bra before unzipping my pants and letting them fall to the floor, kicking off my shoes at the same time. Putting my thumbs in the waistband of my panties, I shimmy them down until I'm standing naked before her.

She licks her lips, and her eyes dilate as I settle between her legs. Pulling her panties down, I lean in and swipe my tongue through her folds before flicking it over her clit. I've become somewhat of an expert at oral sex, and it doesn't take me long to work her into a frenzy.

"Please, Tori, I want you to fuck me," she begs, so I slide up her body, nipping and sucking as I go. Lining my pussy up with hers, I start to move above her, knowing she loves when I do this so we can come together. She moans and groans as our clits collide and our pussy lips slide together. I fuse my mouth to hers as she wraps her legs around my hips and starts to thrust with me. I can feel my orgasm building deep inside, and when I pull away to get a better angle, she latches onto one of my nipples and starts to play with the ring I have through it. My orgasm is just out of reach, and I know what I need to push me over, but Candy doesn't like it.

"Harder," I demand, and she shakes her head.

"No, I don't want to hurt you," she pants.

"Please, I need it," I beg, and she closes her eyes, grabs the ring between her lips, and pulls. It's not hard enough to rip it out, but it's hard enough that the bite of pain pushes me over the edge, and I come with her following just after me. As soon as I feel her body stop shuddering, I slip down again and lap up our combined releases, rewarding her for what she did even though she didn't want to.

Her hands slide into my hair and caress me gently as I clean her up. This is why I know this won't last. We both know it, but we aren't quite ready to accept it. I need something different than what Candy wants to give me. Pain and domination turns me on, and whether I'm giving or receiving it, I don't really care, but Candy is too gentle for that, and I won't ask it of her.

Pulling away, I lean in and give her a kiss. "Thanks, babe, I needed that."

As I climb off her, I think I see hurt in her eyes, but I'm not ready to think about the cause. I use the bathroom off the office to clean up and make my hair neat and tidy again before returning to quickly redress. She's quiet while she dresses. I shove my guns in their holsters and swing my jacket back on. Sometimes I wear an ankle holster with another gun there, but I didn't this morning. Once I'm all set, I head around to the desk, take the computer out of rest mode, and bring up the information I needed. Attaching it to an email, I send it to myself and then stand up, stuffing my phone in a pocket.

"I've got to go. I'll see you later," I tell her, placing a kiss on her soft lips, knowing that will probably be the last time we'll be intimate.

It's been a long time coming, and I think she's started to develop feelings despite me not being her only lover. It was the look in her eye, and when feelings start to develop, I get the urge to cut and run. I'm just not built for emotions and monogamy. The thought of being responsible for someone's life, which is essentially what will happen if I have a relationship, terrifies me, and it's what's stopped me from exploring anything with Sage too. Nope, if I go there, I may not be able to stop, so I stick to women. If I explore the unknown, I might like it too much, and then how would I give it up?

She's silent as I leave, but as the door closes behind me, I hear her scream before something smashes against the door. Yup, pretty sure I won't be doing that again. Patting my pocket, I feel the joint I have in there, but I know I need to be alert. God, I can't wait to get home so I can light up.

Chapter Twenty-Four

A s I walk through the crowded club, I toss my car keys to Poppy, the girl behind the bar. "Give these to Sam and Dean. If they aren't out in five, go get them and tell them to meet me at the Lucky Diamond. She starts to argue, but I hold up a hand. "I don't care if they are balls deep in Lacey, they have had enough time. Oh, and if they scratch my car, I'll kill them." I see her swallow nervously, and I try to put a smile on my face, but I guess it comes off more homicidal maniac than friendly, because she squeaks and runs away.

Damn it. This thing with Candy has got me all fucked up. I throw open the door and it bangs against the wall as I stomp to Gio's car that's idling directly by the entrance. Climbing in, I pull the door closed a little too furiously.

"Hey," he complains as I put on my seat belt. "Easy on my car."

"Oh, blow it out your ass, Gio," I retort and cross my arms, staring out the window.

The car starts to move as he drives us in the direction of the Lucky Diamond. "Aww, what's wrong, babe? Didn't get your weekly orgasm?" he asks sarcastically, and I growl, whirling on him.

"Why were you late?" I snap, watching him carefully and waiting for him to lie.

"My meeting ran over," he replies, not taking his eyes off the road. Hmm, he didn't lie.

"Who were you meeting?" There's a pause, and I know before he does it that he's going to lie.

"Just one of our suppliers, no one important." He tugs on his right ear, and I feel like pulling my gun out and shooting him in the foot. Nothing vital, just maybe a pinkie toe. He can live without that, but fuck, it would hurt.

Sighing, I turn away from him again, but I make sure he can hear me clearly. "You know, out of everyone in our lives, you were the one person who I could always count on to tell me the truth. It kind of makes me feel sick that once again, the person I trusted most in this world is lying to me."

We don't say another word. I can't even look at him, and the tension in the car is thick. Gio pulls into the underground parking at the Lucky Diamond, and we climb out.

"Dad says we're using the limo today and to meet him out front." Gio looks at his phone, and we use the elevator to get up to the main floor. It opens into the middle of the game floor, so it's loud and noisy chaos, but I love it.

"Oh, where are we going for dinner?" I ask him, and he shrugs as we walk across the casino, passing all the tables and slot machines.

"I'm not sure. All he said was that he had an announcement and a surprise." The doors are in sight, and I can see the limo parked in the valet area at the front of the hotel. When we exit the hotel, I see that the car door is open and Dad and Carla are waiting for us. Dad is frowning, but I don't think it's at us, so I turn to look back and see Penelope and Lorenzo following closely behind us. I guess we weren't the only people who were late. Suddenly, Gio stops and bends down to pick up a casino chip from the ground. Just as he does, there is a huge explosion, and we are thrown off our feet. I get tossed backward and hit my head on the ground. Dazed, I try to sit up, but the heat of the explosion and my throbbing head make it hard, and the last thing I see before blacking out is the limo that Dad and Carla had been sitting in consumed by flames.

My mind is foggy and my body aches as I try to wake up. Fuck, what did I do last night? I don't remember going on a bender. But then an incessant beeping noise makes itself known, and I realize my arm is heavy. Struggling, I finally get my eyes open and find myself in a hospital bed with an IV in my arm and a heart rate monitor attached to me.

What the fuck? I freeze as it all comes back to me. Dad! Carla! Gio! Struggling, I reach over to rip the IV out of my arm, but my body doesn't want to cooperate. A hand on mine stops my struggles, and when I look up, I find Sage, his cheeks streaked with tears.

"Let me up. I need to go to the others." I try to fight him, but he sits down on my bed, wraps his arms around me, and just holds me.

His body trembles as he sobs, and I shake my head. "No, no way. No! Noooooo!" I shout, my voice giving way to screams, and I fight against him. "Let me get up. I want to see my dad," I yelp, but he just holds on. Finally, I exhaust myself and collapse into his embrace, sobbing. I know the truth. He's gone. My daddy is gone, and I will never see his smile or be held by his strong arms again.

I'm not sure how long we sit there, holding one another, but when I see movement over his shoulder, I'm completely drained. Sam and Dean are standing guard on either side of the door, and they have stopped the nurse from coming into my room.

"Let me through, you idiots, I need to check on my patient." She sounds pissed.

Sage pulls away, wiping his face with his hands before he nods at them. They step aside, and she bustles in.

"Move out of the way please," she asks Sage in a no-nonsense voice.

He lets go and moves off the bed but keeps holding my hand. The nurse checks all my vitals before speaking to me.

"Hi, I'm Nurse Scott. Do you remember what happened?" she asks, making notes on the chart in her hand.

"The limo exploded," I answer flatly, and she nods.

"Yes, I'm sorry for all of your losses, Ms. Russo."

All my losses?

"Who else?" I demand of Sage, and he flinches but looks me directly in the eye as he breaks the news.

"I'm so sorry, Tori, but we lost Carla too." Just as the final word leaves his mouth, I turn to the side and vomit bile onto the floor. The nurse jumps out of the way, so I don't splatter her feet. I wipe my mouth with the back of my hand, expecting her to scold me, but she just looks at me, her eyes full of sympathy. She tells me she's going to find someone to clean it up and leaves quietly, and Sage returns to his seat beside me.

I have no tears left to cry, and I need to know everything. I channel my anger, refusing to give into the emotions threatening to overwhelm me. I've been taught that this organization has no room for feelings. "Tell me," I order, and I'm not sure what he sees in my eyes, but whatever it is makes him shudder before he starts.

"Before I begin, if it's any comfort, both of them died instantly. Mickey is alive, but he's in a coma. He was standing on the other side of the vehicle because he stepped out to have a smoke when it exploded. He was thrown hard against a car parked on the other side, and he has swelling on the brain. They put him into a medically induced coma after they removed a flap of his skull in the hope that not too much damage would occur. It's a waiting game for him. Gio was here, but he was checked over and then he discharged himself against doctors' orders. He has a few cuts and bruises and a possible concussion as well, but he wouldn't stay. He said he needed to make sure that whoever was responsible for this attempt at a hostile takeover could see it failed. He's in charge now, and he needs to be seen throwing his weight around."

Holy shit, my brother is the mob boss. I'm so numb from everything, I can't even react.

Sage goes on. "Both Lorenzo and Penelope had a few scrapes and cuts that needed seeing to, but they were told to go home. Gio assigned round the clock protection on both you and Mickey, and of course I wouldn't leave you alone."

He's quiet as I try to wrap my head around everything. "What happened? What do you mean hostile takeover?" I ask him, still confused.

Sage does a double take, and when he meets my eyes, his are full of sympathy. "Tori, honey, someone planted a bomb under the limo, and Gio and I think it was meant for all of you. We believe it should have gone off when you were all in it, but it malfunctioned.

This was most definitely an attempt to get rid of the Russo family line."

A bomb? Someone killed my dad and Carla so they could take over our business. The cold fury that has been my constant companion since Stacey's betrayal washes over me, and I yank the needle out of my arm and push Sage out of the way. "Where are my clothes?" I ask when I realize I'm wearing a hospital gown.

He shakes his head, and I know he's going to argue with me.

"Don't, Sage. Just hand me some fucking clothes. I need to be with Gio. We need to work out who did this, and then I will rain hell down on them." I look at my henchmen. "Where is my gun?" They exchange a glance.

"Mr. Russo told us not to give you one," Dean stammers, not meeting my eyes.

I gasp, and Sage grabs my hand.

"They mean Gio. He's Mr. Russo now." Of course he is. I'm such an idiot. I drop my chin to my chest and breathe for a moment or two. The tears threaten to surface, but I let the anger, fury, and need for vengeance wash away the sadness. Steeling myself, I take a deep breath, and when I look up, I'm no longer Mafia Princess, but Azrael, the Angel of Death. Heaven help those who have done this, because I will wash the streets with their blood when I find those responsible.

The last poignant notes of "Hallelujah" float away on the breeze as the singer steps back and the priest moves forward to deliver his sermon. I don't hear a word of it as I study the large gathering, trying to work out if anyone here could possibly be responsible for my aunt's and father's deaths. One by one, I study family friends, business associates, and strangers, all here to pay their respects to the Russo family and their late boss, Stefano. I see a lot of the casino workers here as well saying goodbye to Carla. When they heard that Mickey was in the hospital and not able to attend, they came in his stead as a show of respect to a woman they all respected and admired. Which one of these solemn people is a liar? Which one has perfected their grief mask but is secretly laughing behind it?

It's not until the mourners start throwing roses onto the coffins as they lower into the ground that I realize it's all over and I have missed everything that's happened. Penelope and Lorenzo are the last to throw their flowers before it is my and Gio's turn. Sage offers me a hand to stand, but I shake my head slightly and he drops it. I need to be seen as strong. I can't let anyone think there is any weakness to me. On the other hand, however, they are welcome to underestimate me, because my trigger finger is itchy and my thirst for revenge is fierce.

Finally, Gio and I are left alone. Sage steps away to give us a moment, and I can see various members of our organization staked out around the area, giving us a circle of protection when we are at our most vulnerable. Neither of us will outwardly show our grief. We will save that for the privacy of our own home. Here today, we stand strong and united, even though there is a bigger wedge than ever between us. I outright asked him if this had anything to do with where he goes, and he vehemently denied it. He swore on the family name that it didn't, so I let it go, but it hurt that he won't tell me. That he doesn't trust me with whatever it is.

I release my rose, the thornless stem slipping out of my hand and into the large hole, landing on top of all the other white roses on the coffin. My and Gio's blood-red roses stand out on top, and as I go around to do the same to Carla's, it reminds me of Ed's first droplet of blood on the white tiles of the interrogation room. That feels like so many years ago now.

It's funny how blood has become an integral part of my life. Family first and always is what Dad taught us, and Gio and I are now the last remaining members of our family. Sure, there are a few second cousins and Lorenzo, but he is not to be trusted. I have never trusted him, and it got even worse after the whole incident with the Kitty Cat Club. If I could take the escorts away from him, I would, but Dad told me to bide my time. If he didn't have the escorts, he would be free to stick his nose in places Dad really didn't want him to.

I asked Gio about that tattoo of Dad's he promised to tell me about and never had. *Cruor, Veneratio, Virtus*. Blood, Honor, Valor. It's the Russo family motto and what every person brought into the organization has tattooed on them. A couple of days ago, Gio organized for the Russo family tattoo artist to come and tattoo it on me. I chose to put it across the left side of my ribs under my heart. I had him add a stylized drop of blood to the tattoo as well. Blood over everything. Gio had him add the same thing to his tattoo, and whenever someone swore their loyalty to him, we had them all add the drop of blood to their own tattoos as well.

Funnily enough, Lorenzo didn't have a tattoo. I asked Gio about it, and he said that blood family members were not required to get the tattoo, but most did as a sign of respect. Lorenzo didn't as a big *fuck you* to his father when he wouldn't legitimize him. Once he was dead and Dad offered it to him, he said he didn't want it and never would despite being loyal to the family. Sounds shady to me, but for now, we let it slide.

We say our final goodbyes, turn our backs, and walk away. My hand that isn't in my brother's clenches, the only outward display of anger that I show as I catch sight of the people waiting for us.

Not willing to let us mourn in peace, Penelope taps her foot. "Well, it's about time. The lawyer is waiting to read Stefano's will back at the fortress."

I try to yank my hand out of Gio's and reach for my ever-present gun, but he holds on tight.

"We will follow you," he tells her, and she heads to the waiting limo, escorted by Lorenzo. I watch them both go before nodding to two of the security still surrounding us.

"Follow them." They hurry away as the rest of the guards fan out, walking with us as we move to Gio's parked car. Sage is leaning against it, and he's arguing with someone. It's a woman, but she has her head covered with a black mourning veil. Well, that's certainly dramatic. When we get closer, she turns, and I see it's Candy, her red hair now visible. What the fuck? My hand clenches in Gio's, and he gives me a reassuring squeeze before going around to the other side of the car and flipping his seat forward for Sage. Both give me a false sense of privacy, considering they are just a few feet away, but I appreciate it.

"Oh, baby, I'm so sorry," Candy sobs and reaches for my hand, but I pull it away and glance around. When I look back at her, she appears hurt, but I don't feel guilty.

"Thank you for coming, but we can't do this anymore."

Her eyes fill with pain, and she takes a step back. "But it's alright for you and Sage to be together?" she spits, the hurt turning to anger, and I feel my eyebrows jump in surprise.

"Me and Sage? You think we're a thing?" I ask her, and she sneers.

"I see the way he looks at you, and I've caught you looking at him too."

"I can assure you that is not the case. You're the only person I've been intimate with for a long time, but what's done is done, and it's over. I'm sorry if this hurts you, but it really is for your own good."

"Fuck you, Tori." She spits on the ground and flounces away, and I climb into the car. The atmosphere is tense as fuck as Gio pulls away from the curb.

Chapter Twenty-Five

~∾~

"Wow, you really dodged a bullet there, but I bet she was wicked in the sack. Crazy is always good in bed," Sage comments conversationally, and for the first time since I woke in the hospital, I smile.

Gio chuckles and holds his hand out for Sage to fist bump, and the tense atmosphere dissolves as we drive home. It's silent but comfortable, with quiet music playing, but when we pull into the underground garage, Gio stops the car and breathes out a deep breath.

"Dad's lawyer called me yesterday to give me the heads-up. Penelope is expecting to be in the will, but Dad has left everything to you and me. She has permission to live in the old house, and she gets a small allowance, but apart from that, nothing. So please expect some drama and try not to shoot her."

"That's it?" I ask him, and he shakes his head. "No.

Apparently there is a recorded message we must sit through before the reading of the will, so you need to brace yourself for that."

A recorded message from my dad. How the fuck am I going to get through that without breaking down? I look between the two boys in horror, and Sage pats me on the shoulder. "It's okay, you've got this."

His gentle reassurance helps, and I climb out of the car, sliding my seat forward so he can step out after me.

The two of us flank Gio as we use the elevator to get up to the house. When the doors open, the foyer is filled with mourners who have returned to celebrate Dad's life—or to get a sneak peek inside the house people have whispered about for so many years. Mayor Steel nods to Gio as we pass, as do several other well-connected individuals whom we have blackmail on. Gio was very quick to let everyone know that even though Dad was gone, his legacy lived on through him. After a few well-placed threats, we quickly got everyone back into line before they could even think of stepping over it.

It's not just the foyer that's filled with people, but the entire ground floor. We don't stop to talk. The crowd parts like the Red Sea as the three of us march through it. The reading of the will is going to take place in the secret room beyond the conference room, but everyone is waiting in the conference room when we arrive. Gio moves over to Dad's lawyer, welcoming him as I move to the side and observe the people here. Apart from Lorenzo and Penelope, Ben and Suzie are here as well as Dad's cousin Petey, another high-ranked officer in our organization.

"Can we please get on with this?" Penelope drawls with greedy anticipation, and I keep my face blank despite the smirk that wants to show itself.

"Firstly, I ask Giovanni and Victoria to make their way into the room. Your father left a recording for you to watch." He looks down at the paper in front of him and nods. "And Sage too."

Penelope's gasp of outrage is good for my soul. "Why the hell is he invited in?" she demands, and the lawyer holds up his hands.

"I am just honoring my client's last wishes, Mrs. Russo."

Gio pushes in the eye of the bust, and the door pops open and the three of us descend the stairs. When we get into the conference room, there is a laptop set up on the table, and I take a seat in front of it as the boys crowd in behind me. The lawyer follows us down, making sure the door is closed. I press play on the screen, and my dad's smiling face appears. I can't stop the tears that roll down my cheeks at the sight, and both Gio and Sage place a hand on my shoulders.

Dad's smile is bittersweet as he waves at us. "Hello, my children. If you are watching this, then the unthinkable has happened and I am no longer with you. Know that I love you all very much, and it has been my honor to see you grow into the wonderful human beings you are." He stops and chuckles. "Yes, even you, Sage, although you drive me to drink sometimes. It has been a joy getting to know you over the years, and I hope that by giving you my last name, I have done right by you." The lawyer passes Sage an envelope, and when he tears it open, it's adoption papers saying that Sage is now a Russo.

A gasp escapes his mouth, and I see the tears well in his eyes.

"Gio, make sure he gets the tattoo. He hasn't gotten it yet, but it is time. Look after my children for me, Sage, they are going to need a friend in the future to come, because if I am not with you, it means that the traitor in our organization has succeeded. Although I am no closer to finding out who it is, I leave it in your capable hands to figure it out. I have faith in you all. If Mickey is still with you, use him, trust him, and rely on him much the same way I have over the years, but whatever you do, do *not* trust my brother and do *not* trust Penelope. Both are going to want to wheedle their way into the day-to-day operations of the business, but you must not let this happen. Gio, stand strong and be the leader I know you to be. Tori, my sweet mafia princess, it is time you became Azrael, the Angel of Death, for real." He winks before sobering up again. "You are the underboss now. Show no mercy. Protect your brother, protect Sage, and protect your heart. Trust no one but each other. Find my killer and avenge me, and then move on. Live and love like your mother and I never could. Make the Russo family proud. We will be watching over you from above."

The video blinks out, and I try to swallow past the lump in my throat as I hastily wipe the tears from my face. The lawyer gives us a moment as we sit in a loaded, emotional silence before he grabs the laptop and holds his hand out for us to go back upstairs.

The lawyer fiddles with some paperwork for a few minutes while we get resettled. As I look at Penelope, it's all I can do not to grin with glee as I see her face turn red with impatience at the delay. But finally, he is ready, and the reading of the will is quick. "Ben and Suzie are guaranteed their spot in this house and their jobs as long as they would like. Both have been bequeathed a nice cash amount, which I will disclose to them in private," he starts when everyone sits around the conference table. He looks at Lorenzo next. "Here is the deed to your apartment. Stefano had it signed over to you." He passes over a piece of paper, and I see Lorenzo's jaw clench. Next, he moves on to Penelope.

"Mrs. Russo, you have been given the house that was your previous address. If you choose to sell it, Giovanni Russo gets the first right to buy it back. You may also keep the jewelry, clothes, and car gifted to you by Mr. Russo." Penelope is preening, but her expression drops when he turns to look at us. "As for the remainder of Mr. Stefano Russo's estate, it will be shared equally between his two children, Giovanni and Victoria Russo, as well as an undisclosed amount being gifted to Mr. Sage Russo."

"What the fuck?" Penelope screams, jumping to

her feet as she slams her hands down on the table. "Who the fuck is Sage Russo? He's not a fucking Russo, he's just some trumped-up junky whore Stefano felt sorry for. What about my share of the estate?"

"I already read what you were bequeathed, Mrs. Russo." The lawyer stands his ground in the face of a furious Penelope.

"As his wife, I am entitled to more than that no matter what the will says. I'll sue."

He hands her a document. "You signed a prenup when you got married. You're entitled to only what he allows you to have." Her face pales as she reads the piece of paper he handed her.

Lorenzo gets calmly to his feet and adjusts his suit jacket before looking Gio in the eye. "I will expect weekly reports on everything that is going on within the family business."

Gio snorts. "Yeah, and why would you think that would start happening? Just because Dad is gone doesn't make you any higher on the ladder than you were. You report to me, and you report to Tori. Just stay in your lane and keep your head down, Renzo, and we will all be okay. Enjoy your whores and your coke, and Tori and I will continue to run Dad's empire just like he wanted us to."

The look of pure fury that flashes through Lorenzo's eyes is nothing short of staggering, but instead of arguing, he wraps his hand around Penelope's arm and helps her to her feet. "You two haven't heard the last of me," he growls.

"How fucking cliché," I drawl as he leads her to the door. "Oh, and Penny, darling, make sure your shit is out of this house by tomorrow, or I'll throw it on the front lawn." The satisfaction I feel at telling her that is almost as good as an orgasm. Almost.

A week after the reading of the will, Gio and I discovered who planted the bomb. He was some idiot off the street who didn't even consider how many cameras were situated around the hotel and casino. He can be seen casually strolling up to the limo while it was parked in the underground parking lot and sliding beneath it before emerging five minutes later. Once we had his face, it was just a matter of Gio's tech guys running it through facial recognition before we had a match.

He didn't even bother to hide, and I think it's a genuine surprise to him when, accompanied by my henchman Sam and Dean, I blow a hole through his apartment door and let myself in, passing the shotgun to Dean to hold onto so it doesn't ruin my aesthetic.

"What the fuck? Who are you?" He jumps up from his seat on the couch.

Sam and Dean stand on either side of me while I

wait. I hear one of them mutter, "Fuck," and the other one sigh.

"She's Azrael, the Angel of Death," I hear Dean deadpan dryly. Seriously, how hard is it to get good henchmen around here?

The guy, whose name is Stan, looks confused. "Huh?"

I wait, tapping my foot.

"She's your worst nightmare," Sam mutters, and I throw my hands up in frustration.

"Thanks a ton, assholes. You're really trying to sell the image. How am I supposed to intimidate people when you won't even take this seriously?"

"Well, if you just told them your real name, it would be enough to make anyone piss their pants," Dean snaps back.

"Yup, just hearing the name Russo is enough to make someone fearful, especially the cocksucker who killed your dad," Sam drawls and waves at the guy. "Look."

The guy is now gaping at me, his face has paled, and I can see his hand twitching like he wants to reach for a weapon or something. I pull my gun out of my holster and point it at him.

"I wouldn't do that if I were you, Stan."

"I... I... I didn't know it was your dad's limo when I was paid to do that job. I swear, I just thought it was some rich whale staying at the casino. They pay me not to ask questions, just to do the job. They assured me there were no cameras to catch me planting the bomb."

He's talking furiously now, the words spilling out of his mouth in the hope it might save him. Spoiler... It won't.

"They lied," Sam drawls, shaking his head at the guy's idiocy.

"Now you're going to tell me who gave you the bomb, and maybe we will leave here and never come back." This time it's me who's lying, but the thing about being a woman is that men believe you if you take the right tone. And sure enough, hope blooms in his eyes, and I feel a wave of smug satisfaction roll over me. *Got him.*

"His name's Franz. I don't have a last name, but I met him at Purgatory. It's a bar down on the waterfront and is run by the Horsemen. He told me it was an easy job for easy cash, nothing else, I swear. He didn't even mention who paid him, just that they had paid him to make a bomb that would blow up a larger car and was easy to plant."

Although the Russo's run Suncity, there are always others trying to muscle their way into some of the action. The Horsemen are a biker gang whom we occasionally contract with to protect our trucks on drug runs. We have an easy agreement. We pay them well to protect our drugs, and Lorenzo pays them well to distribute it through other states too. To hear they may have some kind of connection to Dad's death is surprising to say the least, but I don't let that show.

"And he didn't mention who?" I press.

"No, nothing, he gave me the bomb and the cash

in a backpack. His instructions told me where and when to plant the bomb and the license plate of the car."

"And that's it? You can't think of anything else to tell me? What did this Franz look like?"

"I don't know, he was average, about the same height as me with brown hair. There was nothing special about him." I can see the guy thinking. "Oh, wait, yes there was. When he handed me the backpack, he was missing two fingers on his right hand."

Well, I guess that's something to go on, which is more than I had before we got here. I smile brightly at Stan.

"Awesome, thanks for your help."

He visibly relaxes. "So, you'll leave now and won't shoot me?" he asks hopefully.

"No, you stupid motherfucker, you killed my dad." I lift my gun and shoot, watching the round hole in the middle of his forehead ooze blood as he falls to the ground, dead as a doornail. Satisfaction rolls through me as I turn and head for the door. One down, at least one more to go.

Dean and Sam follow me out of the building. I see Sam on the phone, calling in the cleanup crew, as I pick up my own cell and dial my brother.

"Yeah?" he answers, sounding distracted.

"Now is that any way to greet your favorite sister?" I ask him.

"I'm in the middle of something," he growls at me,

and my eyebrows rise in surprise. Gio always makes time for me.

"Well, I have a name. I'll be picking him up and taking him to the warehouse if you want in on this," I tell him, not hiding my annoyance.

"Yes, I do, but I can't get away at the moment," he replies.

"Whatever, nothing is more important than finding out who killed Dad, but you do you, bro." With that last cutting remark, I hang up on him.

"Shady motherfucker," I growl. "Have we worked out where he's been going?" I snap at Dean, who shakes his head.

"No, he's managed to lose every tail we have put on him and found every bug we've tried to put on his phone. He's clever. He's a Russo."

I growl in annoyance. "Once we find out who put a hit on Dad, we are making Gio a priority, even if I have to drug him to get it out of him. I just hope he's not doing the family dirty. I don't want to run the organization, and I don't want to put a bullet in the only family I have left."

Chapter Twenty-Six

Purgatory is in a seedier side of the city down on the docks. It's rough and run-down and stereotypically screams MC clubhouse. It's late afternoon, and it already has quite a crowd if the cars and bikes parked out front are anything to go by. I left the limo behind and took my own car this time, thinking it would fit in better. The Hellcat is the nicest car in the lot by far, and I'm hoping I still have my hubcaps when I get back. I'm also hoping the custom license plate that says "Azrael" is enough to scare anyone off. Down here, I have a little bit of a reputation for being batshit crazy. Even though my henchmen won't play the game, the strippers have been very good at spreading rumors.

The inside of the bar is smoky and smells like beer and piss, and I wrinkle my nose slightly as I look down at my shoes. My poor Louboutins are going to end up scuffed and damaged in this place. Gio better buy me a new pair. The noise dims a little as I walk from the door to the bar with my head held high, not intimidated one bit. I learned early on to fake it until I make it, but to be honest, I'm not scared. I hope someone underestimates me. I'm almost begging for some unrestrained violence. Knowing I'm one step closer to the person who killed my dad brings me some relief, but I won't be completely happy until whoever is responsible is drowning in their own blood.

The noise behind me returns as I step up to the bar, flanked by Sam and Dean, and the grizzly-looking bartender stares down his nose at me.

"Are you sure you're in the right place, little missy?" He raises a condescending eyebrow, and I just smirk.

"Is Franz here?" I ask politely. There's no point in starting off on the wrong foot right away.

The bartender narrows his eyes in suspicion. "Now what could a pretty young thing like you need with a crusty old coot like Franz Three Fingers?"

"Just tell Ms. Russo where he is, and we'll grab him quietly and get out of your hair. If not, the Horsemen may find themselves having their contract renegotiated, if you get what I mean," Dean growls ominously, and it's all I can do to hide my grin. He's so cute when he gets all growly, but it works because the bartender pales and points toward a side door.

"He's in the back with a girl. Room two."

"Oh, are you running whores through here?" I ask him, and he shakes his head hurriedly.

"No, just some bitch he picked up."

"I hope so, because that was not part of our agreement. All the whores in the city go through us. I'd hate to think you were cheating us out of a cut if you were. Please give Slasher my regards, and if anything gets messed up as we bring Franz out, please send us the bill." I lean against the bar, and Sam and Dean go to get Franz. Within seconds, a high-pitched scream cuts through the air, and everyone turns to look at the now open door leading to the rooms. A naked, semi-attractive woman comes running out holding her clothes with a terrified look on her face. She runs into what I'm assuming are the bathrooms. Not long after, Sam and Dean drag out a struggling man.

"Sorry, we had to make him get dressed," Sam apologizes, and I pat him on the cheek.

"Much appreciated." I look Franz up and down, and there is absolutely nothing remarkable about him. He is just plain and average, like Stan said, except for his right hand and his missing fingers.

He spews a whole heap of threats. "Who are you? What the fuck do you want? Get your hands off me. You'll be sorry. I'll find out where you live."

"Well, hello there. I'm Victoria Russo, but you can just call me Azrael, since we're about to become well acquainted." The noise in the bar disappears so suddenly you could almost hear a pin drop. Ah-ha, vindicated, the name does have an impact. "Come along, we don't have any time to waste."

Franz stopped struggling for a moment when he heard my name, but now he renews his efforts in desperation, like a man who knows he's going to the executioner. It's always nice when they aren't stupid.

Gio's not at the warehouse when we arrive with Franz, and a new wave of fury pierces my psyche. I can't believe he hasn't dropped everything for the chance to interrogate this guy.

I have to give it to him, Franz is persistent. He continues to struggle as Dean and Sam get him out of the car, bring him down the steps, and strap him into the chair. We leave him there as we go get a cup of coffee. Making them sweat is half the fun. I wonder if he will have pissed himself by the time we get back.

"What do you think, boys? Should I go straight to the drugs and get as much out of him as I can before killing him, or should I just start with the torture?" I ask my henchmen as we sit on the other side of the two-way mirror and watch him continue to struggle. My coffee is hot and has a shot of whiskey in it. We keep supplies here for just this kind of occasion.

"He looks like a pussy," Dean observes. "If you torture him, he'll pass out before you can get any information from him."

"Agreed. Start with the drugs and get what you need, then you can play with him after," Sam chimes in while taking a sip of his coffee.

I sigh in disappointment at their responses. "Bummer, drugs it is." I stand up and drain the rest of my mug before looking down at my shoes. "Crap. I need to keep another pair of shoes here so I don't ruin my good ones."

"There are a couple of pairs of rainboots in the bottom of the cupboard. I'm sure one will fit." Sam points inside the room.

"Really? That's perfect. Sam, I could kiss you." He blanches, and I frown. "What's wrong with me kissing you?"

He exchanges a look with Dean. "Sage told us if we liked our dicks then we need to stay the hell away from you," he mutters, and Dean nods.

"Yup, I really like my dick, so keep your lips to yourself."

I blink slowly in surprise. "Sage? My Sage threatened you?" I ask them, and they nod in unison.

"Huh." I'm not sure what to do with that information, but it kind of makes me feel warm and bubbly inside. I toe off my shoes. "Let's do this."

We walk into the room, and Franz starts to babble and plead for his life, but I ignore him while I go in search of the boots. Dean and Sam take up posts against the back wall. They know not to get in the way after experiencing an unfortunate incident that saw them both splattered with blood from arterial spray. Just thinking about it makes me giggle. Their faces were priceless.

"You know, Franz, interrogation takes a little planning. I don't like to ruin my clothes or my shoes, and I wasn't really prepared for it today. Luckily we have these." I grab the boots out of the cupboard and slip them onto my feet. "Do we have overalls or something? I hate the feel of sticky clothes when they are covered in blood," I ask the boys, and they both shake their heads. "Well, let's put them on the shopping list. It would make my laundry easier, and I'm sure the girls who do it would be grateful."

Putting my hands on my hips, I look at Franz. "Okay, are you ready to begin?" He's shaking with fear, and the scent of urine permeates the air. "Damn it, Dean, you were right. Fuck, I hate it when you're right." He smirks, and I grumble, "This is going to be fun now."

Turning back to the counter with all the tools laid out on it, I bang them about a bit before turning on a drill and then a reciprocating saw. I let that buzz for a moment or two before throwing them back with the other tools. Don't get me wrong, these tools are great and I have used them on people in the past, but they are messy and usually cause someone to pass out right away. In reality, the saw is only used to dismember them once they are dead.

"Fuck, Tori. He passed out," Sam tells me.

I turn, and sure enough, the asshole is unconscious in the chair. "Shit, now *that's* never happened before," I grumble with disappointment.

"Told you he was a pussy," Dean gloats, and I flip him off before turning back around, grabbing my drug of choice, Trilimide, and filling a syringe with it. Our Colombian friends shipped us some of this when our last shipment of coke came in as an added bonus. It has been very helpful as a truth serum.

"I'll just inject this, and by the time he wakes up, it should be in full effect." I go over to Franz and push back his sleeve, jabbing the needle into his bicep and depressing the plunger. Just as I'm pulling it out, the door bangs open, and Dean and Sam whip out their guns and point them at the intruder.

"At ease, assholes, it's just me," Gio drawls, his hair sticking out at all angles like he's been running his hand through it. The guys relax and put their guns away.

"Well, boys, look who decided to join the party. How kind of him." The sarcasm in my voice is unmistakable, and Dean and Sam know to duck for cover.

"Ah, we're just going to wait out there now that you've got more backup," Sam says diplomatically, and they both leave, Dean sneering at Gio the whole time. I do like loyalty in my men, and Dean just earned himself a big fat bonus.

"No need to be a bitch, Tori." Gio walks over to stand in front of Franz. "This is the guy who made the bomb? He doesn't look like much. And what did you do to him that made him pass out already?" He searches for signs of torture before looking at me and raising an eyebrow.

I roll my eyes and throw my hands up in the air.

"Nothing. The man's a pussy. I just played with the tools a bit and he was out like a light."

Gio frowns. "That doesn't scream hardcore criminal to me."

As pissed as I am at him, I have to agree. "No, it doesn't."

"He's just a patsy. Want to put money on it?" he offers, and I growl.

"No bet. And don't think I'm not going to ask where you've been when we're done here. If I had my way, *you* would be in this chair and *your* veins would be flooded with drugs. I don't like being kept in the dark, Gio. You are starting to look as shady as Penelope and Lorenzo."

He purses his lips and scowls at me. "Just because I want to maintain somewhat of a private life doesn't mean I'm doing anything untoward."

"Whoa, big word, bro, but it also doesn't mean you're not. Think carefully about this. It's always been you and me, together, and that's not happening at the moment. We really aren't gelling."

Before he can respond, Franz groans and rolls his head to the side, peering up at me. "You're hot. Want to suck my dick?"

I hide a snort, but Gio's face turns red and he backhands him. "What did you say to my sister?"

"I asked her if she would suck my cock. It's not big, I'm sure she could do a really good job of it." Franz is wide-eyed and sincere in his declaration.

I can't stop the peel of laughter that rings out as

Gio's mouth drops open in surprise. "Oh my God. Can we send the Colombians a thank you fruit basket or something? This is awesome."

"For fuck's sake, let's get on with it. I don't need to hear him hit on you," Gio grumbles, and I get control of myself.

Pulling up a chair, I turn it backwards and straddle it as I smile at Franz. I may not have to get bloody today after all.

"Did someone pay you to build the bomb that killed Stefano Russo?" I watch him think about it before he nods enthusiastically like a toddler.

"Yes, I got a nice chunk of cash for that job even after I paid that idiot to plant it."

"And who was it?" I ask him, my fingers tightening over the back of the chair in anticipation. This is it.

He shrugs. "No idea. It was posted on an underground message board, and I took the job. I got an email with the details, and the money was wired into my account. The username was DTF, that's all I can tell you."

Gio grunts, and I look at him with a raised eyebrow. "What?"

"DTF. Down to Fuck," he says wryly, and I roll my eyes.

"That definitely has to be a male. Only an idiotic man would use that as a username." I turn back to Franz. "That's it? You can't tell me *anything* else. You didn't meet them or anything? Talk to them on the phone or through text?"

Franz huffs. "Fuck no, people like that are scary."

Gio swears and starts pacing the room. I can tell his anger is riding him. Surprisingly, unlike the first time we did this together, I'm the calm one. His hand twitches, needing to reach for his gun, so I quickly ask another question.

"What message board was it?"

"Hit and Run. It's where anyone who is anyone posts their hits." Well, okay then. That's something I never thought I would hear.

"Excellent. Thank you, Franz, you have been a very good boy." I lean forward and pat him on the leg.

"Does this mean you'll suck my cock now?"

I wrinkle my nose as a bulge grows in his pants. Gio screams, pulls out his gun, and blows Franz's brains out from behind. Brain matter splatters all over my face.

Screaming internally because I don't want to get brain matter in my mouth, I run and grab the hose that's on one wall, turn it on, and spray myself down.

"You fucking asshole!" I scream once my mouth is clean. "Now who is trigger happy? I wanted to hear him squeal." I look down at myself and gag at the smell. "You couldn't have waited until you were in front of him?"

When my eyes meet my brother's, I stop screaming at him. I see the sadness and utter helplessness he feels over Dad's death and instantly forgive him for covering me with a brain smoothie.

"Oh, Gio, don't blame yourself. You aren't to

blame for Dad's death. None of us are. We should have had people inspecting the cars. We will find who did this, and when we do, they will wish they got a death as quick as Franz's." I go to hug him, but he puts his hands up.

"Love you, sis, but this is Dior." He points to his suit. "And I don't want Franz all over it."

"Well, I didn't get a choice, and neither do you." I tackle him, and he can do nothing but wrap his arms around me and hold me tight. I feel him shudder, and a small sob escapes his mouth as we stand there covered in Franz, grieving like we don't allow ourselves to do normally.

I meant what I said. Whoever did this will wish they were never born when we get our hands on them.

Chapter Twenty-Seven

～∽∽～

G io put his tech team on finding the user on the Hit and Run message board, but the profile had been deleted. They then tried to track the money from Franz's bank account, but once again, they came up empty. Gio's tech team is good, but whoever wiped all traces of the transaction is even better.

With no leads to go on, everyday life takes over, and Dad's killer gets pushed to the background for the moment. Gio and I stay busy mowing down other families who thought we'd be easy pickings with Dad gone. They were wrong. Eventually, we kill enough people for them to start taking us seriously, and business continues as usual.

Six more months go by, and I finally graduate from high school. I've decided not to go to college, but Gio is keen to return. He won't be living in the dorm, instead he will return home each night.

Sage has taken over most of the drug branch of the

business, while I handle the casinos and clubs, and Gio does guns and everything else. Between the three of us, we have a handle on things—except for the escorts branch. That's still in Lorenzo's hands. Gio has people trailing him and Penelope daily, making sure they aren't stepping out of line, but I have this funny feeling everything is coming to a head. I thought for sure they would start a relationship now that Dad is out of the way, but their relationship seems to have gone in the opposite direction, and they are barely civil to one another. I had also been expecting a lawsuit after Penelope's threats at the reading of the will, but nothing seems to have eventuated from that. I'm not sure if she was told she had no case or if she's biding her time. Both have been quiet, too quiet, and it has us worried, but all we can do is wait and handle the fallout if it happens.

The club is hopping tonight when I walk through the doors and down the set of stairs. My mask and wig are firmly in place, and my Russo tattoo has been covered by heavy stage makeup. No one would ever know that the woman wearing the slinky red lingerie under the fake black fur coat is Victoria Russo, coheir to the Russo empire.

I have a playdate with a new sub who practically

begged me to take him on after watching a public scene I did with one of my female subs. Normally I don't look twice at men, but there was something about this one. He's all smooth planes and golden skin, so he has so much more landscape for me to draw my blade across. There was also something in his blue eyes that resonated with me, a pain that needed an outlet, and I happily agreed to give it to him. I was pleasantly surprised when I enjoyed it the first time and eagerly agreed when he asked for another session.

Striding through the crowd, I make my way to the bar and order myself a drink, turning to lean against it and watch everything that's going on around me. While some sex clubs are apparently pretty tame, this one definitely caters to the wilder patrons. Although there are private rooms, there are no fucks given about anything happening out in the open either. There's a large center stage surrounded by lounges and booths, and a scene is taking place at this moment. Darkness surrounds the stage except for the spotlight shining down over the participants. A young redheaded woman is bent over with her hands and head in the stocks, unable to move as one man fucks her face and the other one fucks her from behind. All of them are wearing the required mask, but theirs match, so I assume they are together. Patrons are allowed to wear whatever mask they want so long as they don't remove it while in the club. Anonymity is respected here, and though there are those who are in relationships and have dealings outside the club, in here, they must follow the rules.

The sounds of her passion are intoxicating, so I move deeper into the room in the hope that I can get a better look.

The man at her head is choking her on his dick, his ass and leg muscles flexing deliciously with each thrust. I move around to have a look at the man behind her. He's got her hips gripped in both hands and is powering into her as hard as the man in front of her. The tattoos on his arms catch my eye, but before I can make out any detail, I'm tapped on the shoulder.

"Mistress V, your room is ready and Romeo is waiting for you," the staff member informs me, and I lose all interest in the scene behind me. As I make my way through the crowd to the back of the club, I think back to how I ended up here in the first place.

"Fucking hell, Tori," Gio growls with frustration, grabbing his head in his hands as the latest person we brought in for interrogation passes out from blood loss.

When he looks up at me again, I flinch at what I see. His annoyance at me and the fury he felt for the person we had been questioning has been replaced by pity.

"Tori, you need help or a better outlet. You can't keep killing all the people we bring in here just because you like to see them bleed. It's gone too far, sweetie." He comes over to me, takes the knife out of my hand, and leads me out of the interrogation room. "You are banned until you

get some semblance of control. If you want to make someone bleed, I've found a place where you can do that and they will enjoy it. It might be better to have people enjoying you cutting them as opposed to not getting any satisfaction because all they do is scream. Maybe you will find more pleasure in it if they get off on it."

I was so confused when he told me to dress up, and he and Sage took me to my first sex club, one that dealt with a darker side of pleasure. I mentored with a Dom for a few weeks to learn the ropes and get a grip on my control that really had disappeared. There was no choice, killing people at the club was frowned upon. Now I get a rush from the fact that I can control my need for violence and the look in my subs' eyes when I give them exactly what they need.

Blood play is a very specific form of pleasure, and there weren't a lot of Doms who offered it at the club, so when I expressed my enjoyment, it wasn't long before I had a regular rotation of women wanting to feel the steel of my knife—women who don't shy away from the tightly coiled violence in my eyes. Instead, they get wet and purr like kittens as I bring them to orgasm after orgasm.

My own orgasms that I experience as I drag my knife across the smooth skin of my subs and watch their blood bloom on the surface are beyond transcendent.

But my new male sub has been an eye-opening experience. While Sage and I have flirted and exchanged a kiss, it hasn't gone any further than that. There's a level of trust that I hesitate to ruin by making our relationship sexual. He gives me something on another level that I need so badly—emotional stability in a world ruled by chaos. It's something I thought I had with Stacey, and she proved me so wrong.

My new male sub mostly likes me to rub my naked body over his while he bleeds, and he does beg so prettily for my knife. It turns me on something fierce like no man, other than Sage, ever has before, but I worry it's actually the blood and not the man.

I quietly enter the door to my private room where Romeo is waiting for me. The bed is a wrought iron four-poster that allows me to tie my subs up in creative ways. The lighting is dim, and there's a cupboard of new, packaged toys to be used at my pleasure. There's also a little corner with some seating, but I never use it.

The staff knows my requirements for my subs, so he is restrained nicely. The cuffs, which are attached to chains bolted into the ceiling, circle his wrists, suspending him spread-eagle for me. He's naked apart from a pair of tight black briefs that do nothing to hide his delicious buttocks. He's facing away from me, and although he briefly stiffened when he heard me come in, he's relaxed, waiting silently and patiently as he should while I admire his form. Romeo, which is a false name much like my Mistress V, is muscular and has nicely defined thigh and calf muscles, as well as biceps and pecs—all favorite spots of mine to use my knife on. While I love to see the blood well upon his skin, I'm not here to do damage to him, in fact, quite the opposite. My subs bring a feeling of peace to my mind when I am allowed to cut them, and for that alone, I will cherish them and take care of their needs.

I walk forward, the sound of my heels deafening in the room, which is soundproofed from the outside. There is a camera that monitors everything that goes on in the room for the sub's safety, but I ensure that when I leave, the footage is erased. I run my finger along Romeo's back, and a shiver flows through his body.

"Hello, Romeo," I whisper as I lean over him. The soft fur of my coat brushing across his skin, combined with my breath sweeping across his ear, causes goosebumps to cover his body, and I smile. He is so reactive.

"Mistress," he sighs like it's a relief that I'm here.

"I'm sorry I kept you waiting." I move around to the front of him and step back so we can look at one another. Romeo's body is free of any adornment, which makes it an absolute landscape for my knife.

I reach into my pocket and feel for my special knife, the one Aunt Carla gifted to me at the very start of all of this. It's sitting next to my gun, which I refuse to go anywhere without. I slide it out, leaving the gun hidden, before shrugging out of my fur coat and leaving it to pool at my feet. I watch his eyes widen as he takes in my lingerie-clad body. My bra cups barely cover my nipples, and what little bit of fabric exists is sheer, same with the tiny black thong. I wanted to wear stockings and a garter because I know Romeo enjoys how I look, but I like to kick off my heels, so there's no real point anyway.

My eyes trail down his body and stop at the thick bulge in his briefs. "That looks uncomfortable," I say, gesturing to it with my knife. Any lesser person would have flinched, but I swear his nipples get harder and his dick pulses.

"Are you ready for me, Romeo?" I ask.

"Yes, please." His voice is filled with longing.

"Safe word?" I ask him just as I always do.

"Skittles," he answers with a whine of need.

"Good, let's begin." I move over to him and run my hands over his smooth expanse of skin, trailing my fingers lightly across all the grooves and dips in his sublime muscles as I build his anticipation. His breathing starts to get faster, and I can see his fingers clenching within his restraints.

Flipping my knife, I lightly run the blade across his chest. I've become somewhat of an expert on how hard I need to press without doing too much damage. My blade is sharpened to perfection, and I know from experience that the pain is a fleeting kiss before the blood starts to well upon his skin. Our dual groans make my core clench with need as enough blood builds to start dribbling down his chest. It's slow and will clot soon enough, so I move on to the next. One after the other, I cut small, shallow slices across his skin. No words are exchanged, so just our combined harsh breathing fills the room until we're both panting with need. Finally, I can't stand it anymore, so I undo his restraints and help him shuffle back and lie down on the bed. His torso is a bloody mess, and he looks like he's been the target of a serial killer. I almost come from the sight alone.

Feeling a little bold, I remove my bra and crawl across the bed until my body drapes over his, and I ease myself down onto his chest, his lifeblood hot and slippery against my skin. We both sigh as I start to rub myself all over him. I slip and slide as I enjoy the way his body feels under mine, his blood coating my skin as I move. Usually, I lie across him sideways, but this time I lie along the length of him, and as I rub up and down, my core bumps against his dick. I stop, shocked at how good it felt.

His hands come up to my hips. "Please don't stop, use me for what you need," he begs between gritted teeth. I look up at him in shock. Usually he doesn't talk unless spoken to, but I can see how much he wants me to do this in his eyes, and it did feel amazing. It's very different from when I rub myself against a woman.

"Okay, but keep your hands to yourself and close your eyes, no coming," I tell him, trying to keep the need and want out of my tone. His hands quickly drop away from my body, and he squeezes his eyes shut. "Good. If you can keep them like that until I'm done, I will allow you to jack off."

"Can I jack off on you?" he asks, almost too quiet for me to hear, but he keeps his eyes closed.

"If you do as I ask, then yes," I answer, a little surprised at what just came out of my mouth, but as soon as I start to glide my body over his again, I forget about everything else.

I slide up and down, basically humping him as I feel my orgasm build, my eyes locked on the exquisite red color painted all over his body. He has a cut line across his left peck that is slightly deeper than all the others and still oozing, and without thinking, I stick out my tongue and lap at it, the coppery taste and his rock-hard cock rubbing against my clit sending me hurtling over the edge. I can't stop the moan that leaves my mouth as I feel myself squirt, drenching his underwear with my fluids. He had been thrusting his hips the whole time, but at the feel of that, he stops and his whole body tightens up as he grits his teeth. He bites down on his lip hard enough to make it bleed, but I guess it does what he needs it to, and his body relaxes minutely.

"Did you come?" I ask as I shuffle my way down his body, pulling down his drenched underwear at the same time. My eyebrows jump up in surprise as his long, thick length is released. It's my first close look at a dick, so I check to make sure his eyes are still closed before I get a good look at it. Its purply red head looks angry, his veins are large and pulsing, and it's weeping precum from the tip.

I reach over and grab my knife, and slowly run the

flat of the blade along it. I feel him flinch, but when he doesn't use the safe word, I flip it over and very lightly run the sharp edge over a small section, releasing a pleased sigh when a little line of blood appears. I watch as more precum weeps from the end, dribbling down and mixing with the blood. Romeo's head is rolling back and forth now, and while he's distracted, I lean in and run my tongue along his length, gathering up the blood and cum mixture before moving back and letting the flavor spread across my tongue. It's very different from any girl I've tasted, but that could be the mix with the blood. I realize he's dead still, and I chide myself for letting myself get distracted.

"Keep your eyes closed, Romeo, and you may take care of yourself." His hand quickly goes to his throbbing cock, and he groans as he starts to stroke it, his grip punishingly tight. His eyes are closed, so I lean over and position my breasts above his length, and it doesn't take long before his hand speeds up and he moans, shooting thick ropes of cum across my tits, mixing with the blood on my skin. When he's done, I lean back and rub the mixture into my skin with fascination, the cum thick and stringy as it mixes with the blood. Moving my hand down into my thong, I use the mixture for lubrication and rub circles on my clit, and before long, I'm coming again, my soft pants loud throughout the now quiet room.

When the fog of my orgasm clears, I snatch my hand out of my panties, horrified at what I just did. When my eyes go to Romeo, he's still on the bed with his eyes closed, and his breathing is even. Holy shit, did I go too far. I scramble to my feet and hurry into the attached bathroom, running the shower and quickly washing the evidence off my body. Grabbing a towel and a wet washcloth, I rush back to the bed to check on my sub. I notice how sweaty his hair is and how clammy his skin feels, and I panic.

"Romeo, shit, Romeo, are you okay?" I shake him a little, and he rouses.

"Will you be my Juliet, Mistress V?" he slurs as his sub space smile spreads across his face, and I almost collapse to the floor in relief. I allow him to drift as I take special care in cleaning him up. When I've cleaned all the blood and semen, and pulled up the blankets and tucked him in, he rolls over, mumbling incoherently. Now that he's clean, his skin feels normal and he is no longer sweating, so I'm hoping that was just from him trying to control his release. I brush my hand across his blond hair, which is a mess behind his mask, trying to figure out what I'm feeling. This man could be very dangerous for me. He lets me do things that I'm sure not many others would. It's lucky we stick to pseudonyms and anonymity, otherwise I could grow too attached. Leaning in, I place a kiss on his lips, unafraid that he will feel it in his sleep.

"Thank you," I whisper before getting up and finding my fur coat. Removing my panties and picking up my bra, I toss the blood-soaked items into the bin to be disposed of once the room clears and it's cleaned.

I pay the staff extra to burn anything I may leave behind.

Wrapping my soft fur coat around my naked body, I grab my knife, which I cleaned, from the bathroom. After tucking it into my pocket, I send Sam and Dean a message, telling them to be ready to pick me up. I look around the room, checking I've left nothing that can identify me. Opening the door, I signal to the staff member that I'm done. They hurry away to bring in Romeo's designated caregiver, who will stay with him until he is awake and ready to leave.

Normally a Dom would be expected to cuddle with their sub after a scene and comfort them, but in my contract, I expressly state I will not do this and that they are to provide someone to look after them once I'm done with them. What's freaking me out, though, is that I desperately want to go back in there, strip off my coat, climb into bed with him, and watch over him until he wakes. Instead, I wait at the door until a man wearing a black mesh top and leather pants with bare feet strolls toward me. His bright blue eyes hold mine for a moment before they drop to the ground in submission. He brushes past me, and I catch the scent of something familiar, and then it's gone. I guess he must be wearing a cologne someone else I have contact with wears.

He goes in and closes the door, leaving me to hurry to the entrance, my feelings driving me to distraction. It's not until I'm in the car and we are heading home that I realize I forgot to have the footage erased. Fuck!

I lean my head back and close my eyes, trying to avoid thinking about anything but the taste of his blood and cum and the phantom feeling of my body against his. Maybe instead of this, I should be seeing a shrink to talk about all my issues. Or maybe it would be safer to just go back to being Azrael, the Angel of Death.

Chapter Twenty-Eight

Present

After I wash my face and check my makeup, I meet Gio out on the balcony of the VIP area. We look out over Club Hell, surveying our kingdom. I watch, despite the dark club, small drug exchanges take place all within plain sight, but if you didn't know what to look for, you wouldn't see it. I smile, pleased at how well things are going in my domain, but that soon fades as I watch the next group of people enter the club.

We allow anyone over the age of eighteen to attend our clubs, and technically they should be stamped with "underage" if they are under twenty-one, but Gio and I don't give a shit, and we have the chief of police in our back pocket, so they leave us alone. It's funny what a picture of someone in women's underwear will get you.

We often get people we both recognize from school, but the group that enters now has my teeth grinding as I reach for my knife that's tucked into my bra, just like Aunt Carla taught me.

Smiling and laughing like they have no cares in the world, Stacey, Nikki, and their crew, surrounded by James and some of the football crowd, make their way to the bar.

I put up a hand to have them thrown out by security, but Gio grabs it and pulls it down.

"Now, now, let's not be too hasty. I think we need to play with our prey just a little before we kill it, don't you?" My brother has a wicked glint in his eye, and he presses his finger to his earpiece. "Sam, see the group at the bar being served by Tammy? Please show them into the VIP lounge, compliments of the owners." He turns to me and grins like a shark, all teeth. "Come on, let's take a seat and let them come to us. After all, it would be rude not to offer them hospitality."

He leads us to the ridiculous thrones that are in the VIP area. Technically they are meant for people having parties up here or the actual VIPs, but I guess he and I count.

We take a seat, and a waitress takes our drink order. Pulling out a joint, I flick my lighter, lighting it up before shoving the lighter back in my pocket. My gun is secure in the little thigh holster I have it in today, but it's visible because my dress slides up. Leaning back, I take on a casual air just as the group makes their way up the stairs, giggling and laughing.

The noise isn't as loud up here as it is on the main floor, and I clearly hear Nikki when she catches sight of my brother. "Holy shit, is that Gio Russo? I heard he died."

"Nope, it was his dad." That voice is enough to trigger some memories, and they flash before my eyes, causing me to freeze. Gio pinches me in the side, making me unfreeze and glare at him.

"What the fuck, man?" I ask him, and he nods.

"That's better," Gio murmurs.

"Oh, wow, Tori, as I live and breathe. I had no idea you had come back to town."

Rolling my eyes, I turn to face my arch nemesis.

"How did you even get up into the VIP room? Are you here with someone famous?" Stacey looks around, and once again Gio snorts as my mind goes back to that party and her not having a clue, as usual.

Before either of us can answer, a hostess comes over to us. "Ms. Russo, someone is demanding to speak to the owner downstairs." Gio starts to stand up, but I pat his knee.

"Be a dear and wait for the drinks. I'll sort this out." I stand up and straighten my tight dress, not pulling it down over the gun. The group's eyes almost bug out of their heads as I walk down the couple of steps and move past them. A gorgeous redheaded woman and a blond-haired male catch my eye on the way past. They look familiar, but I instantly dismiss them since they are friends with this lot.

"Holy fuck, did you see Tori? She looks smoking hot," I hear James say to one of his friends.

Turning back, I see Stacey stop the hostess who came and got us. "Did you say someone needs the owner?"

The girl nods, and she looks a little confused.

"Tori Russo is the owner of this club?"

"Yes, Ms. Russo is one of the wealthiest women in the state. She and her brother own many clubs, hotels, and casinos."

Her expression as I go down the stairs is priceless, but when I stop, pull my gun out, and aim it at her head, well, that look makes me giggle with glee. I mouth, "Soon," in her direction and put my gun away, hoping she doesn't pee her pants while I'm gone.

When I get downstairs, I go to the main bar and ask one of my staff members who wanted to see the owner. He tells me they are gone but they left a note. He passes me the note, and when I open it, there's a message.

Beware of the fox in the henhouse.

What the fuck? I turn it over, and there's more.

They are coming for you and Gio next.

The end.

Thank you for reading!
I hope you enjoyed the book. It would be super awesome if you could leave a review wherever you bought it, because I love to hear what you thought of the story.

Want more of Tori, Gio and Sage?
Pre order Book Two
Lies Untold
On Amazon now

Want to keep up to date with new books coming soon?
Sign up to my newsletter here
Newsletter

Another way to do that is to join me Facebook group. I drop teasers and giveaways in there all the time. Here's the link
Lexie's Ladygarden

Visit my webpage and check out reading orders and what else I've written.
www.lexiewinston.com

Acknowledgments

Thank you to all the normal crew this book wouldn't be possible without you all.

To SCW Editing and Elemental Editing, thank you so much for your amazing editing skills

Emma for all the late night and early morning chats.

Infinity Book Designs for the cover

My beta team for being super awesome as usual.

Grace and Hope for being my rocks, long live the throuple.

Lastly to you the readers. I'm hoping you guys enjoy starting a whole new series. A little different to what I normal write but I'm hoping you will embrace it with open arms like you did the Neighpalm Series. So thank you to each and every one of you for taking a chance. Thank you to everyone who reviews and recommends it and thank you to all of you who preorder the next

one as soon as you've finished the last. You guys are the
reason I can keep writing this story.
Until next time. Happy Reading
Xoxo

Lexie

Check out something else by me. A Sci-Fi reverse harem romance.

Apprentice
Galaxy Circus 1

Chapter One

"Miss Jenson, did you hear what I just said to you?" Mr. Ryding, the weaselly-looking lawyer, says to me from behind the large walnut desk. He's fidgeting with the papers in front of him, stacking them, picking them up, tapping them, and then placing them back on the desk in front of himself. While I sit there, waiting for him to say more, he straightens the pens in the holder to the right of him. Given he's done this all at least half a dozen times, it seems like he's doing everything in his power to avoid making eye contact with my very confused self.

"I'm sorry. I'm not sure I understand you. I received a letter from your office saying I have been bequeathed something. I was told that I must present myself in person to sign some papers in order to receive it. Now, you are *also* telling me it was from a grandfather I didn't even know existed, one who obviously didn't want me, as I spent the first eighteen years of my life in foster homes."

He looks up, briefly pausing his fidgeting. "Yes, that's correct. Though it's grandfathers. Plural."

Plural? I puzzle internally. *Never mind, I'll come back to that.*

"John, William, and Eric Adams are your paternal grandfathers, and it wasn't that they didn't want you." His shifty eyes soften briefly before he continues. "They weren't able to find you. Your parents were estranged from them, and they were not notified at the time of your parents' accident. When you were placed in foster care, they weren't in the States, making it even harder for word to come down the appropriate channels." He shuffles his papers again. "When they did eventually find out, John rushed back. Unfortunately, you'd been placed in the system and had your name changed, as per a request in your parents' will, by then. You'd disappeared and were well hidden. Due to the nature of their business, they decided that maybe you were better off. Their job required constant traveling, never settling in one place for very long. It was no place to raise a child, or so they thought. They believed you were safe and loved."

I scoff out loud at that one, hitting my limit of holding my tongue. Though I have to give the man credit. Despite his obvious nerves and my apparent skepticism, he soldiers on. "Otherwise, they would have claimed you immediately," he assures me.

"So, why am I finding out about this now? I'm assuming they're all dead, so why leave our estrangement until I had no chance of getting to know them?" I'm trying my best to keep my tone under control, but I'm honestly at a loss. There isn't a part of me that can reconcile these strangers leaving their granddaughter at the mercy of the system, name change or not. There had to be something terribly wrong with them, or maybe they thought there was something terribly wrong with me, if they'd chosen to stay away until we lost the chance to ever have a relationship.

The shifty look in his eyes is back, and the fidgeting obviously isn't cutting it since he gets up from his desk and starts to pace behind it. He marches back and forth in front of the big picture window which holds the view of the river his office backs onto. He stops, takes a deep breath, and turns to look at me.

"Well, actually, that's not quite true. Misters Adams have not passed on. They've decided to retire, and the family business may only pass down to a family member. You're the one that was chosen, so they contracted our firm to find you. It has taken quite a while, I can assure you."

"Excuse me?" I gasp. "Are you saying my grandfathers are alive and want to meet me?" As a little girl, I would have dreams of a relative swooping in to rescue me from the never-ending cycle of foster homes. I had finally given up around the age of thirteen. I wasn't one of those kids who were beaten or abused in care; I just never seemed to fit in. I was never really included or felt like I was one of the family. It would've been nice to know there was someone out there who wanted me.

Of course, my very skeptical nature decides this is too good to be true, turning my surprise into anger.

"Why the fuck am I dealing with a lawyer and not them directly? Can they not even be bothered, or are they too fucking chicken to face me themselves?" I can practically feel the steam escaping from my ears. It takes a lot to get me mad, but when I get there, you better watch out. Mr. Ryding swallows nervously and brings a finger up, trying to loosen his collar.

"Ah... but... They're..." he stammers. The man must be good at his job if he was able to track me down, which was apparently quite the feat, but he's horribly unprepared to deal with a woman's anger.

Taking a deep breath, I try to calm down. *Don't take it out on the lawyer, Lila. He's just the messenger.*

"Why me? I'm assuming there are other family members they could turn to?" I rub my eyes, already feeling a headache brewing. They've steadily been getting more frequent, and this meeting is not doing me any favors.

"Yes, well, no. There *are* other family members, but you are their only grandchild, and they've decided that it's time you join the family legacy. You are to be given the opportunity first. All the details are in the package." He sits back down at the desk and gestures to the stack of papers he'd been fidgeting with. "You're required to spend twelve months within the business, learning all the ins and outs. If, at the end of the twelve-month period, you're unwilling to continue, the business and the role of CEO and all it entails will pass on to the next eligible family member. You will carry on with life as if the previous twelve months had never really happened."

I stare at the package like it's a snake that's going to bite me. I just don't know what to think. Do I ignore it, sign it over now, and wash my hands of the whole debacle? Or do I take a leap of faith and at least meet the men that could be the best *or* the worst thing to happen to me?

"Can I have some time to think about this?" I ask. "It's quite a decision I need to make."

Mr. Ryding shakes his head. "I'm sorry, but this decision needs to be made as soon as possible. Our firm has been looking for you for a while, and I'm afraid we're out of time. You need to be on a plane to London in two days' time. We're going to need an answer now."

It's my turn to start pacing. Jumping out of the chair I've been sitting in, I start stalking back and forth across the room. The pounding behind my eyes has intensified, and I rub my temples in an attempt to alleviate it. What to do? It's not like I have anything keeping me here. I don't really have friends, mainly acquaintances. My best friend and roomie is head over heels in love with her partner, so she'd be ok if I left. I have a dead-end job in a bar that pays crappy but keeps me busy. Looking at the facts of my life, as totally unimpressive as they are, I guess there's nothing specifically stopping me from going. I've always dreamed of adventures, feeling sure that there must be something better in store than the life I've been living.

"All right," I tell him, making the decision, "I'm in. Show me where to sign."

He goes to the stack of papers on the table and pulls some out. "You need to sign here, here, and here. One of them is a non-disclosure form. No matter what happens, from here on, you are bound by a confidentiality clause. Even if at the end of twelve months you change your mind, everything you see and do will be confidential, and there are some very harsh consequences if you break the clause. A plane ticket is also in the pack, in your name, with the details of your flight. You'll be met at the airport by a driver who will take you to where you need to be. For your peace of mind, you can tell people where you are going and why, but there is to be no sharing of any other details. It's actually a good thing that you don't have a huge circle of friends." I'm torn between surprise that he knows that fact and being insulted by the comment despite its truth.

"We've been looking for you for so long I wouldn't hesitate to say we know everything about you," he replies to my look, a little more defensively than I expected the nervous guy to manage.

"Yeah, ok, because that's not creepy or rude," I reply sarcastically.

I busy myself with signing papers, and by the time I'm finished, my hand aches and my head throbs incessantly. Gathering my copies of everything, I shove them in my hand bag; I'll read it all when I get home. "So what business have I just signed my life away to?" I ask Mr. Ryding, thinking this is probably something I should have asked *before* signing. Fuck, I'm an idiot. Why didn't I ask that first? I mentally slap my impulsive self.

"Have you heard of the Galaxy Circus?" he asks, slightly distracted with gathering all his copies of the paperwork.

I nod enthusiastically, feeling more upbeat than I have this entire meeting. "Oh yes, isn't that the circus that claims it has aliens as its performers? It pops up throughout the globe and is always sold out even though the schedule is too random for anyone to know where they'll be next. People have been trying to debunk them for years. I remember reading that PETA was trying to gain access to prove that their animals are mistreated." I laugh loudly, remembering how that particular situation worked out. Apparently, the circus claimed their animals were really shifters, a clever gimmick that allowed them some special dispensation and gave PETA no ground to stand on. Hey, if people were gullible enough to believe it, then that was their problem.

He looks at me, a strange glint in his eye. "Are they gullible or just looking to be entertained?" he questions, his words coming oddly close to the thought I hadn't spoken aloud. "Well, whether they're gullible or not is besides the point. It still attracts huge crowds when it does tour. It is one of the most popular circuses around, even outselling Cirque du Soleil despite having less shows each year."

My heart starts to beat rapidly as Mr. Ryding looks at me with an oily-looking grin, possibly the first time I've seen him smile since I walked in the door. "Miss Jenson, with the papers you signed, you just joined the circus."

Get it here